Angels:

A story about
Fannie & Freddie,
the President,
Blackmail and Murder

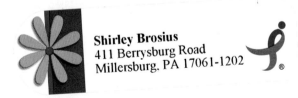

Shirley Brosius
411 Berrysburg Road
Millersburg, PA 17061-1202

By John C. Bieber

PRESS

To Barb –

Thank you for trusting me and believing in me.

Thank you for laughing with me, not at me.

You are my true love and best friend.

"With deep eternal love."

HP

IN THE BEGINNING

He worried that his heart would stop. The stress was coming at him from all sides. Matt could feel every beat of his heart in his upper chest and neck. He knew it was stress and he had felt this several times in his life while going through periods of work pressure, but never like this. He could feel his heart skip beats. The feeling was especially bad while trying to go to sleep at night in his bed next to his wife. Lying on his side with his head on his pillow, Matt could hear the tiny movement of his skin and hairs of his ear against his pillowcase. This magnified the sound of each heartbeat. He would feel his pulse stop for what seemed like two or three seconds, but in reality it was just an instant, a single palpitation. But in that long instant he would sometimes wonder - Will I die now?

In bed, he would roll to his other side or rearrange his pillow to escape the sound. Sometimes he would give up and get out of bed. He would go to his home office and look at his computer or go to the family room and watch TV news until he fell asleep there. Most nights he would eventually fall asleep in bed from exhaustion caused by worry, other times he would pray himself to sleep. That was something he learned from his wife. Many years ago she told him she prayed when she could not sleep. She would pray and imagine herself wrapped in the embrace of God, like a little child safe and warm on the Father's lap. It worked for her every time.

Matt Davidson's business was failing. The Fannie Mae and Freddie Mac disaster exploded in late 2008 leaving the real estate and banking industries in chaos. Matt's real estate company bought houses, fixed them and sold them for a profit. A lot of people called it "flipping" houses. He never called it that because he could not stand to watch those TV shows where people did crazy things under the pressure of artificial deadlines. The house flippers on TV were first-timers and were unrealistic about how fast and easy they thought they could make a lot of cash. Matt had investors that he called partners but they were only involved in the money side and he made every decision for the business. Matt was also a landlord of houses he owned and rented.

The people who bought Matt's houses were mainly first time buyers who now could not get mortgages despite the billions of dollars the government gave to bail out banks to loosen credit. Along with the housing bubble bursting and the banking industry in crisis, the Dow Jones losing half of its value, 401Ks evaporating, an economy grinding into

1

recession, the government taking over corporations, and unemployment at 10%; all seven of his tenants were behind on paying their rent compounding Matt's problems. Two tenants lost their jobs and others had their work hours reduced or were laid off. His rental houses were in Norristown Pennsylvania, northwest of Philadelphia. The rental houses were single family homes rented by middle to lower income families. He was trying to sell some of the rentals to free up some cash, but it was the same slow process for getting those buyers approved and into mortgages. Matt could not sell them to other real estate investors because they were used to buying cheaper than Matt could afford to sell. His company was knocked to its knees because his resources for cash, the life blood of real estate had stopped flowing.

Matt's bills did not stop flowing. He still had carrying costs, mortgage payments, taxes, utilities and insurance to be paid for his properties. His bills at home were piling up also. He cringed every time their furnace or dish washer and clothes dryer make a strange noise because he knew he did not have the money to replace any of them. His truck and his daughter's car were soon both due for state inspections. His wife's car needed new tires and he felt guilty having her drive on them as they were. Matt dreaded phone calls from numbers he did not recognize on his caller ID. Collection companies were starting to call. He was behind on two credit cards he used for buying materials for the project houses. His priority was to keep current with his own personal mortgage. He also had large property tax bills looming in the distance for all of his properties. Matt would pray for wisdom concerning business decisions and he knew he needed God on his side. Matt prayed for help.

***

In the summer of 1990, Matt and his wife Jennifer were at the beach in Ocean City New Jersey with their best friends Mark and Lisa. Jen and Lisa were very close friends since they met in college 10 years before. All four enjoyed spending time together and for this trip they had rented a house for a week right next to the beach. It was a hot, sunny week and by Thursday they were all tan and relaxed. A tropical storm was coming north along the coast. The ocean was already getting rough and the wind had picked up. The waves on the beach were much larger and crashing louder than the day before. When they packed their gear to head to the beach for the day, the guys usually packed the cooler with soda and beer. Today at Lisa's request, they mixed up a one gallon thermos of sea breezes with vodka, grapefruit and cranberry juice.

The four of them spent most of their beach time lying in the sun, reading, sleeping or in the water cooling off. They all enjoyed walking on the beach and they could see Margate and Atlantic City to the north in the distance as the shore curved to the right. It was especially pretty at night. The guys liked to throw a football around and they always brought their baseball gloves and a ball. Matt and Mark liked to dig holes in the sand and build big mounds with tracks and tunnels through it that a pink rubber ball would roll down and into a pit filled with ocean water. They would build close enough to the water's edge in a spot that would eventually have to battle the tide coming in. They would build sand walls and trenches around their creation to protect it as long as possible from the waves that crept closer by the minute. They were engineers at heart. Other people's kids would come over to them and help build. Most of the boys could not wait to take over the project when Matt and Mark were finished with it. Jen and Lisa liked to watch their big boys play.

Jen was an excellent swimmer. "Be careful if you go out past your knees. The water's getting rougher. I had to really work the riptide this time in." she said to everyone as she came up to their beach blanket from the ocean and squeezed the water from her shoulder length hair. As the day moved on, the sky darkened with cloud cover, a solid gray blue neutral sky that blocked the sun and made it hard to tell what time of day it was. Most people had already left the beach. All four of them agreed to do the same and start heading back to the house. The gallon of sea breeze was gone and Matt was feeling extremely relaxed. He decided to hit the water one last time to rinse off the sand.

Matt was doing fine in the water up to his waist and he was moving with the current, leaning into the waves as they hit his side. He went under the water a few times to shake the sand out of his hair and swim trunks. He stepped up onto a sandbar and then fell into a trench that took him off his feet and he had to start swimming. Matt was not a strong swimmer. He liked to tell people that he was slightly more buoyant than a rock, but a rock could hold its breath longer. Matt knew to swim with the current and angle himself toward the beach, but no matter what he did he was still heading out and away from the beach. He was worried. He looked all around him and there was no one near him to call out to. The life guards had already left the beach and apparently Jen and the others were not watching him. At this point there would not be much they could do to help him anyway as he was out of reach and heading

3

further out. Matt was tiring fast and he thought – What a stupid way to die. I can't believe I'm going to drown. Where will they find my body?

Just as Matt felt desperation starting to take him over. A man on a boogie board appeared just behind Matt to his left. Matt yelled over to him "Hey man, can you help me out?!"

"Yeah, let's go." the man said. Matt did not take a good look at the man because he was focused only on not letting go of the board and getting to the beach. Matt kicked along with him and they seemed to quickly make it in to where Matt could get on his feet and walk up through the rough waves out of the water and onto dry sand. He stopped and leaned over with both his hands on his knees, exhausted and out of breath. He turned back to look for the man to thank him, but he was not there. The beach was empty all around him and he did not see the man anywhere. He looked into the surf and there were no people in the water as far as he could see. Matt realized he was at least 200 yards down the beach from Jen, Mark and Lisa.

"Where did you go?" Lisa asked Matt as he walked up to the others who had finished packing up most of their gear. "We didn't see you. We thought you went up to the boardwalk to use the bathroom."

"Some guy just saved me from drowning." Matt said, having still not fully recovered his breath. He described what happened to him "This guy came out of nowhere on a boogie board. There was no way I was gonna make it in." He dried off with his towel and put on his t-shirt. "If he didn't come by, I know I would have drowned."

***

Matt was a believer. Since accepting Christ 25 years ago, he never had one day of doubt in the Lord or of his own salvation. When he started his real estate company he was very confidant. Matt had been a salesman his whole working career. He had worked for three different companies, one small and two large corporations before starting his own business. Matt was always the top sales guy wherever he was. Before he started his company, he sold inventory tracking software to large companies and made enough money to have a very nice lifestyle that included an expensive home near Valley Forge in the suburban Philadelphia area. His family drove new cars. They had been taking two vacations a year. One had to be in the Caribbean because his family loved the beaches and the blue green waters of the islands. They liked to go there over Thanksgiving and it was a good time for the kids being off school and since neither Matt nor Jen had many family members, there was no pressure to do the holiday family visit tour. Their other vacation had to be somewhere in the United States. That started when his children were young. The idea was for them to see the USA, have a great time and being patriotic, Matt liked to spend money in America.

Matt's family was small. He had one older brother who was single and now lived in Florida. Matt's parents were both deceased. He was never in trouble nor was he ever a problem for his parents growing up. He was always a good kid. Matt was a B student in high school and college but he could have studied more and done better. He always had a good sense of right and wrong and he was kind.

Matt was popular during his school years and wherever he worked. He was on the bottom of the "A list" in high school. Girls liked him. He had one steady girlfriend for a few months early in his junior year until one day he realized there were lots of girls at his school. Matt spent most of his free time with the girls he dated, especially in the summer time. Girls kept him off the beer drinking team that a lot of his jock buddies were on. They always asked him to come on their "road trips" or to "go drinkin" but he would say to them, "You guys can have all the cold ones, I want the warm ones."

In high school he played football and was on the track team. He played one year of college football at offensive line. He did not have a sports scholarship so the economics of needing a job kept him from playing more. His parents did not pay for Matt's college. He worked, got a student loan and a few grants to pay for it. After college he stayed in shape by lifting weights in his basement, running and riding a mountain bike. Matt was six foot tall and a fit 220 pounds. His brown hair was graying at the sides of his short haircut, but his face was youthful and people thought he was younger than his 49 years.

***

Matt told no one, not even his wife the extent of his business problems. He felt like he had no one to turn to for help. Friends of his in the real estate business were all suffering and now he did not have the confidence to get involved with any new projects with new investors and he had to keep up a good appearance with the investors he did have. The only thing he told his wife is "It's tight right now. Don't buy anything big". Jen trusted him completely and never got involved with Matt's work or the books of the real estate business. She was truly a gift from God to him. She worked for a very stable company, but they could not support themselves on her income alone. If she were not working they would have been financially finished by now.

Matt was grateful to God every time something went right. His first thoughts when something good happened were "Thank you Lord". He was sincerely grateful for the help even in the little things and he did not take anything for granted, especially now that everything was so difficult.

Matt had never been lucky. He worked hard for everything he had. He could not remember many things that just fell into his lap. He always had to make the extra phone call to close a deal or run some advertising one more week to sell a house. He knew other people who literally stumbled and fell into money all the time. He also knew many financially successful people who were liars and thieves. Men who cheated on their wives, drank too much or used drugs. He knew these people had problems but he rationalized their financial success by thinking they must have made deals with the devil. Matt was frustrated that his work seemed like it was not being blessed. He tried to analyze what was happening in his life. He thought to himself - What am I supposed to learn here? He believed God would provide for him and his family and he knew there were probably thousands of blessings and things and problems unseen and unknown to him that he was likely being spared from. Finances and business were the places where he was most vulnerable and Matt knew that if God wanted his attention, this is where He would work on him. God had Matt's full attention.

Matt's parents were very working class people and he grew up in a small, very clean row house in a steel town west of Philadelphia. His mother died from heart disease one year before he and Jen were married and ten years later his father died of lung cancer. Both of his parents were long time smokers. Matt and his brother did not inherit anything from his father because his father's home had been sold to pay medical bills. Matt was sure of his father's saving faith in Christ. His father had not been a church goer and finally with his own mortality in front of him, he wanted to talk about his faith with Matt. Matt prayed with him in the hospital and he walked his father through a prayer of repentance, acceptance of salvation and confession of his belief in Jesus as Lord.

Jen's background was different. She was an only child and her parents did help her pay for most of college, but Jen always worked to earn her own money. As a high school teenager she worked in a boardwalk t-shirt shop and she waitressed during her college years. Jen's

6

mother was a well known landscape painter who sold her own original beach paintings. Her father was an executive at a large insurance firm in New York City. Both of her parents were killed during the time Jen was pregnant with their first child Abby. They were killed by a drunk driver while they were crossing a road returning from one of their walks on the beach. They had lived in a New Jersey shore town. Jen's only comfort then and now, was that she knew her parents both believed in God and she was sure of their salvation.

Jen's parents had been there for both Jen and Matt when they came to know the Lord. When Jen and Matt starting dating seriously, her father liked Matt very much but he was concerned about his salvation. Jen had accepted Christ when she was a young teenager. Her father sensed where she and Matt were heading together; so on their third visit to her parents home, Jen's father took Matt for a walk alone on the beach after dinner. He explained to Matt what he and Jen's mother believed about their relationship with God and he told Matt about the clear simple path to salvation. It was the right time for Matt to hear it explained so easily and personally. At home at his apartment, Matt had begun reading a Bible secretly, without telling Jen. He came across the verse, Mark 10:15 about having childlike faith. This made perfect sense to him and he believed it. A few days later when Matt was alone exercising, he prayed and asked Jesus into his life. He told Jen and she cried tears of joy. When he told Jen's parents, they said it was one of the happiest days of their lives.

***

It was very late one summer night when Matt, Jen and then two year old Abby were driving home from Mark and Lisa's house after a long day of picnicking, sun, volleyball and margaritas. Abby was sleeping secure in her car seat in the back while Jen slept in the passenger seat next to Matt. At night, Jen usually fell asleep in the car as soon as the door closed. Matt was a good driver and he was alert and in good condition when they started the drive toward home in their Honda Accord. At about half way, Matt felt his eyes get heavy so he kicked off his sandals to drive barefooted, turned up the radio and opened his window to send more air toward his face. This usually helped him stay alert. But a few minutes later he fell asleep at the wheel. He remembered an instant of peaceful rest. Then he heard his mother's voice say "Matthew." It was so clear that it startled him awake and he regained control of his car

7

without incident. It was her voice in the same tone he had heard a thousand times waking him up out of bed for school in the morning at his parent's home. Her voice had saved them and he replayed it over again and again in his head until they arrived safely at their house. When they got there, Matt told Jen he heard his mother's voice and they felt it confirmed their hope that she was a believer when she died. This was one of those things Matt and his mother had never really gotten around to talking about. They believed God would only use her voice if she was in heaven with Him. They were filled with emotion and grateful they were safe and Matt was grateful to have heard his mother's heavenly voice.

COLLEGE DAYS

Matt always said Jen was the smarter of the two of them. He realized that quickly when they were in college. He often told her she should have studied medicine because she could retain all kinds of information on all kinds of subjects and she could memorize. She was your worst nightmare if you played trivia games with her.

Matt first saw Jen in 1981. In college he noticed her at a popular college bar called "The Cellar". It was a basement level bar that was always crowded and loud. He noticed her because she was the leader in a group of her girlfriends that always arrived at the bar together. She was the center of the group and her friends loved her. Matt was intimidated by her and by all the attention she got from everyone, especially from guys. Matt was never interested in any of her girlfriends but he did flirt with some of them, but he only did that to learn more about Jen.

The first time they spoke to each other was on a sunny cool November day at an outdoor ATM machine on campus. Matt was waiting for her to finish getting some cash and it was taking her longer than a typical withdrawal. He did not mind because he got the long unobstructed view of her. If he were a hunter, he had a clear shot.

"You can try my PIN number." Matt called to her from about 10 feet behind her.

"That's OK. I always win at this game." She said as she turned around toward him and waved five twenty dollar bills.

"You're much better at that than me. The most I ever win is twenty bucks." Matt got a good look at her beautiful face and brown eyes.

"I guess you aren't very lucky." She said.

He knew he was staring into her eyes and somehow he forgot how to speak. He could still think though, and he was calculating the unlikely probability of him ever talking to any girl as beautiful as her again for as long as he lived. Jen had her shoulder length blonde hair put up in a high ponytail. Her face was flawless and her neck was long and bare. Matt pleaded with himself - Please brain, help me!

"Me lucky? No my name is Matt. I've seen you at the…"

"The Cellar. Yeah, I've seen you too. How come you never said hello? You don't look like the shy type." Jen said.

Matt was off balance. He was slowly coming back from his vision of Jen bringing him an icy beverage wearing not much more than a smile. He knew he had to kick his game into gear and he was only work-

9

ing at half power on the charming and witty scale. If he ever wanted her to bring him that beverage, it was now or never.

Matt said "Well, I'm not a pushy guy and you always look like you're busy with your friends. Plus I can't remember jokes, I have zero pick-up lines, I'm usually broke, but I do have nice feet."

Jen laughed and looked down at his sneakers.

"Yeah. I believe socks are the key to nice feet. Look. I have good white socks on right now." He pulled up the leg of his jeans to show her. "I rarely go barefoot and my feet don't look like most guys, ya know? Hairy monkey feet." Matt said.

"Yeah, I don't like monkey feet, especially on girls".

"Oh me too. Nothing worse than short skirt, long legs, high heels and hairy monkey feet."

Jen laughed again and looked at him hard. She liked him and knew how important a sense of humor was, and he was very good looking. She wondered if he was a Christian.

"Will you be at the Cellar Friday night?" Jen asked as she took a step toward him. This was the week before Thanksgiving and students were all leaving town next week to go home for the holiday.

Matt said "I think so. I hear they're having a turkey flavored beer, to get us in the mood for Thanksgiving."

"That's great. What flavor will they have for Christmas? Reindeer?"

"That's funny, and a good idea actually. Seasonal animal flavored beer. Cooked or uncooked?"

"Cooked for sure. Ground Hog Day beer uncooked could taste a lot like uh… dirt."

Matt laughed and thought there were few girls he knew that would have gotten his lame turkey flavored beer joke, much less think of something funnier. Jen was beautiful and funny, a rare combination.

Matt and Jen met Friday night at The Cellar. The place was packed with students, all excited to be heading home for the break. College crowds were mainly beer drinkers. Jen did not really drink. At the bar she would have one lite-beer in a bottle and hold on to it all night. Her reason for doing it was she had grown tired of answering the question – Why aren't you drinking? With a beer in her hand, people stopped asking. Jen was very social and she liked to be with her friends; believers and non-believers. She felt that socializing with them where they relaxed and had fun, was one of the most effective places to demonstrate her faith. Her testimony was being a social Christian who was never afraid to talk about her faith and to get into heavy theological conversations. She spent many long nights discussing the Bible with friends who were sober and some who were drunk. One particular night that she always remembered, even many years later, was a long night of talking about Revelation with Johnny, a very long haired art student who was caught up in the end times and was not concerned about the present day.

Matt was not a big drinker in college. He had a rough experience of getting sick a few years before he met Jen, at a party after playing "Quarters". He never had a great tolerance for beer after that.

Jen and Matt talked and danced with only each other all night. When the bar closed at 2AM, he walked her a half mile across town to the apartment that she shared with three other girls. Most students in town walked to the bars because they did not want the hassle of being pulled over by the police who took drunk driving very seriously. It was a warm night for November. Matt took her hand and their fingers found a comfortable way to lock together as they walked. She liked him. He was smart, made her laugh, he smelled good and he had a strong build. She felt very safe and protected walking with him. Matt was six inches taller than Jen. She thought he looked like a football player. At the bar she liked looking at the hairs of his chest at the open top button of his blue oxford shirt. She had thought about his blue eyes since they first met at the ATM machine until they met again this night.

Matt was completely relaxed and confident with Jen. She was so much different than most girls he dated or had as friends. He enjoyed talking to her about any subject because she was so intelligent and he did not feel any sense of her testing him or comparing him to some other guy. There was nothing antagonistic or pretentious about her. He felt like he had known her for years. They agreed on many things from their attitudes about school, their hopes for their careers, music, movies, and food.

As they walked and held hands, Jen asked him where he was in his religious faith. Matt said "I'm really an uneducated Christian." He told her "I went to Sunday school a couple of time when I was a kid. That's about it. I've honestly never just sat down and really considered what I really think about Jesus. I believe he is who everyone says he is, but I would have a hard time explaining why to anyone. I'm pretty theologically immature. I know I have to sort it out, but I don't know where to start."

"I truly do believe Jesus is my savior. I'd like to talk about it with you any time you want." Jen said.

"Are you one of those extremely good looking Christian women who lure poor guys like me into a level of acquiescence and then thumps them with your Bible?"

"Do I look like I'd thump you with a Bible?" she said with a big smile and a flutter of her brown eyes.

"No, but think like you could be dangerous." Matt said with a big smile.

Jen lived in the second floor apartment of an old Victorian house on the main street in their college town. There was a big front porch four steps up from the sidewalk that went around one side and into a spot that was dark and out of the glare of the streetlight. They walked to that spot and stopped in the shadow and stood close together, face to face.

"What day are you leaving to go home for Thanksgiving?" Matt asked.

Jen's home was with her parents, about a two hour drive from campus. She was from New Jersey and grew up on the beach in Seaside Heights. "Wednesday morning. I'm driving with my roommate Mary Lynn and dropping her off at her place. She lives about twenty minutes from my house".

Matt said "I have to work tomorrow and Sunday with this guy who hangs sheetrock, you know, drywall? I'm supposed to meet him in about five hours."

"Then you better go home and get some sleep mister."

"Yeah, but I really don't want to go." He pulled her to him, his hands around her waist. She put her arms up over his shoulders. They could see each other's face from the amber glow of a light through a window left on in the first floor apartment. She pulled him closer and they kissed.

"You have to go." She whispered in his ear.

"I *really* don't want to. I can stay awake till I have to go work. We could go get some breakfast and I could drink some Cokes and pour extra sugar in them for energy. An energy drink, lots of sugar and caffeine. Wow, I could make something like that and sell it to people who needed a jolt of energy. I could call it Mr. Perky. Ya know, like Dr. Pepper? Mr. Perky. Hey I think I just invented something. I'd be alert and perky, in great shape to work."

"Did you say perky? I love that word. But I think you should go home and get some sleep, Mr. Perky."

"OK. I guess you're right." He paused then said "I'll be around Monday if you want to call me."

"Oh, I'll call ya. Now get going".

With a big sigh Matt said "Goodnight, I mean morning... uh, you know." Then he stepped toward the porch railing, put his right hand on the porch railing and swung his legs over and made a perfect landing on the sidewalk four feet below. He waved goodbye, turned in the direction of his apartment and started a quick jog home.

Matt missed her already. Jen knew that he was the guy for her.

WHAT HIS SINS WERE

Matt started his real estate business because he was frustrated and tired of working for other people. As a salesman he was tired of other people, project managers and support people not caring about the product he sold. He could develop the account, form the relationship with the customer and close the deal only to hand the project off to a project manager who just did not care as much as he did.

When he started his company the housing market was strong, money was everywhere and easy to get. For the first few years business was good and he enjoyed it more than anything he had ever done in his working career. He enjoyed the freedom to work on the deals he wanted to, no one else to blame or depend on. He liked to talk about the business and he was proud of the company he was building and proud of himself. He resisted the feeling that he was a little bit better than the average Joe types he saw trudging off to some hourly job every day. Matt was never a boastful man. He knew that cockiness was wrong and he felt like he kept it in check pretty well. When business was good he never bragged about how much money he made or what kind of new toy he just bought like a lot of other guys did. He never liked being around those types of people.

Maybe it was pride that kept Matt from telling Jen about the trouble he was having or asking for help. He was very private and did not want to appear stupid or weak, especially to Jen and his family. He felt that the only one he could ask for help was God and he did that, shooting up prayers to heaven all day long. Matt also prayed long difficult prayers asking God to help him. He did not want pride to be a barrier between God and him. Matt knew that pride was a sin.

Matt thought he knew what his is sins were. He had once promised God that he would give ten percent of the profit of a sold house to the church. When the house sold he rationalized the profit so low that he made a deal with God that he would get back to him on the next one. He promised to tithe and never did. Matt would drop the F-word occasionally when he was with his contractors. He always regretted it as soon as he did it and he thought swearing made him sound ignorant. Matt fudged numbers occasionally with expenses on a house. He looked forward to a Friday evening bottle of wine. He thought Jesus made and drank wine. He also knew God did not like drunks and Matt never thought of himself as one even after a third bottle and when he could hear himself begin to slur his words. And then there was YouTube. Friends would send him funny or political videos that he would look at and forward along to other friends. Matt's problem was that with every YouTube video the screen offered, there were related videos and it was easy to veer off and find something nearly pornographic to look at.

The pressure of his failing business and the humiliation he feared was so great that he felt it in his every waking moment. The weight of failing his family was so intense that he felt out of control. He considered suicide as a way out. He knew the idea was insane but he thought that if his back was up against the wall hard enough, he would be able to kill himself, and he was certain he could make it look like an accident. Matt set a scene in his mind where he would be alone at a house he was remodeling and he would stage an accident. He imagined that he could set up a situation where he was cutting a board by hand with an electric circular saw and he would saw deeply into his thigh, stagger around to splash some blood as if he were trying to save himself then just lay down and bleed out. He thought of removing anything from the house that he might use to stop the bleeding, like paper towels or rags and rope or wire that he could use as a tourniquet. He would leave his cell phone in his truck and not tell anyone he would be at that house. He imagined it to be painful but he thought it would not take very long to die.

However, Matt knew he had ruined the suicide option by letting his million and a half dollar term life insurance policy lapse because when the bill for the premium came, he did not have the money to pay it. He pushed it off one too many weeks and it was cancelled. Even months later he did not have the money to get a new policy. He thought suicide would have been a real option had there been adequate insurance money to rescue his family. He worried about what his death would do to his wife and children. He wanted to grow old with Jen. He cried himself to sleep a few nights considering it. Matt believed that if he did take his own life, as a believer he would go to heaven, but his eternal reward would be less. That made him sick thinking that even in heaven, for all eternity he would be embarrassed about his low rank and be labeled a loser. Matt knew without insurance money, he could not end his life because his family would be worse off with him dead and without cash, and at least if he were alive he had some chance to keep their home and some financial stability. Things could get better, but he could not imagine when.

Matt prayed constantly. He always prayed for God to bless his business and family. Now he felt himself talking to God and praying about everything all day. In the car, at this computer, in the shower, on top of a ladder, while standing in front of someone in the middle of a conversation he would pray. At the last closing for a house he sold, Matt told Jen he had prayed during all the paperwork and up until the time he left there, went to the bank and deposited his check. Whenever he felt the need for help, or the need to help someone else he prayed. He felt God pressuring him to focus on Him.

When Matt got so tense, nauseous and worried that he felt he could not take it, he would get on his knees with his face on the floor and pray. Sometimes it was violent prayer. He would cry, get angry and vent to God. He often felt like a little boy crying to his Father for help. But he felt alone and unanswered. Always on the edge, credit used up, barely making it month to month. Matt prayed at home in his office every time he went to look at his bank accounts on-line. He would log-on, enter his password and close his eyes and pray until his account balances appeared on the screen. He prayed that he did not bounce any checks or get over-draft penalties. Knowing he had gone through all his resources he recently started looking for a job back in the corporate world. He called old contacts and told them he was looking for work. They all told him about layoffs and cutbacks their companies already made and how they were worried about being cut also. The job market was a dead end especially with unemployment heading to ten percent and the stock market losing half its value since the new president took office. Timing of everything in his life could not be worse. Matt felt the need to shield his family from all this. He kept up a good front at home.

Matt was good at that. The year before Matt started his company, he had an affair with a woman he had known in college. Jen never knew about it. Matt met Pam at the self service gas station near his home where he usually stopped three or four times a week for gas or coffee. One afternoon Matt and Pam pulled up at the opposite sides of the same gas pump. They got out of their vehicles at the same time and looked right at each other.

"Matt is that you?" Pam said taking off her sunglasses.

"Pam! What are you doing here?" Matt said and he went around the pump and gave her a hug. He thought - Man, she feels good.

"I live here, about a mile from here. Do you work nearby?"

"No. I live a mile that way, off of Old Forge Road." He said pointing the opposite direction and taking a good look at her. It was 1PM on a hot July day. Pam was wearing shorts, a sleeveless tank top and sandals. Matt was wearing a neck tie with his long shirt sleeves rolled up. He thought she looked fantastic, even better than he remembered. He thought she was a year older than he was because she graduated the year before he did. They were not intimate friends back then. She always liked Matt but he never asked her out on a date. Matt had known Pam for two years at college. They were friends who shared a few classes and went to many of the same parties. Matt had seen her get drunk several times and that kept him at a distance. They had not spoken or had been in contact in over 20 years, but he was happy to see her now.

Matt said "I've lived here for 10 years and I've never seen you around".

"We moved here 6 years ago. I come here all the time to get gas and coffee."

"That's crazy! How did we never see each other? Pam you look amazing! You said "we moved" does that mean Mr. Pam?"

"Yeah Kevin and I've been married 7 years. He works in the city. Matt you haven't changed a bit! I'm so glad to see you!" and she hugged him again.

"Me too. Can I buy you something to drink inside? Oh and I guess we both need gas."

They filled their gas tanks and went inside the GasQuick together. They walked to the back of the store where the cold drink refrigerators with glass doors were. Pam lead the way making sure Matt had an opportunity see that she was in good shape. Together they reached for the same type bottled water and laughed and Pam leaned into him for a moment. Matt paid for their water and they walked back outside to their cars. As he opened his car door Matt said "Pam, I gotta get going but let me give you my number". He grabbed his business card from the compartment between his car seats and handed it to her.

"Thanks! Let me give you my number."

"No, really I gotta go. You can call me and leave a number or email me."

"OK. Matt it's so good to see you." She gave him a third hug and said "I will call you. I promise!"

With that they parted, got in their cars and headed off in different directions. Matt wondered how many times they must have just missed each other passing on these roads, at the malls, restaurants, grocery stores, the movies. They probably passed within a couple of feet of each other driving in their cars over the 6 years she lived in the area. He also thought about how good she looked. She was not the pretty girl he remembered from college but now she was a mature beautiful woman, and he knew the difference.

Pam kept her promise and the next day she left a voice message on Matt's office phone. He listened to it from his cell phone in his car when he called the office to check messages. "Matt, it's Pam! I was so excited to see you! I'm calling to give you my cell number, its 555-465-6123. Give me a call and I'll buy you lunch. Do you like the Iron Grill at Colonial Mall? I love it there. Call me! Bye!"

Matt got a feeling he had not felt in a very long time. It was a combination of nervous excitement with a dose of the butterflies. He listened to her message 10 times until he called her three days later on Friday. He called her at 1PM because he thought if she had been free on Monday at 1PM she would probably be free same time Friday. It was also after lunch so she should be available. He did not want to call too early or too late. He called from his cell phone in his car not from his office where someone might hear him. He found a place away from his office, and parked his car under the shade of a tree. He did not want to be interrupted. He also knew if this was an innocent return phone call, the time and day and where he called from would not matter.

He made the call. "Pam, it's Matt."

"Matt! It is you! Hi!" she answered. She was excited and had been hoping he would call.

"I got your message about lunch. That would be great. I know the place, I've never eaten there but if you like it, it must be good." He was trying to speak in a calm voice even though he could feel his heart beating in his neck.

"I'm so excited! You'll love it. The food is wonderful and it's beautifully decorated. When can we meet? How about Monday? Monday at 2:00? It's not so crowded then."

"Well yeah, I could make two o'clock. That sounds great. Should I meet you inside?"

"That would be perfect. Oh Matt, I can't wait to sit and talk to you about the old days and get up to date on what you're doing now."

"Me too Pam. OK. I'll meet you Monday at 2:00."

"OK, bye Matt!"

Now Matt had something to think about all weekend and he thought about Pam a lot. He knew there was no legitimate reason for meeting her, especially being a married Christian man. Why not tell Jen and invite her along? He could just as easily invite Pam and her husband to his house for a nice cookout with his wife and kids. Matt thought he was enough in control of himself to get close to the edge of this cliff of adultery and take a good look over the edge without falling. It was as if his moral compass fell to the floor and cracked. He was quickly taken in by the anticipation of what might be. Matt imagined how this lunch could play out. They could have a nice chat about old times, catch up on what was new with the both of them, talk about the spouses, kids and then decide to get together again soon with Jen and Pam's husband. Or they might meet, talk, have some flirty banter and realize that is not the right road for them to go down. Matt mostly thought about a third possible outcome which was for this to be the opportunity to indulge himself with another woman.

Monday came and Matt was in the restaurant parking lot 30 minutes early. He parked at the furthest edge of the lot away from the entrance where he would have a clean view when Pam arrived. He wanted her to enter the restaurant first. Matt put on sunglasses, lowered the car sun visor and he even brought along a newspaper that he could use as a shield in case Pam spotted him early. He also traded cars with Jen that morning in case Pam would recognize his car from the GasQuick.

Pam arrived at 2:01. She pulled up in a red Volvo sport utility wagon, the same one she had when they met last week. He could not see her get out of it because Matt was parked on the opposite side of her driver door, but he watched her come around it and walk across the lot and walk into the restaurant. All he really saw was her short skirt, legs and high heels.

Matt wanted her to have time inside to gather herself and set whatever scene she needed, so he waited three minutes before he drove across the parking lot and parked two spaces away from where she parked. He wanted to appear cool about this. He checked himself in the mirror, straightened his tie, took a couple of deep breaths, grabbed some Tic-Tacs and went in.

It took Matt's eyes a few seconds to adjust inside the darker restaurant but he kept his sunglasses on until he spotted Pam on the far left side of the main dining room at a table against a long window. She waved to him as she sat facing straight toward the entrance where she could see everyone entering. No one was seated at tables anywhere near her. Matt walked toward her removing his sunglasses on the way. She stood up and hugged him and kissed him on the cheek. "I'm so glad to see you. Oh Matt, you sit here." Pam said as she motioned to the seat to her right. They had a smaller square table that sat four people.

"I'm sorry I'm late. Have you been here long?" he asked as he immediately began to take in the view she provided. Pam wore her light brown hair up off of her neck in a bun. She was tan and it made her green eyes look greener. Pam's white sleeveless silk top plunged in front to provide a line of cleavage that was garnished with a diamond pendant necklace that worked like an arrow pointing to where his eyes wanted to go.

"No. I really just sat down. I didn't even have time to order a drink. Thanks for meeting me! I'm sure you're busy with work."

"Well today I made sure my afternoon was open." Matt said with a smile.

"Good. Then we can talk!" Pam waved to the waitress who came over to them with menus. She ordered a glass of wine and Matt ordered a Vodka and cranberry juice. Matt could handle vodka all day with hardly any effects and years ago he read in a men's magazine that vodka and cranberry juice was not supposed to leave an odor on one's breath.

The waitress brought their drinks and they both ordered salads with grilled chicken. Over the weekend Matt had even thought about what he would order for lunch. He knew he did not want to order anything heavy like a big cheese burger and fries – the last thing he wanted to do was look like a slob, and if he got the chance to get close to Pam he did not want a full stomach slowing him down.

Pam told Matt her life story. Everything since the day she packed up at college to go home after graduation until today. She was now in her second marriage to a lawyer who worked 65 hours a week in center city Philadelphia. She had no children and said she was never interested in having any. Pam did not work but several days a week she went to the large popular fitness center in their town. Matt got the impression that Pam spent most of her time trying to look good, and she did a great job at it. She only asked Matt a few surface questions about his work and they reminisced about some friends they had in common at college. She did not ask about his wife, even though he saw her look at his wedding ring several times. The conversation was flirtatious. She complimented him about how he was in such good shape and she made a fuss about his graying hair and how she thought it made him look like George Clooney. She told him about some of her relationships with men including her former and current husbands.

Alarm bells were ringing in Matt's head and he knew the direction this lunch was headed, but he did not want to stop. He was enjoying her. He hoped for this and he knew it was wrong. He thought about Jen in flashes. Pam was so different from Jen. Matt knew it was not too late to pull himself back from making a huge mistake, but he wanted to be close to her and he loved whatever her perfume was. She was beautiful and he felt intoxicated by having all of her attention. He loved the idea of being pursued. Matt was feeling overwhelmed and stimulated by all the things she brought to him, all the things he desired. They kept tight eye contact and he watched her body language. Pam touched his hand often. She pressed her hand on his thigh a few times under the table. She inched her chair closer to his and he did the same. She was giving Matt all the right signals. His head was buzzing and his mind racing a million miles an hour. After they finished eating and the waitress brought them their third round of drinks, Pam moved closer to Matt and told him she had a dream about him two nights ago. In her dream she was alone in a dark room, cold and nude and after a time Matt came into the room, gave her his warm coat and walked her out of the room. She said that was all she could remember. He did not know what to say but he clearly knew she wanted him.

"Pam, you know I'm married." He said as he looked into her eyes and slowly pulled his hands back closer to himself.

"I don't need to know anything about that. I'm not interested in your wife. I'm interested in you Matt."

He said "I wasn't sure where this conversation would lead but I admit I sort of wanted it to go this direction. I thought about you all weekend, I even got here a half hour early and just waited in my car. You're a beautiful woman, and I feel flattered that you still like me. What did you think would come of this?"

"Be with me Matt. We can steal some time here and there. Matt I always wanted you, even way back at college but I could never get you to ask me out. I guess I should have just jumped your bones." she said with a smile and she rubbed his leg with her leg under the table. "When I saw you last week I felt this flood of old feelings. I've been thinking about you constantly since then. I'm sorry but I believe in following my emotions and Matt I'd love to be with you. You look so good. Oh Matt."

She took his left hand with both of hers and kissed it. Matt scanned the dining room to see if anyone saw them. No one was near them or looking their way.

"Pam, I have never done this before. I've never cheated. I look at women a lot, too much, but I've never pursued anything with anyone, ever."

"Matt I know you're a good guy. You always were and that's one of the reasons I'm attracted to you. But I believe I'm only here in this life for a short time and I deserve what pleasure I can get and give."

Matt could not believe how easy this was. She came to him. Pam was doing all the work. He could have sat there through lunch and not said a word and come to the same ending. This was happening so fast. Years ago with Jen it was slow and built over time. Pam was available right then, that minute. He knew all he had to do was say yes, and at the very same time he was thinking about the millions of reasons why he should walk away, and he was also wondering if she could keep this a secret.

Matt signaled the waitress to bring the check. After he paid, they got up from the table and Pam said she had to use the ladies room. He walked with her toward the hall around the corner from the main dining room where it was. He leaned his back against the wall and waited for her. When she came out she walked up to him and put her right hand on his left cheek then moved it behind his neck and pulled his face down to hers and she kissed him. Matt did not resist. He returned the kiss and breathed in her fragrance, touched her skin and pressed her body.

The affair lasted three months and then it ended as easily as it started. Matt stopped calling her and she stopped calling him. Several times they had talked about the need to end it, and then it did. It just ended. He could not even remember their last conversation. It ended cleanly and he never saw her again, never even in passing at the GasQuick. Afterward he looked for her every time he went there. For months he expected to hear her voice in his voicemail at work, but she never called. Jen never found out about it. He felt like he got away with something huge. There seemed to be no consequence, or visible damage from the affair. Matt prayed about this affair hundreds of times, telling God he admitted he sinned and asked God to forgive him. Even though the affair ended five years ago, Matt thought about it almost daily, wondering if this was an unforgiven sin that held him back from God's blessing. Was that the invisible damage?

OFF TO CHURCH

Jen often said that Sunday mornings were sometimes the worst for Christians. Satan would do everything he could to keep them out of church. Their household got cranky nearly every Sunday morning when it was time to get ready. Their daughters Abby and Erika would argue about some piece of clothing they both wanted to wear. Tommy could never turn off Sponge Bob and get in the shower on time. Matt could think of a dozen things he would rather be doing instead of spending 90 minutes in church. Jen was the spiritual leader of their family every Sunday, but Matt knew he should be.

Matt often prayed during the drive to church for God to keep the voices of distraction out of his head. Matt knew the sounds of the evil wormy voices of condescension and arrogance that he heard in his mind. It was as if they were talking into his ear at church – Where did this guy learn how to park a car? What the heck is she wearing? Why do those people always get here late? When will he stop talking? What makes him think he can sing? Why is that girl playing with her cell phone? Who is kidding who with another mission trip to Hawaii? I can pray better than him. Why can't those people keep their kids quiet? Don't they know I'm praying here? Wow, Mrs. Jones really has been working out! Why is that family always at the altar praying? Oh, look whose back. I guess they got tired of St. John's church. That guy wears the same suit every week. I wonder who paid for those flowers. I'm glad I got out of usher duty this month. How can she afford more tattoos, she barely has a job? What is he wearing? Didn't he know he was going to church this morning? Should I show him how to put his cell phone on vibrate? I can't believe how much they paid for that new organ. I wonder who really gives the most in the offering plate. Why do they ever let that guy speak at the podium? Those kids really are ugly. Time to wrap this thing up. Boy, am I hungry. I wonder who the Eagles are playing today?

***

Matt knew he was supposed to listen for God. He would pray and get thoughts in his head but sometimes he could not tell if they were his own or God whispering to him. He did know that if it was biblical it could be God, but he prayed for something more definitive. He did not need a burning bush but he was looking for just a signal from God to let him know he was not alone. There were many times when he would sit out on their patio at night alone and look at the stars. He was always amazed at the miracle of God's creation, the expanse of the universe. He would think and wonder about what his own small part of it was. Matt had a theory that because the universe was so big, part of the work God had in store for believers after the second coming of Christ, would be to travel to all parts of the universe, to all the worlds unknown to spread the Gospel. Matt was a Star Trek fan so he loved the idea. Every time Matt looked at the stars he prayed for God to send a shooting star right at that moment just to show him God was listening. It never happened that way, but he asked every time he looked up.

TUESDAY

On Tuesday morning, Matt was still at home in his office after everyone else was off to school and Jen had gone to work. He was feeling the stress heavily on his chest and shoulders. He was worrying about some bills he needed to pay. Matt had one finished house on the market to sell for over four months and he had one rental house empty too long because he could not find a tenant that had a real job or could afford the first month's rent and a security deposit. He also had two houses he was remodeling which were taking too long to finish and they were draining cash.

The day before, Matt had spent two hours with a Christian contractor named David who used his "Christianity" as a shield to defend his poor and slow work performance. Matt felt conflicted when he would talk to David about why work was not getting finished and he wanted to be a good example of a Christian with this fellow believer. All of that unraveled when David put the blame for painting work not being finished onto his helper named Walter. Matt reminded David that when they started spray painting the rooms, no prep work was done, no spackling or filling cracks, no sanding, no taping of the wood trim, and they over sprayed onto areas not to be painted. Matt made David re-do it properly. Walter said, "David told me to just spray it to make it look like we did a lot of work." David told Matt that Walter was a liar and a drug addict. Matt stepped between the two to keep them from hitting each other. Because of David, this house was three months behind schedule. Three months the house was not bringing in rent, three months Matt was paying holding costs. Cash is the blood of the real estate business and fast turnover is critical. He felt like he was dead in the water.

Matt got down on the floor in his office and he prayed. Matt always began his prayers with thanking God for all the blessing he had received. He knew Jesus would not abandon him but waiting on God's timing was nearly too much and he did not know how long he could stay on his knees. Matt asked the Lord to look into his heart and take away what was not of God. He wanted to be part of God's will and he asked for God to take away any desires he had that were not part of God's plan. He laid his soul open to Christ and prayed for help and restoration. He called out to God and cried like a child longing to have the touch of his Father.

At the end of his prayer Matt was emotionally spent and he calmed himself with deep breaths. He opened his eyes slightly and through the blur of his tears, in front of him less than six feet away he saw a large and tall figure in a shining pure white robe standing before him. His eyes instantly opened wide. He gasped and jerked himself backward and caught himself with his hands behind him on the floor. Shocked and scared he knew what he was looking at but checked his sanity at the same time. "My God, an angel." he whispered. Matt pushed himself forward and grabbed hold of the desk with his left hand to get his balance while still on his knees. The angel was silent and ominous. He filled the doorway, as tall and as wide and he had a radiance all about him. The angel had brown hair and the irises of his brown eyes looked somewhat larger than a human's. His eyes penetrated Matt's. Matt looked away and closed his eyes for a second as he tried to clear his head. He could physically feel the presence of the angel and Matt looked at him again, his eyes racing, looking from head to foot trying desperately to process what he was looking at. The angel did not speak, he only looked at Matt and he sensed the compassion the angel felt toward him. Matt knew he must pray and thank God that this must be God answering his prayers. He exhaled deeply and on his knees, trembling, he thanked God for showing him that he was not forgotten, and that God knew he needed help and sent this angel to him. Matt prayed and when he lifted his head and opened his eyes, the angel was gone.

Matt was not surprised the angel disappeared and he felt completely exhausted and physically heavy. He was dizzy and could barely get to his feet. He got up and sat back on his desk chair. He looked around the room, the floor and doorway for some sign, or some mark of evidence that what just happened really happened. His mouth and lips were dry and he was thirsty but too tired to move from the chair to get a drink. He needed to check all his senses and try to remember every detail of what he experienced. He sat for a long time and then tears came as he started to weep with joy, overwhelmed that he was visited by one of God's messengers. He could feel in his soul that the angel had been real. He felt washed with God's love and he cried, joyful and relieved and he was no longer afraid.

Matt lost all sense of time. The last he remembered, it was about 10AM. He looked on his computer screen and now it was 1PM. He laughed to himself and thought about what he would tell his wife. Would she really believe him or get mad at him for making a bad attempt at a joke. She had a great sense of humor. A sense of humor that kept them from arguing for the 26 years they knew each other, but Jen never joked about God.

It took Matt another hour to get himself out of the house. He was completely distracted from what he had planned to do for the day and thought instead he would do something simple while he could just think about what he saw in his office and try to figure out why. He needed time to clear his head and pray. He decided to go to one of his houses being remodeled where no contractors were scheduled to be. Matt could take his chain saw there and cut up some dead fallen trees and scrub bushes that needed to be cleared. This would be mindless work that he enjoyed. "No heavy mental lifting" he liked to say. He left his house through his garage and grabbed his saw, his 5 gallon gas can and the smaller two-cycle engine gas can on the way out. He needed to stop for gas for his saw and for his silver gray Ford F150 truck with a crew cab that was parked in the driveway.

He felt dazed as he drove down his driveway and onto a small road that led to one of the main roads and then to the highway. Several cars passed him going the opposite direction. When he stopped at the first intersection, a dark blue older Ford Taurus passed in front of him making a turn. From out of Matt's daze, he saw an angel in the passenger seat of the Ford. He blinked to clear his eyes and turned his head fast enough to see the angel look directly back at him. The driver of the car was an old man who looked to be in his late seventies. Matt felt his heart race. He thought - Am I really seeing angels? Could I be losing it? Is stress getting to me so badly that I'm imagining them? He felt doubt for a moment. A car had pulled behind him and blew the horn to tell him to move out. Matt waved a quick "sorry" wave and took off.

The area where he lived was fairly rural, mostly suburban in between two smaller towns just outside Valley Forge National Park in Pennsylvania. There were many beautiful and some very old historic stone homes. The area had people living here, only 25 minutes from center city Philadelphia, since 1682. Two miles down the road a school bus was stopped with red lights flashing delivering a kindergarten child home in the afternoon. Walking across the street in front of the bus with the child was an angel. Matt saw one other angel standing inside the bus with the other children. It was becoming hard for him to breathe.

A few miles down the road, he pulled up to the gas pumps at GasQuick self service gas station. He immediately saw other angels. One was walking out of the GasQuick store behind a young woman dressed for office work and another angel was standing near two men who were filling gas cans and gas tanks on a trailer full of paving equipment. In the sun the white of the angels robe looked much brighter than the one he saw in his office and they had a shimmering glow about them. Matt could see they were wearing robes over tunics that were floor length. He could not see their feet and they had nothing covering their heads. Every angel he saw was male. They were all tall, at least 6 foot, 9 inches and were broad shouldered with strong necks. They looked like professional football players, about thirty years old, handsome with perfect facial features. They had different colored hair and skin tones, the same different colors as humans have. He found himself just staring at the angels, who were not seen by anyone else.

Matt remembered what he was doing and got out of his truck and opened the back to get the big gas can out. He filled the truck tank and the gas can, and then went inside the store to get a drink. His mouth was dry and he could feel his heart beating fast. Inside the store was another angel standing off to the side watching the customers come and go. Matt made eye contact with the angel and the angel responded with a nod of his head. He carefully walked toward the angel. The idea came to Matt to pinch himself as if to make sure he was not dreaming, so he pinched his thigh through his pants pocket and it hurt. He thought - I guess I'm awake but why did I have to do that so hard? He stopped next to the angel and faced the wall as he spoke to him so no one would see Matt talking to himself. It took Matt a few seconds to muster up the courage to speak to him, and then he asked "Why can I see you?"

"We serve God." the angel replied.

"Am I crazy? Are you real? Should I see a doctor?"

"No. Yes. You are not ill."

Matt laughed out loud. "I can't believe this." he said. He paused for a moment. "Who will believe me? Who can I tell about you guys?"

With a motion of his head and eyes, the angel indicated to Matt that someone was watching him talk to himself. "Oh yeah." Matt said and pulled his cell phone out of his pocket and held it to his ear pretending to talk on the phone. Matt turned and stood beside the angel now both looking the same direction at the customers. The angel did not look directly at Matt and he could not look directly in the angel's eyes because the angel was watching the people in the store. Matt was intimidated by the size and physical presence of him standing so close. He asked "Are you here for me or for all these people?"

"We minister to God's children."

"Can you tell me anything about what is happening to me?"

"You are known to God. Attend to your business."

***

Matt got home at five o'clock that evening. Erika, his 15 year old daughter was home with her brother, nine year old Tommy. They were watching TV. Abby was at her part-time waitress job a few miles from their home. She was nineteen and attending college locally and living at home.

"What's for dinner? We're hungry." said Tommy. He was in 4th grade, big for his age and that pleased Matt very much.

"Feed me Seymour!" Erika said quoting the line from Little Shop of Horrors.

"No soup for you!" Matt said back to her with his best Soup Nazi accent.

One minute later his wife entered from the garage carrying a plastic bag from the local market. "Frozen pizza! Come and get it. No... let me bake it first." Jen always joked that if they had a family crest there would be a pizza in the middle of the design.

Matt calmly waited until they had eaten dinner and the kids were doing homework and on the computer before he approached Jen. He watched her while they ate and thought about how she would react to his angel story. "Jen, come downstairs with me to talk. I gotta tell you about something that happened to me today."

"Is it serious? Do I need a glass of wine or a box of tissues?" she said smiling.

"No. Really, I need to tell you about it."

"OK" she said and they went downstairs to a beautiful game room, media room that he built six years ago. Every time he went down there he thought the room never got used enough. They sat facing each other on a couch in front of a big screen TV.

Matt said "I really want you to listen to what I'm going to tell you and if I look or sound insane, tell me right away."

She put the back of her hand on his forehead. "Well, no fever so you probably aren't delirious". He smiled, took a deep breath and began to tell her about the angel in his office, the angels at the gas station, the one he spoke to and the others he saw the rest of the afternoon.

She let him tell the whole story without stopping him or asking questions. He told her how he was praying that morning and then everything that happened after that. He told her what the angel said and he described each angel he saw, where he saw them and what they were doing. Her eyes were big and on his the entire time. When he finished, she was silent for a moment, then quietly she said "I believe you. I'm a little shocked, but I don't think you're insane." She paused, taking time to carefully choose her words. Matt did not say anything. He waited for her, needing to hear her thoughts. He trusted her completely and she was always his wise counsel. "You know I truly believe in God, in Jesus. You know I believe angels are real. Nothing you've told me is inconsistent with anything in the Bible. People have seen and have been helped by angels since before Moses. Why shouldn't you see angels? I wish I did, but it is you who was given this gift. What does it mean? Have you been praying?"

"I've been praying my brains out constantly for months. You know I've been praying about the business and really, things aren't doing well." He thought to himself - Why can't I still just tell her everything?

"Then that is why you've seen them. You prayed. They're here to help you. But what will they do? Are they here to protect you, us? And to see so many angels! Something is being revealed to you. God does this for a reason. There is nothing random about how God works. You, we better pay attention to what's going on in the world and around us and the kids. With all this bad economic junk we are in…. maybe this is a warning."

"Should I just call the mental hospital and have the white coat guys come and pick me up? Do I have any clean underwear? I have to pack." Matt said, trying to release some of the tension.

"Look, I said I believe you." She took his hand. "This just does not happen to anyone. Angels visited Daniel in the lion's den. They visited the Virgin Mary."

"Oh great, If I'm pregnant…."

"Ya know, even Balaam's donkey saw and angel so don't get too full of yourself."

She smiled and reached out to hug him. They held onto each other and they both felt safe. Jen asked him questions about all the angels he saw. They had talked for half an hour when Tommy came down to them and asked if he could have ice cream. Jen said yes, but only if she could have some also. Matt did not want any. His stomach still had a nervous tense feeling. Tommy ran back upstairs to the kitchen.

"I'm not telling the kids about this and I don't know if there is anyone we can tell. Do you think Pastor Chuck could…"

"You know I'm not wild about Chuck." Jen said.

"You're right. It's just you me and the angels for now until I get further instructions from the boss." he said pointing toward heaven.

"Have you seen any more angels here in the house since this morning?"

"No, and I hope that's good. If I saw them here all the time I'd get pretty concerned, like something's gonna happen."

Tommy yelled down the stairs, "Mom, do you want your ice cream up here or down there with Dad?"

"I'm coming up." she replied.

Matt stayed behind and sat back into the couch. He felt much better after telling Jen about the angels but he still had so much emotion in him and so many questions for God. He also thought he just needed to rest his brain for a few minutes. He found the TV remote under a pillow where Erika usually hid it. He flipped on Fox News. Matt let the weight of his head lay back on the pillow behind him and he closed his eyes and just listened to the background noise of news and commercials for a few minutes.

The news anchor's voice caught his attention, "Dramatic footage of a fire rescue today in south Florida where an elderly couple was forced to jump 30 feet into an inflatable rescue mat from their burning condo in the retirement community of "Seven Palms". The screen showed news video from ground level outside the building. The couple was standing on the outside ledge of their fourth floor balcony as smoke poured out the door behind them. The husband gave his wife a push to send her to the mat below. The instant she was free of the ledge, angels appeared holding both of her arms as she fell and landed perfectly onto the mat. The camera went back up to the husband who himself was now flanked by two angels. He readied himself and jumped while angels went with him and steadied his fall. As soon as they hit the mat, the angels vanished.

They showed the video again in slow motion. Matt was now on his feet. He yelled to Jen to come to him. She came quickly and he told her what he saw. "Did you see any others, on other channels?" she asked.

"No. Not yet." And he started flipping through TV news channels to see it the report again. He stopped at ESPN and saw video of a soccer match and there were at least one hundred angels spread out around the stadium, in the stands standing and watching the crowd. "They're in the stands! There are dozens of them. Oh it figures, the British are playing the Germans".

He watched for a while then flipped to some other channels. A commercial for laundry detergent came on and in the shot, behind a woman pitching soap, he saw a solitary angel standing in the background. Then

33

Matt said, "I'll bet they are all over the History Channel."

"Go back to the news" Jen told him while she sat down and pulled a fleece blanket over her lap. She had left her ice cream in the kitchen. Matt was still standing. He went back to Fox News.

"Holy crap! Oh, sorry Lord. I mean Wow! Jen, I see angels standing with these soldiers. There are a few in with the civilians, the locals too. There and there." He stepped toward the big screen and pointed to where they were. The screen had video from Afghanistan. The shot was mostly American soldiers being interviewed, walking and riding in armored personnel carriers.

"Oh Lord, I wish I could see them." Jen said.

Matt smiled at her and said "I wish you could too, but I'll tell you about everything I see." He found another news channel where angels were at the site of a train crash in India. The angels were kneeling at the sides of a few wounded passengers on the ground.

In a TV news live shot from a street in New York City, the camera panned away from the reporter to show a group of people standing behind him, and in the group, Matt could clearly see a tall, magnificent angel looking right into the camera. "Wow." Matt said, in a whispered half breath. "Dear Lord, what a beautiful creature."

He continued to flip through the TV channels and he would stop at places that seemed likely he would see an angel. He did not see them everywhere but he saw them regularly in some surprising places. Jen brought her Bible and their Strong's Exhaustive Concordance of the Bible down to the basement to have them handy for reference. While Matt surfed the channels, she looked up verses about angels. The initial trend Matt observed was that he saw most of the angels on news video rather than regular produced TV. Documentaries were the next most productive. He told Jen that anything with real life video was best. He did not see any angels on the Cartoon Network.

Matt went to their powder room for a break. While he was seated, he picked a magazine off the top of a small stack on the table next to him. He flipped through some pages and saw an angel in a photo. It startled him and he almost dropped it. He asked himself - Where will this end? Will this work for any photograph?

Matt grabbed the entire stack of magazines and ran up to his office. He went to his book shelves. Matt loved to read biographies, but of mostly historical or political figures of World War II back through the American Revolutionary War. He grabbed some books with photos to see if the same held true as it did in the magazine he just saw. He grabbed A History of Vietnam, two books about FDR and Churchill, Stephen Ambrose's book "The Wild Blue" about World War II bomber pilots, Ric Burns "The Civil War" and David Mc McCullough's "1776" just to make sure angels did not show up in historic paintings. He took all the books back downstairs to be with Jen, who was still watching TV. "Jen, now I see them in photos too."

"Matt this is a miracle. God needs you to see this stuff. We have to figure out why. Tell me if you see any in that book." He was fanning through the pages of photographic journal of World War II.

"Oh my good Lord." Matt said. In the book he found a black and white photo taken from inside a Higgins troop landing craft at Normandy. The photographer was facing forward toward the beach. The boat looked to be at least 100 yards out. Clearly visible was the beach with the iron obstacles in the sand ahead of them. The photograph is primarily of the men in the craft waiting in full gear, helmets, packs, rifles four abreast waiting to stop and have the door drop open. The photo looks like it was taken over the shoulders of the last row of soldiers. But Matt could see three angels in the craft standing in front of the soldiers also facing the beach. The angels were holding tall rectangular shields and their powerful wings were half expanded as if poised to fully open when the landing door dropped open. These angels were there to protect the soldiers from enemy fire and deliver them to the beach.

Another photo from the flight deck of an aircraft carrier, showed a priest kneeling at the side of a wounded sailor who was lying on his back. Matt recognized this photograph because he had seen it dozens of time over the years. The priest and the sailor were both protected by a standing angel whose wings were spread wide around them both and the angel's head was bowed in prayer. It made his heart swell to see God's angels here on earth protecting American service men. He described to Jen everything he saw. She was amazed and excited. His descriptions and the knowledge of this divine angelic protection made Jen cry.

"Matt, maybe you'll see angels in some of our photos. I'll go get the photo albums, and we have hundreds of family pictures on the computer."

"Well yeah… let's try." Matt said. Jen left to get the albums and bring them to him. He thought that it might be nice to look through their own photos, but he was sure that was not the purpose for having been given this ability. When she came back, he sat with her and looked through them right away. Jen brought six albums and her reading glasses. They looked at them in order of oldest to most recent. She missed her parents very much and she was hoping Matt would see angels in a photo with them. The second album had pictures from the vacation with Mark and Lisa in Ocean City, New Jersey. They saw a picture of one of their sand creations. The photo next to it had Mark and Matt posing behind it, the ocean and the beach were behind two of them.

"Jen, there is an angel, right there." He pointed to the spot on the photo where an angel was standing on the beach, knee deep in water looking out into the ocean.

"Matt… that's the day you nearly drowned."

Matt got goose bumps and his eyes got misty. "I guess God's been watching out for us for a long time."

They looked through all the albums and the last one was out of order. It was from the years when Abby was pre-school age. They were both disappointed that Matt had not seen more angels with their family, but neither was surprised. He said "I think catching an angel in a photograph is like catching a flash of lightning. But unless you're photographing something dramatic happening or taking photos of a serious situation where people and believers need help, then you'd be more likely to get an angel in the shot. But that's crazy because no one can see angels so they don't go looking for them. I guess it's not like you can set out to catch them on film because I might be the only guy that can see them anyway."

Jen flipped to some pictures of when Matt's father was sick with cancer. There was a shot of five year old Abby, and Erika who was one year old, with Matt's father on his hospital bed before he died. In the corner of the room was an angel.

***

Matt was also seeing dark smoky swirls around some people on TV. He described them to Jen as looking like ghostly veils of black and gray gas, swirling and half transparent. Occasionally they had the shape of a head and face at one end. He got a clearer look at one that had deep dark black holes where eyes could be. They seemed to intermittently have arms and hands. He did not see any legs or feet attached and they were always in motion and they never touched the ground. They looked to him to be about six feet long. He told her they could not be good and the more of them he saw the more certain he was that they were demons or fallen angels. He knew they were evil. He saw one on a crime scene report and another in an infomercial about buying real estate for no money down. Matt thought that was hilarious and said to Jen, "I knew it!" After a few hours he told Jen it seemed like he was seeing two angels for every one dark figure. Matt started calling the dark figures "gasbags".

He saw the demon gasbags on a crash disaster TV show. On one video clip two appeared at the side of a drag racer right before a car exploded at the start line. As quickly as the flames surrounded the car three angels were with the rescue men who extinguished the fire and pulled the driver from the car. There was one following an accused killer doing the perp walk into a court room. He flipped the TV channel to some old film of Joseph Stalin. There was one large dark gasbag hovering beside him as he waved to a crowd. A popular rock star had one with her as he watched a clip of her at an awards show. He saw two gasbags with a group of congressmen addressing reporters about how the Federal Reserve and the FDIC must buy as much as $1 trillion dollars of toxic assets from banks.

At a different press conference on another news channel the junior senator from Michigan, Anika Hannan was announcing a stimulus program taking place in her state. Several dark figures swirled around her and also around some members of the press who asked questions. Hannan was in the national news regularly as she had become a very visible and vocal supporter of the president's economic recovery plan. Being from the hard hit Detroit area, the president felt she would be an untouchable defender of his policies.

Matt and Jen spent the next eight hours looking at TV and paging through books. The kids asked what they were doing and they told them they were looking for a certain picture Jen needed for a report she was doing for work. They drank three pots of hot tea and they finished a bag of orange Milano cookies and the ice cream Tommy started. Jen wanted to keep notes of what Matt was seeing and how he described it to her but he told her not to bother. "If I'm crazy I don't want you to document it. If this is real the only one who matters is God, and God doesn't need notes."

They stayed up as long as they could watching TV and looking at books. Three hours after they finally went to bed, the alarm clock woke Matt at the usual time, 5:51 AM. It was not enough sleep but it was good and he noticed that he woke in the exact same position he fell asleep. He did not remember any dreams; he just had bone-resting sleep.

WEDNESDAY

It was still dark outside when he got out of bed to wake his daughter Erika for school. He was wearing sweat pants and a t-shirt. He found his slippers on the floor in the dark right where he left them, side by side. He always put them at the same spot because he was organized and he hated to feel around for them on his hands and knees. Whenever he had to leave early in the morning, Matt would put his clothes on the chair by his bed so he could find things in the dark. He would rather get dressed in the dark than turn on a light and wake up Jen.

Matt walked down the hall past the bathroom his daughters shared. Erika's bedroom door was slightly open and it looked like some different light was on inside, not the usual blue glow of her clock radio. As he pushed the door open, he saw an angel sitting on the floor next to her bed. It was not the same angel he saw in his office. The angel's back was against the wall and his eyes were closed. The angel seemed to have a softer white glow about him in the dark. Tears came to Matt's eyes. Silently he thanked God the angel was there. The angel looked at him, smiled, got to his feet and vanished.

Matt stepped into the room and knelt at the side of Erika's bed. He felt the carpet where the angel was sitting and tried to detect some heat or evidence that he had been there. Erika, rolled over to face Matt. She was surprised and half asleep she said, "Daddy what's wrong?" She saw his tears as he wiped his eyes.

"Nothing, I just love you. I'm just feeling mushy."

"Geez you scared me."

"Sorry. Time to get up. Let's go."

She was usually the first to take a shower in the morning in order to get the school bus on time. She was easy to get out of bed compared to her sister. Abby was a three trip wake up. The last year of high school Matt started calling Abby's cell phone from his bed to wake her up. Both of his daughters always slept with their phones. The last thing Abby usually did before she fell asleep at night was text message a friend or her boyfriend.

Matt said to Erika, "You know God loves you?"

"Yeah, I know. He loves you too."

"Boy do I know it." Matt said with a deep sigh, still feeling the emotion going through him.

Erika got moving and Matt went to his office to gather himself and pray. Twenty five minutes later he heard Erika in her bedroom and went over to her. She was finishing doing her hair. The style was with long bangs combed over to one side crossing in front of one eye. He thought she probably moved her hair away from her eye at least 500 times a day.

"Would you please get that hair out of your eye?" he asked.

"It is. I can see."

"How about if I shave that side of your head while you sleep? It was a cool look in the 80's."

"How about not?"

They both went down stairs and she gathered up her things to leave. He could hear Tommy already in the shower. Some miracle must have happened for him to get up by himself. Angelic help, he wondered. Abby would be next to get up and get ready for her first class at the Penn State - Brandywine campus, 30 minutes from where they lived.

They were in the kitchen and Erika's book bag was on the floor by the door to the garage. "Do you want to eat something? Pop Tart or toast. I can make oatmeal." Matt asked.

"No. You know I don't eat breakfast."

"I'm just trying to fulfill my parental responsibility. Hey it's cold outside. In the 30's and will only get into the 40's today. Why don't you wear the new coat you wanted so badly?"

"No. It's not that cold." Erika said while seated at their kitchen counter tying her sneakers.

"Exactly why did you want the coat? Just wear it. A few more degrees and its cold enough to snow. You wanna get sick?"

She pulled on her hooded sweatshirt, zipped up the front, grabbed her book bag and purse, and then headed for the door.

"Do you need any money?" he asked her as he looked into the kitchen catch-all, junk drawer and saw his wallet and keys.

"No."

"Good. Have a good day. I love ya."

"Me too. See ya." she said, and in a rush and a spin she was gone. She was a good girl. Funny, very smart, good grades and she had bundles of energy. She was a slow starter in the mornings but by the time she would come home from school she would be full of stories about what happened with her friends and teachers. Matt often thought what a blessing she was to him and Jen. They were blessed with a chatty daughter.

Matt started a half pot of coffee on the coffee maker and went upstairs and told Jen about the angel in Erika's room. "We have to pray Matt." Jen said as she was finishing getting dressed for work.

Matt was on the bed, lying facing her on his left side holding his head up with his left arm. "Yeah, let's pray in the office."

They waited until Tommy had just walked out the door to get the school bus and Abby had left a few minutes before him. They were alone. Last night Matt showed her exactly where he was in the office when the angel appeared yesterday. Again she stood in the spot where the angel was and she began to cry. She was overwhelmed by the presence of God. "This is like Holy ground. Matt this is so important. We are so blessed. God knows us, he knows our children and he wants to reveal something to you."

They each sat in a swivel office chair and rolled them toward each other. They sat face to face and held hands and bowed their heads. Matt prayed, "Lord Jesus, heavenly Father, we thank you Lord for this day. Lord you are the creator of the universe, all the heavens and the earth. We worship at your feet. We praise your name and thank you for your mercies and blessings. Lord you have blessed me with an amazing gift. Lord I have seen your angels! Your mighty servants here in our home, right in this house Lord! I am humbled and not sure what to do. Why me Lord? Lord please make it plain to me why this is happening. Give me clarity to see all that you want me to see and the wisdom to be able to deal with this gift and be able to know what to do, who to tell and when to tell it. Lord I'm overwhelmed by all this and I want to follow you, to do what you want. Lord I need to hear from you or please have your angels speak to me. Have them tell me what I am to do. We love you Lord. Help us, bless us and give us the courage to deal with what you have planned. Have mercy on me because I'm no Moses. We pray in Jesus' name, Amen."

Jen squeezed Matt's hands and then stood up. She remembered to look on their book shelves for Billy Grahams' book "ANGELS" that she had read and hi-lited a few years ago. "I want to re-read this." she said as she pulled it off the shelf. They walked out of the office and went downstairs to the kitchen. "Oh, I wish I could stay with you today but there is no way I can get out of my regional meeting. Call me or text me if anything happens."

"Don't worry I'll call. Hey maybe I can get an angel to pose for a picture on my cell phone camera. Oh sorry Lord, just kidding." Matt said as he looked toward heaven.

"I should be home by 5:15 and no one has to be anywhere tonight. No meetings or practices. Could we go out for a drive looking for angels?"

41

"Sure. Just me and you, or should we tell the kids? Otherwise if they go with us they are gonna think we're nuts." Matt said as he poured a cup of black coffee.

"Uh yeah… we need to think about that huh? Anyway, remember Matt, God has blessed you and given you a gift. Stay alert and be careful. There has to be a purpose for this."

"Well I really don't think any harm will come to us. We have the best security team in the universe." And with a kiss and a hug, Jen was on her way to work. Matt got himself ready to go and was out the door twenty minutes later to meet a carpenter named Dave.

***

Matt had arranged to meet with Dave about a kitchen where he needed cabinets installed. They decided to meet for breakfast at a diner where they had met several times before. Driving to the diner, Matt did not see any angels or demon gasbags. He theorized that maybe angel and demon activity might be like the weather, some days cool and calm, other days dark and stormy. Matt walked into the diner and as soon as Matt sat down at the table with Dave, he said, "Aw nuts. I forgot the plan for the kitchen. I left it in my truck. I'll go get it."

"Don't worry about it. Let's eat then I'll look at it when we're ready to leave."

So they both drank coffee and ate. They talked about the slowdown in business, politics, some people they both knew and some of the other jobs Dave had done for Matt. They finished eating, paid the check and walked out to Matt's truck. They walked toward the passenger side door of Matt's truck. "The plan is on the floor by the front seat."

Matt had brought his Bible with him this morning. He wanted to do some reading about angels, the accounts he knew well. He also knew he would be doing a lot of praying, and reading his Bible usually helped him to focus his prayers. Dave saw Matt's Bible and said "I didn't know you were a church man."

His comment took Matt off guard. He thought about it for a second and said, "Yeah, I'm a Christian and I'm ashamed that you couldn't tell."

***

While Matt was driving across town, his phone rang. It was a realtor who wanted to tell Matt about a house for sale. Matt pulled his truck over and parked on the city street near an intersection with a traffic light. While they talked, Matt noticed two young men in a low-rider car with loud sound system that slowly went by him and turned at the traffic light. He did not think much of it until the same car came around the block again. This time Matt looked to his left and saw two young teenage girls across the street walking in his direction. The girls were escorted by two angels that walked close behind them. The low-rider car moved slowly at first but did not linger to look at the girls as it did the first time. They accelerated and moved along quickly. It seemed to Matt that the angels must have been visible in some form to the men in the car. He tried to imagine what the angels looked like to the two young men that made them move off so hurriedly. Matt thought they probably looked like large protective fathers.

***

While working and going about his business, Matt found himself to be almost totally distracted by the angels and demons. He saw several of them out during the day and he wanted to watch as much TV at home as he could. He knew he could see more of them all over the world by watching TV and that God would lead him to what he needed to see. Matt wrapped up early and when he got home, he grabbed a handful of pretzels and a drink and headed straight for the basement. He found that he would usually see angels where he did not expect to see them. The demon gasbags were more predictable. He watched a news story of a teenage boy lifting a car off a man who was under it when a tire jack fell. The event was captured on home video. The story was about the boy's amazing strength and an expert commented that rare occurrences of super human or hysterical strength were not recognized by medical science because it is difficult to gather evidence. She said it had become common to credit adrenalin for these feats of strength. What only Matt could see in the video was the lone angel who helped the boy lift the car.

After Jen got home, she joined him back on the couch in the basement. She was ready to settle in for a night of TV and looking through books. With the remote control in Matt's hand, he searched constantly for scenes he would quickly scan and then move on looking for the angels and gasbags. He found video of the January 28, 1986 space shuttle Challenger crew walking to the Astrovan for their ride to the space craft for their launch from the Kennedy Space Center. Matt stopped and watched. Knowing the fate of the crew made it more intense and he prepared himself to see the explosion after liftoff. He watched the famous launch that the entire world knew so well. Three seconds before the voice of Commander Scobee was heard saying "Go at throttle up", Matt saw bright lights streak onto the screen, fly behind and catch up to the shuttle. They seemed to enter into the crew compartment of the Challenger before it exploded. Matt saw the crew compartment fall and over the course of several seconds those same bright lights left it one at a time and streaked away into the heavens. The video continued on and ended with President Reagan's speech to the nation that same day, quoting from the famous poem "High Flight" by aviator poet John Gillespie Magee, Jr. Reagan said the crew of the space shuttle Challenger "slipped the surly bonds of Earth" to "touch the face of God."

***

Later that evening, Matt found Senator Hannan in a taped interview inside the Capitol rotunda. He could see three different gasbags all around her. Matt watched her closely. She was pitching the president's economic recovery package. "The Democratic Steering and Policy Committee is intent on a recovery plan that will work." She paused long enough that it looked like a demon was telling her something. She continued "We need people to be confident that it will work. We have made the choice to create jobs as soon as possible. We may have to spend to get the stabilization we want, but that spending will be targeted." Hannan said.

"Jen, this woman and these things around her just scare the crap out of me. Is she one of them or just under their control? I've gotta see more of her. This is so evil and everybody loves her... at least the liberals think she's miss wonderful."

"You've got to see more video of her on the Internet. We can go find stuff of hers on YouTube."

"Yeah, we can trade spaces with the kids. Let's go throw them off the computers for a while. They should be in bed soon anyway."

They found several clips of Hannan on the Internet and in every one, there were demon gasbags with her.

THURSDAY

Matt was a regular customer at Walmart. He went there often because he liked their prices and he discovered their paint department a few years ago. Matt used most of the same paint colors on his remodel house interiors. They were contemporary colors that he and Jen picked and they always got good reactions from buyers. It made his life simple and he could take the same leftover paint from one house to the next.

On this day, Matt needed two gallons of an exterior paint for a rental house. A city codes inspector told him needed new paint over 2 windows and a back porch railing. Matt had a handyman, Jake, who did small paint jobs for him. Jake did not have a car so when Matt had work for him, he would pick him up at his apartment, buy him a hoagie and a Coke, drop him at the job with his materials and pick him up at the end of the day and take him back to his apartment and pay him.

Matt noticed how busy the store was when he went to get paint. The people seemed to be wound up and cranky. He saw gasbags around the store whispering into the ears of some shoppers and swirling around others. The number of gasbags startled Matt, but he did not fear them because he knew they were already condemned and on the wrong side of God. He sensed that the demon gasbags were aware of him, just as they could see all the other people in the store, but he believed they were unaware of his ability to see them. They never came close to Matt, not like the way they swirled around and whispered into the ears of some people.

There was tension in the air of the store and there were children crying and people arguing. No one was smiling. He saw a man giving a cashier a hard time. People were having trouble with the credit and debit card swiping devices. The store looked messy. He saw a teenager knock over a display, laugh and just walk away from it. A woman looking at a blouse on a hanger missed when she went to put it back on the rack and it fell to the floor. She did not bother to pick it up.

Matt watched the gasbags and the discord they caused among the people, and he felt dirty. He hurried and got his paint and made his way to the checkout. While standing in line, Matt saw two angels appear standing toward the front of the store. Suddenly the angels streaked out of his sight and there was a low rumbling noise from deep below the store. All the lights flickered and went off for a few seconds. Then people all heard the sound of thunder outside. The gasbags disappeared. The rumbling made all the people quiet for a moment. Matt heard people say

"Was that thunder? That wasn't an earthquake was it? Are you OK? It can't be thunder it's a sunny day. Can I help you with that?" At once the mood changed. They were distracted from their own miserableness. It was as if the air was now cleaner and a blanket of calmness covered them all.

***

For Matt and Jen the big news on TV Thursday night was another economic stimulus initiative. The president recognized Senator Anika Hannan's ability to articulate his vision and she had emerged as his best spokesperson. She was articulate and never used a teleprompter. She was so well versed on so many subjects that the press loved her and could always count on her for a good quote or sound bite. The president knew Hannan's natural beauty appealed to everyone and people seemed to never tire of seeing her. She was the only Democrat in Congress whose poll numbers actually went up since last October when the mortgage bubble burst. As his job approval numbers continued to fall; the president reached out to her like a drowning man grabbing for help. Hannan's new point person status angered most of the others in the Democrat leadership. They were jealous of the increasing face time she got on the news networks and she was scheduled to be the main interview this Sunday on "Meet the Press".

Today's announcement was made in the East Room at the White House. The president asked Hannan to introduce him. He controlled every public speaking event he was part of. He decided who said what and who stood where. Today he was surrounded by the Democrat house and senate leaders. The speaker of the house hated Hannan for her beauty, poise, media presence, and her fast rise to prominence on the economic issues. The senate majority leader felt the same way about Hannan and privately referred to her as the Muslim Barbie doll from Detroit. He was worried that he would have to fight her for the senate Democrat leader position one day. The secretary of treasury was also there with them for the announcement. It was his plan they were announcing but the president did not give him a speaking role. The secretary looked like a man whose time was almost expired.

Matt and Jen watched the news after they had dinner with the kids. The report showed video of all of them standing with the president on a raised platform. Hannan gave her introduction and then the teleprompters were raised for the president's announcement.

Matt watched the demon gasbags swirling around all of them. One looked as if it had to be screaming in the ear of the speaker of the house.

Another flew back and forth in front of the entire length of the platform. It looked like it was guarding them, waiting to prevent anyone from approaching from the front. A few gasbags were winding their way through the press corps, stopping here and there chewing on ears. When Hannan spoke one gas bag was around her head. It was occasionally reminding her of what to say. Matt never saw angels speaking directly to people.

Matt told Jen everything he saw. He was sickened by the sight, "Jen I think I'm gonna throw up. Really. This is so evil. I feel nauseous. It looks like the gasbags are telling her what to say! Who are these people?"

"Do you see any angels?"

"No. I don't see any and I've looked at this same story on the other channels. Did you see that!?!" Matt pointed to the TV screen. "The treasury guy just waved his hand like he was swatting at a fly or a bug. It was a demon and it spun around him and took off toward the ceiling...Wow!"

Matt watched the same scene again on the other news channels. He watched the speaker of the house later on TV with Larry King and Matt did not see any gasbags with her. He noticed that the president did not have them near him every time he saw him on TV, but Hannan was surrounded by them wherever he saw her. They seemed to be in a frantic and defensive posture near her. He watched TV as long as he could take it. He stood up and said "I can't look at this anymore. I'm gonna see what the kids are doing." and he went off to find them.

Jen stayed on the couch staring at the TV. She closed her eyes and prayed "Dear Lord Jesus, Mighty God, Heavenly Father. Lord I pray for Matt. I love him so much. He is a good man and he loves you Lord. Please Lord protect him, guide him. Give him wisdom and vision to see the path that you light for him. You have given him this amazing gift and only You know for what purpose. Lord, keep Matt strong and true. Protect him from evil. Bless him, Lord please bless him. Amen."

It seemed clear that the focus of Matt's attention was being pointed toward Senator Hannan. He saw the evil gasbags around her each time he saw her on TV and the Internet. They would seem to always be telling her things or whispering into her ears. As attractive and charming as Hannan appeared on camera, the flurry of the evil around her was overwhelming to Matt. He asked himself - What could she be up to? Who is she connected to? He did as much research about her as he could.

SENATOR ANIKA HANNAN

United States Senator Anika Hannan was the second term junior senator from Michigan. She was elected to her first term in 1998. She was the first Muslim American female elected to the US Senate. Hannan made her way to Washington after serving in the Michigan State Senate from 1995 to 1998. Hannan had won a special replacement election to fill the seat of a senator who was killed in an auto accident. That senator died after he drove his car into the base of a concrete highway bridge while returning to his home late one night. Police said he survived the crash because of his seatbelt and air-bag, but they theorized that he got out of his car on his own after the crash and walked 40 feet before he died from a severely broken neck. They found paint from another car on his driver side doors and they were never able to explain how he got out of his car and walked that far with his head twisted backward.

Anika or "Niki" Hannan attended private Muslim schools in Ann Arbor, Michigan and then graduated in 1985 from Smith College, an all women college in Northampton, Massachusetts with a BA in intercultural studies. She then received a law degree from Stanford University Law School in 1989 and afterward returned home to live with her parents in Ann Arbor. She worked in Detroit as a community activist and organizer while also working toward a doctorate in public administration. She earned her PhD in 1994 from the University of Detroit. She was very active for Democrat political causes and worked hard on making herself very visible in her state senate district. She never married or was ever linked romantically to anyone. The perception of her was that she was a dedicated, tireless and driven worker.

Anika Hannan was the first generation American daughter of Iranian immigrants. Her father and pregnant mother came to the United States in 1967, the same year Rezza Shah Pahlavi, staged his own elaborate coronation ceremony, calling himself "Shah en Shah" - King of Kings of Iran. The Shah of Iran was placed into power by the British and the United States. The Shah became an indispensible ally of the West. This western interference earned the US and Britain the lasting hatred of large sectors of the Iranian public and it helped to unite Shiite clericalists, communists and nationalists behind hatred of the perceived foreign intrusion. The Shah's departure in January 1979 from Iran to seek medical treatment opened the door for the return of Ayatollah Khomeini to Iran on February 1, 1979. That year, the Islamic Republic, appeared on the ballot unopposed, and was approved by 98% of the voters in nonsecret elections. Khomeini incited Iranian militants to attack the United States on November 4, 1979 and the American Embassy in Tehran was overrun and 52 employees taken captive. The American hostage crisis began and lasted 444 days.

Anika was born in Detroit in 1967, two months after her parents arrived there. Her father left Iran out of disgust for the Shah and the ruination of his traditional Muslim beliefs. His breaking point was the Shah's White Revolution, which included land reform, the extension of voting rights to women, and the elimination of illiteracy. As much as he hated the west he was also a businessman and he saw opportunity in America and was encouraged to go there by his religious leaders.

Her father worked very hard in the automobile business and by 1979 he owned his own very successful car dealership near Ann Arbor, Michigan. Mr. Hannan joined a secret Wahhabist group of Muslims in the Detroit area. He tried to distance himself from other Muslims who were less extreme, but because he was a business man in a very public business, he struggled with the need to deal with non-Muslims and less fundamentalist Muslims. He justified working with them all because the work he was doing to influence other American Muslims to Wahhabism was the purpose of all of his work.

Over the years he stayed connected to the new fundamentalist Muslim regime that was regaining authority in Iran. In the 1980's he wanted to play a part in restoring his conservative sect in Iran and considered returning there when the Ayatollah Khomeini took over. He was persuaded by the religious hierarchy to stay in America where he could be useful in the effort to make America pay the price for their interference in Iran. In 1980 he joined a group in America whose purpose was to financially support Iran in their war against Iraq and Saddam Hussein. Iraq was supported by the United States. He secretly worked with that group until the end of the Iran Iraq war in 1988. Mr. Hannan then moved his support to the remnant of the Mujahideen in Afghanistan which became Al-Qaeda. Al-Qaeda's mission is to overthrow and destroy non-Muslim countries i.e. America, western nations and Israel. In 1989 he joined the secret group called Arish-Asad, an American wing of Al-Qaeda. He would continue his personal holy-war.

***

Samir Omar was placed with Anika Hannan by the Arish-Asad at the time she was told by her father to run for the state senate seat opening in Michigan. He moved on to Washington DC with her. Omar had no particular skills only his extreme devotion to Al-Qaeda. Omar came to the United States in 1982 by himself from Saudi Arabia. He claimed to have a degree from King Saud University in Riyadh, but no one could ever confirm it. He was fluent in Arabic, French and English. He had no family. Omar had a medium build, black eyebrows and he shaved his head. He was shorter than Senator Hannan and when she wore heels she was always at least four inches taller than him. Omar could act. He was able to play the part of an efficient assistant. He was polite but distant to all of Hannan's office staff. His official position with her was Assistant to the Senator.

Amy Grace Daly was Hannan's Chief of Staff in her Washington office. She had all operational responsibility for the office and the six home state offices in Michigan that also reported to her. Amy was a fun, full figured, single red head. She was a long time law student who was a little messy and always had a small spill, stain or some noticeable wrinkle on her clothes. Amy idolized Anika Hannan. She loved her natural beauty and style. She envied Hannan's ability to speak extemporaneously, her poise and her strong media presence. Amy was the keeper of Hannan's schedule and she traveled with Hannan and kept her on time while on the road. Amy enjoyed being with Hannan and felt that working for her was her dream job. However, Amy was not included in policy or issue discussions. Hannan kept all of that to herself and the senator also wrote her own formal speeches and press releases.

Omar and Amy almost never spoke to each other. They communicated almost exclusively by email even though their offices were next door to each other. Omar kept his office door closed when he was in it and Amy's door was always open. It did not take new staff long to pick up on Omar's vibe and when they would eventually ask a senior staff person about him, they would say that Omar was "from the dark side."

***

Matt's neighbor Rob had a TiVO recording device he did not use. Rob once complained to Matt that his former wife bought it to record soap operas and home decorating shows. Since she had moved out, the TiVO sat under his DVD player and reminded him of his ex-wife every time he looked at it. Matt remembered that while he was wishing he had one to catch anything interesting during the day when Matt was out. He thought he would record certain news shows on TV where Hannan would likely appear. He asked Rob if he could borrow it and Rob was more than happy to lend it to him.

***

Matt and Jen spent most of the rest of the evening watching TV news searching for anything they would see of Hannan. Jen brought her laptop to the basement. If Matt saw some activity, they would usually be able to find the same video on the Internet and take a second look. They could also look for additional videos of that person or event.

The evening turned into a long night, and Matt was tired and his brain was on overload. Jen had fallen asleep right next to him on the couch. He got up from the couch slowly so he would not wake her. He had to stand up and stretch his stiff knee. As he stood he turned away from the TV looking past Jen, to the back of the room where the lights were turned down low. There in the corner stood an angel. His head nearly touched the ceiling and he was surrounded by a soft white glow of light.

Matt gently woke Jen and with a calm voice so as not to startle her, he said "Jen... there is an angel with us right now." He pointed to the back corner. He spoke in the same quiet voice he used when they walked in the woods and spotted an animal he did not want to frighten away.

Jen sat up and turned around but saw nothing. The angel looked at Matt and then looked at Jen. He smiled, bowed his head and vanished.

"Jen he looked at you...he saw you and he smiled." Matt's eyes moistened with tears and his throat lumped up so he could barely speak. "Jen, God knows us. His spirit is in our house." He had to force out his words in a whispered voice as he got on his knees in front of Jen who had sat up on the couch so she could turn around to look. He hugged her and they held on to each other feeling the joy of the presence of the angel and the Holy Spirit. Then they prayed together.

IRAN

In the spring of 1980, one year after the Ayatollah Khomeini rose to power in Iran, thirteen year old Anika Hannan traveled to Tehran, Iran with her father. Her mother did not make the trip because her father said it was not worth the expense to bring her. Anika was the only child of her parents. Her mother lost the ability to have more children when Anika's father kicked her mother in the stomach during a beating when she was pregnant with their second child. It was the beginning of the fourth month of the pregnancy and they did not know she was pregnant. The baby was stillborn. It was a boy and when he found out he had lost a son, he beat his wife again.

Mr. Hannan was a sadistic husband who never hesitated to punish his wife for the slightest infraction of his rules. Anika's mother submitted to his will and resolved herself to that kind of life with him. Her only wish ever for herself was to not die a painful death.

Anika's father wanted to go back to Iran to meet with his contacts and find out for himself what he could do to help the militant Muslim cause. He also thought it would be an opportunity to take Anika away from the Muslim school she went to in Ann Arbor and give her a more intense experience with the Ulama, the scholars of the Koran. Anika could speak Farsi – the most widely spoken version of Persian Arabic as well as English and was also studying French and Spanish in school.

As a girl she was not allowed to be in a Muslim classroom with boys, but Mr. Hannan bribed the teachers and arranged for her to hide in a closet in the classroom for five hours every day the classes were held so she could listen to the teachings. Her father would place her in the closet, give her some water and a piece of flatbread and tabrizi – white cheese and lock her in before the others arrived. There was barely enough room for her to sit on the floor of the closet so half of the time she would stand and lean against the back wall. She often fought off sleep and frequently felt like she would suffocate from the lack of air flow and the heat. When the class was ended for the day, she had no choice but to stay there until he came for her. Her father was often late.

The Mu'allim, the teachers, taught Sharia and the sunnah, the ways of the prophet. The teachers were all men and there were several of them. There came a point when Anika's father asked the Mu'allim if she was learning. None of them had ever spoken to her or helped her privately as it was not allowed. Whatever Anika gained from the class was her responsibility. Four of the teachers suggested they test her. They insisted on testing her alone in a hotel room. The teachers said they would return her to him afterward.

The testing was brutal. They spoke to her in a different dialect of Farsi she did not understand very well. They hit her when she did not give a proper response. One teacher claimed that she made a sexual advance toward him right there in the hotel room. They all agreed that she had done it and individually they each succumbed to the sexual advances of this thirteen year old girl and each of the men raped her.

When they returned her to her father, they insulted him and beat him and told him how his American whore daughter had seduced all of them. They threatened to tell everyone about his filthy daughter and they told him how he should be filled with shame. The teachers also explained to him a way he could redeem his honor. Mr. Hannan accepted everything they said. Later he beat Anika severely.

The technique was old and it was the same one used to turn some Muslim women and girls into suicide bombers. They would rape the girls and then tell them they have no worth. Shame and guilt would be heaped on them and their families and they would be convinced the only way to restoration was to become a martyr for Allah in the fight against the infidels. The Mu'allim told Anika's father that his honor could be restored by her service to their cause. Two weeks later when the bruises on Anika's face had healed enough, they left Tehran to go home to Michigan. They had been in Iran for six weeks.

The emotional damage done to Anika was devastating and she never recovered. Her defense to the stress her father put her under was to concentrate on whatever task she had at hand. Her school work, studying, forced prayers or chores at home. There was no pleasure or joy in her life. She became detached from her own existence. She felt like a distant observer to what was playing out in front of her every day. Her conversation and responses became automatic and she showed little emotion until her college years when she realized that without social skills she would never be able to achieve what her father wanted. She pushed herself to interact with American adults and students her own age.

Anika Hannan became the center of a plan that would weaken America and buy back her father's lost honor.

FRIDAY

After three nights of watching TV until late with Matt, Jen was tired and she was forcing herself to stay focused on what she had to do at work. She was a regional vice president of a managed health care company and she spent most of her time negotiating contracts with health-care providers. She also did presentations to hospitals and large companies to explain changes in benefits and coverage from the provider and the consumer sides.

Jen was naturally disciplined. She always ate well and tried make sure her family did also. In high school, Jen was a track team distance runner and that is how she still kept fit. She ran a 2 mile course around their neighborhood nearly every day, in all weather. When it was cold, and if Matt was home he would always have a hot cup of tea ready for her when she finished her run. As a runner, she was always able to push herself to put on her running shoes and go out the door for a run. She felt bad when she did not run and she would feel runner's remorse, a feeling of guilt from missing a run. She knew it had to do with an effect almost like withdrawal when the endorphins put in her system during a good workout or strenuous run would begin to decrease. She liked it because it was a physical reminder to go run.

Lately Jen was feeling sleep deprived from staying up late every night with Matt watching TV and looking through all kinds of books that had photographs. Jen brought books and magazines home from the library about American politics, the Middle East, Israel, Iran and anything related to current events.

With all the things swirling around them, Jen stayed in the Word. She made time to read her Bible because she wanted to hear directly from God. The Lord did softly speak to her through His Word. The message she was getting was to wait on the Lord. Jen liked to read in the Old Testament and then as she felt led, she would go to the New Testament to read and then meditate and listen. She felt the sense of peace she needed and received the guidance to stay where she was and wait to be led.

1-800

Matt was anxious about the situation he was in. He knew that worry was an insult to God but his emotions and not knowing what the purpose of all this was, was getting the best of him. While parked in his truck writing a check to the electric company for a bill that was past due, he heard a news radio report about an anonymous tip line the FBI had established and how successful it had been. Over the last few years they had received thousands of tips that led to hundreds of arrests, convictions and deportations.

Matt thought that the FBI could be where he is being led. He wondered - Did God give me this news report to hear? I've been praying for guidance and God uses all kinds of things to guide His people. Matt wanted to tell someone about what he had been seeing. Matt and Jen had some good friends at church he wished he could talk to about this but he thought about how he would react himself if one of his friends told him the same thing. Matt doubted he would believe anyone who said they could see angels on a daily basis. He knew he would want proof and Matt could not provide any kind of evidence, even to Jen. Matt also did not know how long he could keep looking at the gasbags because he sensed evil growing and their intensity level rising. Matt had a headache everyday and he knew it was from the stress of seeing the demons and the overload of information coming at him. He felt like his mind was not getting any rest.

If Matt were to call the FBI, he did not know what he would tell them. He had no facts or anything tangible, but at that moment he felt like he would burst. He thought - What else would God expect me to do? I'm not going to physically do anything to a United States senator. All I can do is tell someone else to do something. He used his cell phone and through information, he located the FBI tip line and made the call. He got a recorded message with instructions and a personal ID number to protect his anonymity. The recording told him to write down the number and leave a voice message at the tone. He painfully started to speak, leaving his message. As soon as he said "Senator Hannan" a live person came on the line and spoke to him.

"This is Special Agent Rogol with the Federal Bureau of Investigation. May I have your name please?"

Matt was startled and he did not want to say anything.

"We know who you are Mr. Davidson, our database is pretty extensive. Your call is being recorded and will be treated confidentially, but obviously we know who calls us."

Matt thought he should just hang up but since they already knew who he was he continued "Well... I called because I've seen patterns of activity around Senator Anika Hannan and it looks bad."

"What do you mean by "bad" sir?"

"I don't think she's telling the truth when she speaks. There is something sinister about her."

"You would be surprised how often we hear that about politicians."

"Look, she... I mean her parents are from a pretty hostile country."

"Do you mean to say her parents are from Iran, Mr. Davidson?"

"Yes, she is a Muslim."

"Are you a Christian Mr. Davidson?"

"Yes. Evangelical Christian."

"Do you have a problem with other religions and other faiths? How do you feel about Mormons, Hindus, Quakers, Sikhs, Seventh Day Adventists, Rastafarians, Catholics and Jews?"

"Hey, I don't have a problem with any.... Look, I'm not a racist. I don't care that she's a Muslim."

"But you brought it up sir."

"Yeah, well I guess I did and I'm sorry. What I was trying to say is I think she has some connections to some bad guys." Matt could not believe he just said that – bad guys?!?

"Mr. Davidson there are a lot of, as you say, "bad guys" in the world. Could you be more specific?"

"I've seen some things swirling around her when I see her on TV." Matt wanted to stay away from the word demon. He felt himself drowning in his own pile of crazy.

"Do you mean ghosts Mr. Davidson?"

"Well kinda, they look very unearthly."

"Mr. Davidson, I'm sorry to say that Skully and Mulder no longer work here."

"This was really a big mistake. I'm sorry I called."

"Thank you for calling the Federal Bureau of Investigation. Please call again if we can be of assistance."

Matt shut his phone, leaned his head way back against his truck head rest, closed his eyes and said to himself out loud "I am so stupid."

While Matt was on the phone with the FBI, Jen was at her office gathering her materials for a presentation she had to make that afternoon to a company across town. Her office was on the second floor of a large old mansion that was converted to commercial office space. The building had beautiful woodwork, doors, hardwood floors, window trim, moldings and wood balusters and railing up the stairs to her office.

Jen had her computer bag with shoulder strap over her left shoulder and around her neck. Her arms were full with a box of printed materials and her purse strap in her right hand. As she moved to the top of the stairs the strap of her computer bag got caught on the top baluster post. Jen stepped off the top step and at the same time an invisible angel, gently flipped the strap up and clear of the post. Jen rushed down the stairs safely and took her things to her car.

***

Matt knew he acted hastily. The call to the FBI was him reacting emotionally to his situation. He did not first think about what might happen or how the FBI would respond. Most importantly, Matt did not pray first or seek Jen's council before he put himself on the radar screen of the FBI. He figured that now they knew him as a nut. Some kook who sees ghosts. He did not know where all of this was leading, and if he would really ever need the FBI, how would they respond now that he was on their list of racist nut jobs. He called Jen and told her what he did.

"Hey Jenny, ya busy?"

"Yeah and I've got a headache brewing. I really have to get out tonight and go for a run. I am so tense." She was in her car driving to her meeting.

"Guess who I talked to today."

"Oh I don't know…God?" He could hear a smile in her voice.

"No, but almost as powerful. The FBI"

"And why would that be?" now her voice was frowning.

"Because I'm an idiot." Matt explained what he did. She could hear that he was beating himself up over it and she told him it was OK. She said that no matter what happened or whatever mistakes they think they make along the way, it is all part of God's plan and He was in control. Matt really needed to hear her say that and he thanked God for her.

***

The routine for Jen and Matt had become - dinner with the kids at about 6PM and then the two of them would head to the basement to watch TV and catch video of Senator Hannan, check the Internet and look through books and news magazines. This was the fourth night in a row Jen and Matt wanted to be in the basement. Tommy and Erika were upset about their parents' new intense interest in the news. They had always watched some evening news before, but now the six or seven hours a night routine was getting old. Abby was not effected as much because she was usually out evenings working her waitress job, studying or with her boyfriend. When the kids joined them to watch TV, Matt developed a few facial signals to let Jen know when there were angels or demons on screen. Tommy did not have enough interest in news to hang in there with them very long but Erika was a news junkie in training.

A program about space flight caught Matt's attention and he listened to "Buzz" Aldrin, the second man to set foot on the moon, discuss the flight and moon landing of Apollo 11. Included were all the famous photos and film clips. They ended the Aldrin interview with his photo standing on the moon with the American flag. Behind Aldrin, in the distance, stood a solitary angel on the surface of the moon. Matt jumped off the couch and yelled "Yes!" and cheered he like he was at a football game.

"Dad! What is up with you?" Erika said. "Even I've seen that picture a million times. Settle down dude."

Matt laughed at himself and at Erika. "Hey... you know I love space stuff. Gimme a break."

Jen was laughing at both of them. "I think we all need a break. I know. Let's go load the dishwasher and do some laundry!"

"Are you kidding? This is Friday night. You people really are domestically obsessed." Erika said rolling her eyes.

"Yeah, maybe. But at least we will have clean dishes and clothes. Go get your laundry basket from your room." Jen said.

Matt added "And tell that boy, you know, your brother... what's his name, to bring his stuff too."

DEALING WITH STRESS

Senator Anika Hannan had almost no outlets for stress, but she did have her car. Hannan usually drove herself to her office every day and to her personal business around Washington. When she was in law school in California, her father finally agreed to allow her to get a driver's license and he bought her a car. Her first was a Mercedes-Benz station wagon. As large and un-sporty as it was, she loved the independent feeling of going wherever she wanted to go, and she liked to drive fast. Hannan was excited by speed and she drove fast every time she was behind the wheel. In Washington DC, Hannan had a special Michigan license plate as a member of the United States Senate with the designation USS 2, United States Senate and the number 2 because she was the junior senator from Michigan. All police recognized the license plates and usually gave the drivers only warnings or undeserved breaks from traffic and speeding tickets. Hannan had been stopped at least once a month since being in Washington DC. Fortunately for her, her habitual speeding stayed out of the newspapers.

Hannan's car was a powerful black 2006 Mercedes-Benz CLS Barabus-D custom V12 sedan. It was elegant, thick and powerful and she felt safe in it, even at 140 miles an hour. It was her only personal luxury. On some stressful nights, she would get onto Interstate 295 and race north to Baltimore and back. If she had more time she would head south to Richmond Virginia on Interstate 95 and try to make the 220 mile round trip back to Washington in under two hours. On straight stretches she would exceed 160 miles per hour. Hannan would escape into the hypnotic night time rhythm of the highway. She burned a CD with heavy metal music. Songs with heavy fast base lines and intense electric guitar that she played loud as she raced with the reflective road markers and the surface lines rushing past her, all made visible in her head lights. She imagined herself streaking past stars through the blackness of space. She could break away from Earth in her car. Three times she had forced cars off the road that were trying to get out of her way. In her rear view mirror she watched the accidents that she caused as she accelerated away. She had several other close calls and incidents with other vehicles and deer on the highways, but when she was driving she did not care about accidents or the potential for her own destruction. Hannan felt alive while driving fast and she craved the feeling of control over speed, when she had very little control over her own life.

SATURDAY EVENING

Most of Saturday evening was spent with Matt and Jen still watching as much angel and demon activity as they could find on TV. Abby usually got home from her waitressing job around 11:45PM or midnight. Matt was still not comfortable with her driving her car late at night. He just felt she or any woman was vulnerable at night on the roads. When Abby walked in the house, she found Jen in the living room sitting in the center of the couch with a big pillow on her lap where she had her Bible open on top of it and her concordance open on the couch to her right.

"I thought you'd be in the basement with Dad watching TV. What is it with you two anyway, watching so much news lately? I'm surprised to see you sitting here." Abby said as she sat down on the love seat opposite the couch.

"Yeah, I know. We seem to be a little media intense lately, huh?" Jen said as she slipped off her reading glasses and rubbed the bridge of her nose. Jen did not enjoy that encumbrance of middle age.

"I'll say. It's like you two are on a mission."

Jen laughed and smiled. "It feels like we are. Let's just say Dad and I are really concerned with what's going on right now with the economy, Dad's business, all the stuff going on. Life is very intense right now."

"Hey, don't I know it. Tips at the restaurant are really down. People are ordering fewer entrees, more appetizers and less adult beverages."

"Poor girl. You just have to flirt more. It always paid off for me when I waitressed."

"That only really works with the guys. Half my customers are the girlfriends of the guys. Where's Dad? Still in the basement?"

"No. He went up to the office."

Abby stood up. "I want to feel him out about me going with Josh's family to the Outer Banks." She had already told Jen about the idea. "They rented a really cool house on the beach and it looks huge, six bedrooms and a pool. Wanna see it? I can show it to you on some rental website. You'll love it."

"No. Show me later. Go talk to Dad before he goes to bed. I did talk to him about it and he's pretty OK with the idea."

"Yeah, I'll go talk to him now." Abby said and she went upstairs.

Matt was at his computer printing out a lease for a possible new tenant. The office was half dark with only two desk lamps on and light from his computer screen.

"Hi Daddy." She came in and sat in a chair at the desk next to his.

"Hola chica bonita. Donde es el quarto de banjo?"

"Your Spanish is getting worse." She said very matter of factly.

"Was I speaking Spanish? It sounded Japanese in my head."

Abby laughed "Daddy, you're so silly."

"As the great sailorman Popeye said, "I yam what I yam and that's all what I yam."

Abby sat and watched him finish what he was doing before she said "Dad, Mom told you about Josh's family asking if I can go on vacation with them to the Outer Banks. What do you think? Is it OK? They rented a really great place for the first week in June."

Abby and Josh had been dating for almost a year. Josh was her first real boyfriend and the two of them always handled themselves maturely and to Matt, they seemed to truly care about each other. He turned to face her and said "I'm fine with you going with them, really. You and Josh have been very reasonable together. No emotional chaos, like some of your friends seem to go through on a weekly basis. He's a good guy. I like the way he treats you and I'm sure he knows I'd destroy him if he ever hurt you, so… it's all good."

"Josh likes you a lot too. Except for the destroying thing."

"Abby, as casual and as expected and normal as your relationship with Josh may be to you, it affects me too. I'm just speaking for myself, not for Mom, but I realize the time has come when you will start having more people in your life. I think I'm ready. I mean, we will have to start sharing you with other people who love you, new people who will love you. You will someday be a full member of another entirely different and separate family from ours … but you're still my girl, and I will always, always, always love you."

Abby stood up and went behind Matt's chair and hugged him from over his shoulders. "I love you Daddy."

SUNDAY

The first time Matt went to church after he started seeing angels, he thought he would see them everywhere. He expected even the parking lot to be filled with them, but as he and the family arrived, he did not see any. When they entered the church, he saw one angel in the lobby. It looked like it was praying while standing beside two older men who were talking to each other. Matt told Jen he wanted to sit further in the back so he could look around and watch the entire sanctuary. They usually sat in the fifth row front left. When Tommy ask why they were not sitting in their usual spot, he told him that he thought he may have to get up and go to the men's room and didn't want to disturb anyone. In the sanctuary he saw three angels. One angel was seated next to an elderly woman who Matt knew was having health problems. Another angel was standing to the far right next to a window along a wall. The angel stood there the entire service and never moved. The third angel sat in the front pew, just right of center and he looked like he was praying with his head bowed the entire service. Matt never saw him move.

The gasbag demons were already there when Matt and his family arrived. He spotted six and they were relatively calm. Not frantic like others he had been seeing everywhere else. The gasbags left the sanctuary when the preaching became stronger and when the name of Jesus was proclaimed. The demons believe that there is one God and they tremble at His name. They would flee as if they could not bear to hear His name. And then they would slowly reappear later like sneaking rats.

THE FRENCH CONNECTION

Victoria Renard was a 45 year old French citizen and former fashion model living in Paris. She was discovered in 1987 when she was nineteen years old attending college in the United States studying English literature at the University of Southern California. Her modeling career took off quickly and she had a healthy athletic look that was popular then. She worked with top fashion designers in commercial modeling and haute couture. Victoria Renard became one of the elite models in the world but never quite in the supermodel category. By 1993 she was doing most of her work in Europe. Around the same time she had opened her own modeling agency in Paris. Tall with raven black shoulder length hair, she was recognized everywhere she went and she loved the attention.

Antonio Jurado was a handsome Spanish Formula One World Race Championship Series driver. He met Victoria at a fashion show in Milan in 1994. Their romance ignited as fast as he drove his cars and by the end of that year they were married in a lavish event in his home city of Barcelona.

Together they lived a glamorous lifestyle. Three beautiful homes, one in Paris, one in Barcelona, and an apartment in New York City. They traveled the world with his racing tour and went to America often. Victoria was most comfortable in her expensive world. Lack of money was always a concern for her but neither she nor her husband had any skills for investment. They were young and beautiful and felt they could always earn what they needed.

In January 1996 Victoria gave birth to twin sons, and the fashion media celebrated them as the perfect family. Antonio was a proud father of his sons. Victoria had done modeling work through most of her pregnancy and even in the late months. She was praised for bringing glamour to the pregnant mother.

Victoria Renard was intimately familiar with all the important social circles of Europe. She partied and spent weekends with royalty, billionaires, prime ministers and movie stars. She had even closer relations with her own French society elite. She had friendly contacts with Saudi Princes who offered her the world to be with her. She always flirtatiously turned them down but in her mind she thought of their proposals as money in the bank, her personal rainy day source of money.

After the Clinton sex scandal became front page news all over the world in 1998, the leadership of Al-Qaeda realized how easy it was for a woman to have access to the President of the United States. A woman with close personal contact with any man could do anything from influence him on any given subject to commit blackmail or be in close enough proximity to murder that man. They believed that with a well planned effort, any male figure in American government would be reachable in the same way. Al-Qaeda was determined to establish female contacts with American political figures and they needed a recruitment process for convincing women to cooperate. Because of familiarity with Victoria Renard through Saudi connections, she seemed the perfect tool.

Al-Qaeda studied the men on the American political landscape and tried to determine who would most likely, in the next cycles of presidential elections to have the best chance of winning the Presidency of the United States. They produced a list of twenty names. Their method of creating the list was sophisticated. They hired a New York public opinion polling company and they consulted Las Vegas odds makers. They knew their list must be flexible and some names would be added as new faces appeared as rising stars. Others would be taken off the list forever like Howard Dean and John Kerry in 2004. They code named this effort - Planted Garden.

***

The Monaco Grand Prix at Monte Carlo was Victoria Renard's favorite race. It was nonstop partying and she would meet with all her friends from all over the globe. It was a week of glamour, fashion shows, beautiful people, politicians, celebrities and paparazzi. It was the most glamorous race venue in the world. Antonio Jurado loved the atmosphere and he loved the race course because of the challenging turns, hills, the tunnel and the straits where they could accelerate. The race at Monaco gives the advantage to the skill of the drivers over the power of the cars. The backdrop of the beautiful boulevards and harbor filled with luxury yachts and the historic city of Monte Carlo made it the most popular race in all of Formula One racing.

The 1996 race was as exciting as any other. Victoria watched the race from a suite in a hotel looking down at the start finish area. She preferred to be with Antonio at the starts to kiss him good luck and to be at the end with him in the pit or the winner circle, but from track level the noise of the race made her uncomfortable and she could only see a small fraction of the race course.

Early in the race, Antonio was in twelfth position, running strong and moving up. The fastest part of the course was between Sainte Devote and Massenet at turn two called Beau Rivage where speeds reached 170 miles per hour. The race is run on the city streets, and along the Beau Rivage was a ten story apartment building with an unobstructed view of the race course. An Al-Qaeda operative rented two end apartments on the top floor from where the race could be watched. Because the apartment was rented well in advance of the race, he had to pay a high premium price to get them both.

Two men took positions in the end apartment three days before race day. They provisioned themselves with food and supplies so they had no need to leave the apartment. These men were French sharpshooters who were hired contract killers. They did not know who they worked for. They only knew who their target was and they were paid twenty five thousand dollars each in advance and would be paid the same again after their work was complete with the result their client wanted.

The shooters camouflaged an area on their apartment balcony by using the lounge furniture to block all possible views of their weapon. One was the shooter and the other his spotter. They practiced their gun sighting on several cars going past them at top speed during practice laps and during the first laps of the race. On lap thirteen, Antonio's black Ferrari with the red number 75 flashed past their apartment at 169 miles per hour. Two cars followed him close behind. The shooter fired at his open wheel left front tire causing it to explode and send his car wildly out of control hitting the retaining wall and launching his car into a horizontal spin. It flipped upside down and slid on Antonio's head for 160 yards where it was struck by one of the trailing cars ripping Antonio's car in half and sending debris of both cars all over the road. Antonio was dead.

Victoria did not see the wreck happen. She was told when she got to the hotel room where she had planned to settle in for the race. She collapsed when she saw the video replay.

MONDAY

Monday morning, Matt pulled into the GasQuick at 9AM to get his usual 20 ounce cup of black coffee. He remembered that he forgot to bring his water bottle from home. He normally took his bottle everywhere during the day. Jen got him used to drinking water for all the 100 same reasons she did. Matt walked to the back of the store to the cold drink section and picked up a bottle. He turned to his right and there walking straight toward him was Pam, the woman he had an affair with five years ago. Matt saw a demon right behind her, over her shoulder.

"Hi handsome." Pam said. Matt instantly noticed that she looked great and better than he remembered. He noticed a few laugh lines at the sided of her mouth that were not there before and her hair was longer and lighter colored. She had a reasonable fake tan, not one of those hideous "Shake & Bake" tans Abby and Erika could spot from a mile away.

"Pam, hey it's nice to see you. It's been a while." Matt was within two feet of her and he noticed himself backing away from her and the demon.

"It's been more than a while." Pam said "Matt you look great. A little grayer, I like it. I always hoped I'd bump into you somewhere around here."

"Well I guess this is your lucky day."

"Wanna get lucky?" she said in her flirtatious way.

"No, I'm sorry, I didn't mean it like that..." He wanted to distance himself from the demon that was within feet of him. The demon was unaware that Matt could see it. It looked at Matt a few times, studying him. Matt felt as if he was trying to calmly ignore a tarantula or a scorpion crawling on his own face.

"Relax Matt. I was just joking. Are you OK?" Pam noticed his unease. To her he seemed tense and distracted, not the funny, steady and unperturbed man she had once been passionate about.

"I'm fine. Just some work stress." He was looking past her at the demon when he spoke.

"Who isn't stressed now days? My husband is a mess. I don't even..."

"Yeah, but how are you?" He didn't want to hear about her husband but he felt like he had to ask her about herself even though he did not want to hear the answer. He just wanted to get away from her and this hideous thing slobbering over her. He could see the demon push her toward Matt as she stepped forward. The demon's hazy transparent black hand, guided hers as she adjusted her blouse to expose more skin around her neck and chest. The demon focused on her, whispering to her, tempting her with memories of their old affair. Matt barely heard a word she said. It was like listening to two people speak at once and hearing neither.

Matt prayed for help and decided to hold his ground with the demon and talk to Pam about the Lord. "Pam, I told you I was a Christian. I believe in Jesus Christ." Matt stopped speaking to watch the demon that bristled at the word Christian, and swirled around Pam like a tornado and fled when he named the name of Jesus. Matt stopped. He must have looked surprised because Pam said "Yes... and... you were saying... and that's good for who, me or you?"

"What I meant was I'm OK, because I've given up all my burdens to Christ. I've put everything in His control."

"Well that's nice for you but I'm not really anywhere close to that." Pam looked like she suddenly changed mood and said. "Well I really have to get going. Take care." And she left the store without buying anything.

When he got in his truck he prayed for her to be free of this evil demon that was influencing her. Matt believed that the demon had guided Pam to him. This was a temptation for her and him. Matt was vulnerable to sin like any man but he was especially weak with Pam, and the affair was the sin he most regretted in his entire life. The demon gasbags knew this and it made sense that Satan would attack him there.

Matt now felt sure demons were not aware of his ability to see them. He suspected it before while being near them, but now after being within inches of one he was certain. Another of God's provided mercies.

When he met up with Jen at home that night, Matt told her about being up close to a demon gasbag. He changed the scenario of what happened and told her it was a female real estate broker he ran into instead of Pam. He told her about the demon all over her and how it fled when he spoke about the Lord. He explained to her his theory of demons influencing thoughts and he told Jen about how he tried to deal with his own sinful and lustful thoughts. He theorized that since he has seen no demons near himself he was convinced his own sinful thoughts were his own.

Jen told him "I have often thanked God that you are a good faithful man and you never cheated on me." Matt told himself long ago that he would never tell Jen about the affair he had with Pam. He had admitted it to God and asked for God's forgiveness hundreds of times in the past. Matt had buried it and he prayed that God would leave it alone.

MR. LANDLORD

Most of Matt's tenants were good people who worked and tried to do their best for their families. He always felt vulnerable when he signed a lease with a new person or couple. Matt did all the normal background checks to verify employment, income, credit and he spoke to past landlords and references. Matt had discovered the best way to check out a potential tenant was to visit them where they currently lived. After Matt received a completed application, he would stop by unannounced at their current address the next day or soon after to ask them one piece of incomplete information or something he was unclear about. He would knock on the door and say he was nearby and thought it would be easy to stop in and take care of the question he had. A few of Matt's houses were in below average neighborhoods. His real reason to stop was to verify they actually lived there and to see inside the house or apartment. If their place was a mess or if there was a dog or some animal living with the people that they did not tell Matt about, he could confront the problem and make a better informed decision whether or not to take them as a tenant.

Occasionally he was faced with a surprise when a tenant turned bad. This was the case with Nelsa Lopez. When he rented a house to her and her husband eight months ago everything seemed fine and rent was being paid on time. Over the winter, rent payments became late and then one very cold day in January he received a call about a leaking pipe in the basement. Matt went to look at it and discovered they never ordered heating oil for the hot water boiler to heat the house and the cold temperature froze a pipe that broke under the kitchen crawl space. They had been heating bedrooms with electric space heaters. Nelsa told him that her husband had left her two months ago and that is why her rent was late and she could not afford to pay for heating oil. Since then her mother moved in with her. The mother was arrested five weeks ago and more of Matt's rent money went to bail her out of jail. Matt told her he was willing to work with her to get caught up if he at least saw some effort from her to pay something. She seemed grateful and they worked out a plan where she could stay in the house.

Nelsa Lopez called him late in the afternoon to say she was moving out of the house right away and leaving town so he should come to collect the last bit of rent money she had for him. Matt hesitated but knew this probably was the only opportunity he would have to get at least part of the rent and he wanted to look at the house to find out what condition it was in. It was almost dark when Matt parked his truck across the street and uphill from the house. There was an old Toyota pickup truck in front of the house and three men were with Nelsa loading furniture and boxes. Matt walked up to them and Nelsa told the men who Matt was.

"Almost finished?"

"Yeah. Just these boxes to load." Nelsa said pointing just inside the front door.

"Do you mind if I go take a quick look around before you go?"

"No. Sure go look. I didn't get to vacuum everywhere but all the stuff is out."

Matt first went upstairs to the attic. The light there did not work so he flipped open his cell phone to get enough light to see his way up the stairs and get around to take a look. The attic was empty so he made his way back down stairs and through the rest of the house. Everything looked as well as could be expected. In the bathroom he turned the faucet on but there was no water. He thought she may have turned it off in the basement. Matt checked the kitchen and there was no water at the sink either. He flipped on the lights to go into the basement. As soon as he hit the bottom step he noticed the copper water pipes had been removed. The water meter was also missing – a $500 item only the city could supply. Copper was stolen from many unoccupied city homes and thieves sold it to scrap metal dealers for cash. Matt let go a heavy sigh and his shoulders slumped as he felt the tension in his neck. He knew he was probably going to get into some sort of battle when he asked her about the pipes. He thought about ignoring it but he was now out at least $1,200 worth of repairs. Matt went upstairs to the living room of the house near the front door. He placed himself between the men with Nelsa and the door.

"Nelsa, we have a problem in the basement." Matt told her.

"What are you talking about?"

"The water meter and the copper pipes are missing. Someone took them all out. Cut them out."

"I don't know nothing about that." Nelsa shook her head.

"You didn't notice that you had no water?"

"I haven't been here for a few days. I didn't know."

The three men who were with her were not large or individually threatening, but Matt knew that in the city everyone could be armed and Matt was not. He silently prayed that nothing bad would happen and that they could resolve this.

74

One of the men spoke up and said "I know who took the copper. It was my little sister. What are you gonna do about it?" The other two men laughed and Nelsa was smiling.

A second man stepped toward Matt, "Yeah Mr. Landlord, what are you gonna do about it? I guess you better call the police or maybe you should call an ambulance cuz you might need one, huh?"

If Matt had a weakness, it was that sometimes he had difficulty walking away. This was one of those times. "Look Nelsa, guys. I came here to get the rent money and that's it. But now your friend told me his little sister took my copper pipes. I think he should pay me for the pipes." He took two steps toward the big brother. "You can get your little sister to pay you back. That's fair isn't it?"

At the same time, and unknown and unseen to Matt, two angels in street clothes came through the front door and walked up behind Matt and stood there looking at Nelsa and the three men. One angel wore jeans, white shirt and a black full length leather jacket and the other angel wore a dark brown leather jacket, white shirt and jeans. The four of them looked at the angels and their attitudes diminished.

"I think that's fair." the big brother said while nodding his head.

Matt was very surprised at his agreeable response, but he kept his serious game face on. "Good. When can you pay me?"

"I can pay you now. How much do you need? I don't want no trouble."

"$1,200 should cover it."

He pulled a wad of cash out of his pants pocket and counted off twelve one hundred dollar bills and handed it to Matt.

"Nelsa, what about your rent?" Matt asked.

"Michael, give him the rent money too. $500." Michael took $500 from a different pocket and handed that to Matt also.

"Thank you Michael. I appreciate you doing the right thing. Nelsa do you want a receipt?"

"No, that's OK." She said politely.

Matt said "Can I have the keys? It looks like you're all finished here."

Nelsa gave Matt the keys and she and the men left the house without saying another word. Matt stayed behind to look again at the repair that needed to be done and make sure all the windows and doors were locked and the lights were off before he left. He walked through the empty house thanking God this situation worked out as well as it did. It was an answered prayer.

THE WORLD TRADE CENTER TOWERS, NY, NY

Matt felt like there were not enough hours in the day to see what he was being shown. He and Jen were both exhausted but alert. Jen was by his side as much as she could be. While flipping through TV channels, they caught the beginning of a documentary about the September 11th World Trade Center attacks. Matt told Jen he was almost afraid to watch. He had seen reports and the videos of the planes crashing into the towers many times over the years. Now he would see the invisible work that only God, angels and demons have seen.

The first shot from the video was taken from street level looking up seconds after the first plan hit the North Tower. He saw the explosion of orange flame and black smoke and from the midst of it; he saw what he knew were angels emerging as bright balls of white light that streaked out of the building up into the bright clear blue sky. Matt knew these angels were escorting believing souls to heaven. He watched the tower burn and more angels emerged from the building from all directions heading skyward. He described as much as he could to Jen. He was on his knees in front of their big screen TV pointing where he saw the angels and showing her which directions they went. Demons were flying around the outside of the burning tower but angels chased them away.

The video moved on to show the second plane approach and hit the South Tower. Before the plane hit, demons were flying circles around the tower close to the area the plane would hit. Matt could see a group of dark demon images flying along side of and behind the 767 jet and they flew straight into the building with it. Immediately angels emerged from the flames carrying more souls to heaven. At the same time, other angels drove off the demons swirling around the outside of the building between the 77th and 85th floors of the South Tower.

While both towers were burning, different views of them on video showed angels going in and out of both, taking away more believers as they perished. There was video of people jumping from where they were trapped by the outrageous infernos. Matt watched one person who, at the moment he jumped, a white light appeared at his side as he fell and then they disappeared out of the view of the camera. They watched the people being evacuated from inside one of the WTC lobbies. Angels were there walking with and among those exiting the building. They were among the firefighters, police and rescue workers.

Seconds before the South Tower fell, more angels went into it on dozens of floors. As it fell, the grey fountain of debris peeled itself open to reveal an invisible column of death where hundreds of angelic lights rose up and out of it, taking more souls to be with the Lord in heaven.

The same pattern was repeated when the North Tower collapsed. As colossal dust clouds cascaded through the city canyons and down the streets, angels could be seen flying up and out of what would be called Ground Zero. Matt saw video shots from street level that included angels walking with people who were completely covered gray in dust. Angels were with the firefighters as they recovered from the devastating collapses. He saw an angel standing over two policemen who were sitting on a curb trying to regroup. Matt saw an angel who stood with a group of shocked and crying people watching the destruction from across the Hudson River.

Video from the first hour after the second tower fell, showed a soul being taken from the bottom of the massive pile of wreckage. On the video from the recovery effort days later, Matt saw angels around the site. Some were standing motionless. Some angels looked like they were praying near and with the recovery workers. Demons patrolled slowly over ground zero occasionally harassing rescue workers in the smoking pile of dust and steel.

Matt described to Jen everything he saw. They watched the murder of 2,753 people in that small area in that short amount of time. Jen listened to Matt and watched the video. She imagined what he saw and cried.

VICTORIA'S SECRET

No one knew Victoria Renard's husband was murdered. His exploded, shredded tire was never closely examined. All agreed that his tire simply blew out and no one ever thought otherwise.

Victoria captured the attention and sympathies of the world as the beautiful widow of the handsome race car driver. She grieved for the loss of the man she truly loved and she grieved for the father her two sons would never know. Her friends gathered near her and supported her while she did not want to be alone. She had family, her retired mother and father who lived on the north coast of France near the port city of Le Havre, but she felt closer to her larger than lifestyle friends.

Immediately Victoria began to worry about money. She and Antonio spent money as fast as they made it. Her modeling career had peaked three years ago and it was difficult for any model to stay at the top earnings level with all the intense competition for jobs and the stream of young new faces and bodies every year. Victoria was offered a deal to write a book about her and Antonio's life together, but his family claimed to have rights to his name and wanted 70% of any profits from the book. It became a bitter argument that she saw no end to and she abandoned the idea. Her modeling agency had never made a profit. For her it was a status symbol and it was expected of her as a way to stay visible in the fashion industry. She was addicted to her standard of living and she was anxious about providing for her sons.

Al-Qaeda felt that they needed to weaken Victoria and make her needy in order for her to consider what they would offer. They had hoped the death of Antonio would damage her spirit, and it did. They had investigated her true financial resources and they were inadequate for the lifestyle she enjoyed.

Victoria was approached by a man she knew, Jules Aimee, who was an attorney that represented a friend of hers, a Saudi Prince and his real estate interests in Paris. She agreed to meet the attorney for lunch at Restaurant le Meurice in Paris to discuss a business proposal. Jules Aimee was 50 years old, average height and he looked middle aged. His face was clean shaven and he had a head of thick wavy gray hair with a few streaks of black. He arrived to lunch wearing a Jean-Paul Gaultier grey sharkskin suit, royal blue shirt and bold yellow tie. Victoria was at her elegant best and many people on the street and in the restaurant recognized her. They met at 2PM and enjoyed a pleasant conversation in

French about their mutual acquaintances and friends. When they finished their lunch and several glasses of champagne, Aimee told her "Thank you for your patience but I do not like to speak of business while enjoying lunch, especially with a woman as beautiful as you."

"Thank you. I do enjoy your company and I agree there is always enough time to take care of business afterward." She smiled and sipped from her glass.

"Victoria, there is a group who would like to offer you an exclusive position with their organization." He sat back in his seat and lit a cigarette. "This is a very wealthy and private group who believe you would be able to help them in a recruitment effort here in France and in the United States. It would be a type of free lance work but they do have an agenda and they will need to know progress is being made at a reasonable pace. Are you interested?"

"What type of recruiting?" she asked as she accepted the cigarette he offered and lit for her.

"They require attractive professional women to develop and maintain relationships."

"With whom?" she asked.

"I cannot say at this time."

"How much can your group, those you represent, afford to pay for my service?"

"They will offer you $150,000 each month paid in cash and $10,000 to cover any expenses you incur. I must tell you that if we continue this conversation further we will pass the point where you must accept the offer."

"An offer I cannot refuse?"

"Just like in the movies." He laughed, nodded his head and looked at her squarely in the eyes so she understood he meant what he said.

Victoria asked Aimee to tell her the details. She accepted the offer without hesitation because she needed the money. He made it clear from the start that there was no way for her out of their arrangement. This was permanent and she now worked for forces that were well funded and far reaching. Her employers would not hesitate to do anything to ensure their interests were protected and kept secret. Aimee told her "The people who pay us will pay us well, but they do expect progress to be made. They will hold us and our families accountable. Do you understand what this implies?"

"Yes." She said as she took in and exhaled a large breath of cigarette smoke.

Over the next several years they would work together, Aimee was her only contact with her employers. She was never clear who they were and she did not care. She suspected who it may be but she never let herself think about it for long. She knew it was not the wise thing to do and she created a mental barrier to separate herself from the job and the money. She looked on this work as purely business and survival for her sons. The work gave her the financial security she needed and it was easy for her and it fit perfectly into her lifestyle. Initially, Victoria was presented with a short list of French and longer list of American men in government. Aimee only communicated with Victoria verbally and in person because he wanted to be sure she understood her instructions and selfishly, he enjoyed being with her and being seen with her. He was not concerned how she conducted the operation because he and Al-Qaeda were confident there was no hard trail back to them. She made her own notes whenever Aimee gave her information. Anything Victoria could ever tell anyone was her word against his. The cash she received was all unmarked and untraceable.

Victoria Renard's mission was to make contacts with attractive women who were either current or past employees or had otherwise close relationships with a list of men in American and French government. She was given the names of the men ranked by priority. Al-Qaeda created the list based on those who were most likely to be elected to the presidency of their countries. She was never told the purpose for making the contacts. In Paris it was easy for her to operate. In the United States, most of the contacts she needed to make were in Washington, DC.

Victoria Renard was a familiar name to most American women because of her modeling fame. She continued to do a modest amount of modeling and as recently as 2007 she had appeared as a guest judge on "America's Next Top Model" and on "Operation Runway" in 2008. She wanted to stay in the public eye to keep her celebrity status.

Her primary recruiting technique was to get close to a high ranking staff member, male or female, of the target official. Victoria's story was that she was recruiting women to work in advertizing at a start up fashion magazine in New York City that had a political edge to it. Most of her contacts were somewhat star struck and no one refused a meeting with her. Victoria asked her contacts to keep their meeting private and she would imply that they could become good friends. She knew they would all talk to some extent, but it made them feel like insiders with a celebrity friend. They all responded with more names and information than she could use. Victoria recruited a few of these first contact women as the direct connection to the targeted men.

The women candidates were all flattered by the invitation and excited about the opportunity to meet with Victoria Renard. The meetings were always over lunch at one of the best restaurants in the particular city. Victoria made the women feel good about themselves. She complemented them and talked about the wonderful things people told her about them. They discussed fashion or whatever the prospect wanted to talk about as long as it kept them comfortable and it allowed them to relax. She would use their vanity against them. As they talked she would watch the women surrender to the dream of working in and associating with glamorous people like Victoria. The greed part came next as she described how they would be very well paid. This was a feeling out process for Victoria and if she felt she was speaking with the right type of woman, she would go to close the deal and tell them the fine print of the offer. She told them the true purpose of their work was to maintain the relationship they had with their respective men and to develop it to an even closer level. They were to work themselves into positions where a sexual relationship could be implied or proved with these men. Only a few were shocked by the offer, but even those women saw the easy route to a considerable amount of extra cash. They were told they were not required to have sexual relationships, but they would be paid more if they did and if they could prove it by gathering DNA evidence, finger prints, documents, photographs, video or sound recordings where and whenever possible. Three women had told her that they were in fact already having affairs with these men.

The money always sealed the deal. At the table she would hand them an envelope that contained a bank bundle of $100 dollar bills, $10,000 cash as a signing bonus. She offered them between $5,000 and $10,000 each month depending on how deeply they became involved. Every month their money was to be simply mailed or shipped by UPS or other carrier to their home in cash, and always sent from different addresses in packages of various sizes. The only thing the women knew was the day to expect the delivery. Victoria warned them not to expand their lifestyle too noticeably. She told them to explain any rise in income to friends as an eBay business, inheritance or a good real estate investment. None of the women were aware of any of the other women doing the same work. Most of them used the money to support their children and families and it took the financial pressure out of their lives. Cash gave them security but it came at a very heavy and unspoken price. Victoria told them that there was no way out of the arrangement and it would only end if the employer ended it. The women never knew who the employer was. Over time some thought it was a foreign government, Russians, North Koreans or the opposing political party of the man.

Over the years, two women decided to end their relationship with Victoria and told her they wanted out. One of women was killed the next day by a hit and run driver while she was jogging and the other was robbed and killed by a masked man while she withdrew cash from an ATM machine. The only woman who rejected Victoria's offer right at the lunch meeting never made it back to her office that afternoon. She was killed as she walked back to work by a man on the street that shot her six times at close range.

As some men fell off the political map and it was clear to all that they would never again be in a position to achieve the presidency, the women with them were eliminated from the payroll and killed.

By 2009 Victoria had sixteen women planted with thirteen men of both major political parties in the United States. Three men had two women planted with them. No one on Victoria's side ever anticipated the fast rise of Sarah Palin and they had no contingencies for a female vice president or president.

To Al-Qaeda this was an inexpensive operation that could yield the greatest rewards.

LE PRESIDENT DE FRANCAIS'

After September 11th 2001, Victoria was instructed to personally get close to the President of France. She had met him many times over the years and she had been at du Palais de L'Elysee for formal French state celebrations. Al-Qaeda wanted to strengthen every level of protection France would give Muslim countries in the event that George W. Bush would retaliate for the September 11th attacks. Victoria was very influential with the French president. She met him many times socially and privately and he always gave her as much time as she wanted. As a result of her persuasive talents, France became a leading voice resisting the Bush Administration's conduct toward Iraq. The French President threatened to veto the UN Security Council resolution authorizing military force to remove Iraq's weapons of mass destruction. France also had their own interest to protect with the extensive oil contracts it had with Saddam Hussein.

INSIDE THE FBI

Michael Rashid was 31 years old and had been working for the FBI as a translator since February 2002. After September 11th, the FBI was desperate to hire Arabic speaking employees. Rashid was straight out of college, smart, needed a job and he spoke Arabic since he was a child raised by his parents in Baltimore. His parents were first generation Pakistani Americans who loved America and were very patriotic. They also believed in the value of speaking several languages, so they taught Michael to speak Arabic, English, Spanish and French.

Rashid's background checked out perfectly during the FBI hiring process. However, the checking did not look deep enough into his mind and heart. While he was in college he became interested in the first Gulf War, Saddam Hussein and the politics of the UN sanctions that were in place at the run up to the war. Rashid became sympathetic to the militant Muslim point of view. Because his point of view was not popular in America, he kept his ideas and opinions secret from everyone, especially his parents.

Three years after he began working at the FBI, he considered that his position there would have some value in militant Muslim circles. He very carefully and secretly reached out to them and made himself known. He spoke to a few mature Muslim community leaders and he used the most veiled terms to describe his interests and abilities while still being certain he was understood. He expected the FBI to hear about his activities and he was prepared to tell them that he was only curious to find out if there were any groups locally. He would say he should have known better and he was stupid to do this and beg to keep his job. After three months of inquiries, Rashid was contacted and word of mouth introductions were made. An arrangement was made for him to be a set of eyes and ears inside the FBI and he would deliver any information, at his discretion, however broad ranging that he thought might be of interest to those in authority, the Arish-Asad. Rashid was paid $2,000 a month. This was enough extra cash to cover his car payment and make it easier to afford a nicer apartment in Alexandria, Virginia. Rashid was never asked by the FBI about the contacts he made, but that did not mean the FBI did not know.

Rashid was smart about what he was doing. He was an excellent employee at the FBI and always received outstanding job performance reviews. By 2007 he was transferred to the Investigative Computer

Training Unit at the FBI Academy in Quantico, Virginia. He worked in data analysis and spent half of his time teaching classes on how to use computers as research platforms, investigative tools, and as tools for analyzing digital evidence.

Rashid never used his cell phone, personal email or the Internet at his apartment for anything the FBI would consider suspicious. He did not subscribe to any controversial magazines and was careful not to watch any television programs or rented movies at home that would draw anyone's attention. Everything related to Muslim events worldwide or specifically the Middle East that he wanted to look at or read was available to him on the Internet or in the databases at the FBI where he was encouraged to read and look at it. That was part of his job. Rashid liked getting away with something. He thought it was fun and he thought he was smarter than most people. He also knew that he could never quit working for Arish-Asad. There was no way out.

Matt Davidson's name turned up in a two line comment in a summary report of calls made to the FBI tip line. This was the first time Rashid had seen Hannan's name appear in one of these reports. He saw it because he did searches of reports based on keywords. One of the keywords he routinely searched for was Hannan. Rashid's FBI supervisors had approved this because he was also searching for threats toward Hannan along with any unusual Arabic words that might be part of the reports. Because Hannan was a prominent Muslim American, he knew his contacts would be interested in information about her. He did not know they were part of the same organization.

Rashid never took any documents or computer discs from the FBI and he never emailed anything to himself. It was against FBI policy and would be careless of him to do so. He memorized whatever he thought had value and later wrote that information into notes at his apartment that he passed along. Rashid made sure there was no physical link from him to the notes he passed. He always wore golf gloves to avoid fingerprints when he prepared his notes. He had thought about using latex surgical gloves but realized it could seem suspicious to anyone looking through his trash why he regularly threw away a pair of latex gloves. In order to explain why he had the golf gloves in his apartment he bought a set of golf clubs and occasionally took them to a driving range to hit a bucket of golf balls. He became a bogey golfer and regularly played with his FBI co-workers.

Rashid wrote the notes in French and he wrote left handed to further disguise his true right handed penmanship. It looked like a child's writing, but it was readable. The notes were placed into cheap white letter sized envelopes and on the outside of the envelope he wrote "Personal Information" and the date. He then completely taped the envelope closed with clear two inch wide packing tape. The receiver of the envelope recognized the writing on it, and the tape made the envelope tamper evident.

Rashid had pre-arranged meeting times with a delivery contact at 6:00PM every Wednesday at one of four rotating locations. Rashid knew nothing about his delivery contact, he only recognized his face and they never spoke to each other. Rashid knew nothing about where or to whom his information was given. The information that he passed on about Matt Davidson was his name, date and nature of his call, home address and his cell phone number. The information was delivered to the Arish-Asad commander in Washington who read it and decided to have Matt killed. Their policy was to eliminate any known or perceived threat or obstacle to their operations, "remove weeds to prepare for a good garden". There were things in play and they were waiting for an opportunity very soon to reap the reward for years of patient planning. They could not afford anyone or anything however small to impede their plan.

The militant Muslim chain of command was rigid and orders only flowed down hill. No one ever questioned the authority above them. The organizational command was simple and mission failure or disobedience was not tolerated. Policy and objectives came from Iran – the high level leadership in Tehran. That leadership included President Ahmadinejad, the ayatollahs of the Guardian Council and the supreme leader Ayatollah Ali Khamenei who held almost limitless power over Iranian affairs. Communications between Tehran and Arish-Asad in America came through Yemen to France then to Washington, DC. Messages were delivered either verbally by scrambled cell phones or person to person. Coded radio similar to Morse code, and encrypted coded messages on CDs were used. Friendly Al-Jazeera reporters transported messages and Al-Qaeda had hundreds of Internet websites where messages flowed back and forth. American intelligence spent millions of dollars chasing these messages and trying to keep up with the changes that occurred daily.

The vast majority of operational cash for Al-Qaeda and Arish-Asad came from Saudi Arabia. Wahabbists like the Saudi royal family had unlimited funds. The only thing they were concerned about was the speed of the operations. They did not want to move too quickly and they did not want to dominate the world news. They were very image conscious and sensitive to America's reactions to the price of Arab oil. As much as the wealthy Wahabbists claimed to believe in the Twelfth Imam returning and wanting to bring peace to a world totally under Muslim control, they enjoyed their extravagant lives and the pleasures their money could buy. They were in no great rush to give it up. When suicide bombing became prominent and the claim that martyrs for Allah would receive 72 virgins in paradise for their sacrifice, many of the wealthiest Saudi men decided to each purchase and violate 72 virgins right here in this world. They joked to each other, "Why wait for heaven if you can pay for it in on earth?"

Money wire transfers were easy between Saudi Arabia and any of the hundreds of accounts and business entities they created in France. Because of the success of the Patriot Act and the ability to track electronic money transfers to the United States, it became necessary for Al-Qaeda to send actual shipments of cash in American dollars. Cash was sent from France to Canada and then to the United States and Washington. Bundles of 10,000 dollars all in 100 dollar bills were sent, usually one million dollars at a time.

The Washington Arish-Asad commander received regular cash deliveries at his heating, ventilation and air-conditioning company office in Beltsville, Maryland outside Washington, DC. At his discretion he paid his entire organization. He was the authority in the United States for all Arish-Asad operations. He was an Iranian immigrant with loyalties and sentiments similar to Senator Hannan's father. Trained as an engineer in Iran, he came to America in 1967. He had financial backing from investors in Iran to start his business and in over forty years his American roots were well established and he had a good business reputation. His HVAC company was a regular bidder on all size projects in the Washington, DC area. This included a great deal of government work. His largest project was part of new construction of the Ronald Reagan Building and International Trade Center in 1996. His business gave him access to many key buildings in the American capitol and he used that access for placing spying equipment.

The Washington commander never met with Hannan's man Omar personally. They communicated by cell phone and usually spoke to each other in French. When the decision was made to eliminate Matt, the commander assigned the hit to one of his cell leaders. The man who received the orders was known to his men as "the Boss." One of his men was able to easily find information about Matt on Matt's own business website. "Matthew Davidson, he must be a Jew." he told the others. They found a photo of Matt from an article about flipping houses that featured his company. The Arish-Asad man found the exact location of Matt's home with a satellite photo map and a street level photo of his house. "I love Google." the terrorist said.

TUESDAY – THE SECOND WEEK

Every day Matt felt the need to pray about seeing demons. He was concerned that seeing them for so long now and so often that these glimpses of evil would affect his mind and drive him crazy. There was so much of it, but at the same time he was sure God had purpose in allowing him to see them and he would be kept from harm. But Matt knew he still had to put on the full armor of God every day and he made sure to spend time reading God's Word. One morning he climbed into his truck and before he started it he sat and prayed about this. He prayed silently for a few minutes and when he finished he opened his eyes and an angel was seated next to him praying. Matt started the truck and the angel looked at Matt, gave him a comforting smile and vanished.

***

Matt's house was located in a beautiful suburban part of Pennsylvania, very close to Valley Forge National Park. There were many exclusive and prestigious homes near his with several parks and wooded areas. Matt's property was in a mature, heavily wooded section called Tory Hill. At the back of his yard about 200 feet from the house was a section of dense evergreen trees and a mix of native elm, maple and tall tulip poplars. His house was a five bedroom, two story house with lots of windows that they had built in 1995. From inside their home they enjoyed seeing the trees in all seasons of the year and very few of their windows had drapes or blinds. Because no one lived directly behind them, Jen and Matt never felt the need to block their view. They had all the privacy they needed. There was a large sliding glass door from their kitchen that opened onto a back yard patio.

Sunset came at 7:15PM. From the cover of the trees and through the scope of his silenced rifle, a sniper watched through the windows as Matt and his family moved from one room to another. He would wait until total darkness before he would take his shot. The sniper wore some hunter's camouflage and took a seated position at the base of a tree. Even at ground level he had an unobstructed view of Matt's kitchen area. There was the normal family activity in the kitchen this evening, dinner and the clean up. Matt's son was sitting at the kitchen counter doing something on a laptop computer. Jen walked in and out of the room frequently. The sniper checked his weapon, silencer and ammunition several times while waiting for a cover of darkness that satisfied him. He checked the night vision goggles that he would wear when he walked through the woods and neighboring properties on his escape route to the highway. There he would take a bus to the mall where his car was parked.

The sniper watched Matt walk through the kitchen and exit through a door the sniper thought led to a garage. Several minutes later he saw Matt in a second floor bedroom window but he quickly disappeared from view. The sniper knew he must act soon or he would likely miss his opportunity for the night. He assumed the family would settle down before long and eventually go to bed. Matt returned to the kitchen and sat beside his son to look at the laptop. The assassin put Matt's head in his sight and fired. He took the recoil of the gun and waited a moment for a puff of smoke to clear from his silencer muzzle. Without taking his eye from the scope he saw Matt still seated next to Tommy. The glass door on the patio window was not broken. The gun did fire. He checked the ejected bullet casing and it was hot and empty. He was confused but had no time to determine what went wrong. Matt was still seated and the assassin fired again with the same result. The sniper frantically reloaded his bolt action rifle.

Stationed outside Matt's patio door, were three invisible angels standing guard. Each carried a tall rectangular shaped shield three quarter as long as the angels were tall and as wide as their shoulders. The angels had blocked the bullets and they were easily absorbed by the shields. The sniper fired a third shot also blocked by a shield. The angels looked at each other and the middle angel said, "Enough."

Now in a half crouching stance with his right knee on the ground, the sniper's heart was pounding and he began to sweat. His hand shook as he reloaded. He thought about what would happen to him if he failed this mission. He raised the gun to his shoulder and found his target in his sight again, when suddenly he saw a monstrous flash of fangs and a blood red mouth charging him. The sniper fired his weapon off target and dropped it as the demon Aeshma bowled him over and pinned him on his back against the ground and held him with his long claws. The demon had run at him on all fours. It had the body of a small extremely muscular man but he was the size of a large heavy dog and covered with long coarse black hair. The assassin could feel the heat and smell the stench of the demon's breath as it screamed in his face "Do not harm the man!"

A light rain woke the sniper eight hours later where he had passed out under a tree. It was 3:30AM. Matt's house was completely dark, and nothing was visible inside. He tried to clear his head and thought he could possibly enter Matt's house to complete his assignment, but the only weapons he had was his rifle and a hunting knife. He had no tools for breaking into a home. He also assumed correctly that Matt's house was alarmed and he did not know if Matt had any weapons of his own. The sniper disassembled his gun and gathered his things. When he put the strap of his bag over his shoulder, he saw three parallel cuts, claw marks, in his jacket where the demon grabbed him. The demon had terrified him and now he had to sort out in his mind what happened. The sniper staggered through the woods and found his way to the bus stop. The busses were not running at this hour so he walked three miles to the mall to get to his car. As he walked away thinking about how he would explain why he failed, he became fearful of what awaited him.

***

Anika Hannan spent her entire life obediently doing what her father told her to do. His discipline was fierce. Since her experience in Iran with him in 1980 she was told by him every day that she was the cause of all the trouble in his life and she had caused him a burden of shame because of her immoral behavior with the Mu'allim. He convinced her that she was defiled and no man would want her as a wife. He told her that her only chance to redeem her life and to make herself right before Allah was to do as she was told. She believed that with Allah's help she would be given a way to make things right for her father. For 29 years she lived this every day. Her life was dedicated to lifting the weight of disgrace from her father. She loved him and she longed to please him and have love returned to her. She was unquestioningly obedient to him and to Islam.

***

When Hannan and Omar needed to discuss something privately, they would occasionally walk outside on the noisy city streets. It was 11AM and they walked on Constitution Avenue between the Russell Senate Office Building and the Capitol. Omar said "All things are moving forward as we hoped. You must be prepared to meet privately with the president. Take the first opportunity that comes. Have you practiced what you will say?"

"Yes, many times." She looked straight at the pavement as they walked.

"You must be perfect. You must be convincing. He must realize the gravity of his situation."

She nodded her head and they kept walking. She hated Omar. He was never helpful to her and he never had one original thought in his head. He was only a nagging watchdog. "There is a man in Pennsylvania who made a call to the FBI regarding you. A Christian man who thinks you are surrounded by ghosts. His name is Matthew Davidson. We must now eliminate every threat or distraction to our operation. The decision was made to do away with him. For some reason the attempt to deal with him failed, but that will be corrected."

WEDNESDAY – IN PHILADELPHIA

In a row house in a rough part of north Philadelphia, four Arish-Asad men, and the sniper waited for their boss to arrive. The house was dark and all the windows were covered by drapes or old bed sheets to keep anyone from seeing inside. Four of them stood around the kitchen leaning against a wall and against the sink. At the table in the middle the sniper sat on a chair with his head down. There was one low watt light bulb turned on to illuminate the kitchen. It hung from a broken fixture on the ceiling.

To a Muslim, cocaine is considered an intoxicant or khamr. When someone who uses khamr says they are a Muslim they insult Allah and bring dishonor on Islam. The boss had a $1,000 a day cocaine habit. If his superiors knew, they would have him killed. Because of his addiction the boss's behavior had become erratic and paranoid. He spoke rapidly and was constantly in motion.

The boss was in a fury when he arrived at the house by himself. He walked quickly through the front door to the kitchen in the back. All the men including the sniper stood up straight when he entered the room. The boss was shorter than all the others and he had a thin build with black hair and a short neatly trimmed beard. "Who is Nazim?" the boss spoke in Arabic.

"I am Nazim." the sniper said.

The boss stepped directly in front of the sniper and they stood face to face. "What do you say happened?! Why did you fail?!"

"Sir, I fired three times. Three shots. Each one did not penetrate the windows of the house. I saw no damage. Nothing. As if my bullets had vanished." He kept his head down looking at the floor, not looking the boss in the eyes. "I know my weapon. It functions perfectly."

"You are a liar!" and he slapped the sniper hard across the face. "If your weapon functions how do you explain your incompetence?"

"Sir I cannot. But I did see something. It was a warning."

"What kind of warning?"

"After my third shot, the demon Aeshma attacked me!" the sniper said. According to Muslim legend, Aeshma is the Muslim demon able to make men perform cruel acts.

"Aeshma knocked me to the ground and screamed at me "Do not harm the man!" I soiled myself and lost consciousness." The other men in the room smiled and laughed. The boss looked at them and they became silent and looked away.

97

"You are a liar and a coward!" the boss yelled and he drew his 9mm pistol from his jacket and shot the sniper between the eyes at close range. The bullet went through the sniper's head and hit the man standing behind him in the throat below his chin. Blood splattered over him and the wall. The sniper's body fell straight to the floor face down in a clump. The man shot in the throat grabbed his neck with two hands while choking and squirting blood. The boss looked down at the dead sniper. Blood flowed from his face into a large pool on the floor.

"Clean up this dead pig." The boss said calmly and then he left the house as fast as he arrived.

MOUNT PENN

One night Matt was watching the 11PM local news and they showed a live shot from one of the tall buildings in center city Philadelphia. The view was looking north on Broad Street and Matt noticed two bright white objects in the distance flying from street level up into the sky and out of camera range. It looked unusual, the direction, speed and shape. It made him think it could be two angels with the backdrop of a night-time city street.

The next day he checked the Internet to find out if one of the tall sky scrapers or the newest 50 story Comcast building in the city had an observation deck open at night. He could not find any, so at home that evening he asked Jen if she wanted to go for a drive. They were in their kitchen and Matt was taking a tray of chicken breasts out of the broiler. "Jen, I want to go to the Pagoda up on Mount Penn. Let's go, just you and me. I want to see if we... if I can see angels flying over a city."

The Pagoda is a Shogun style Japanese seven story building built nearly 900 feet above the city of Reading, Pennsylvania on Mount Penn. It was built in 1908 to be used as a restaurant and hotel. It is the most famous landmark of Reading and offers a beautiful 20 mile view of the entire city and beyond. Matt and Jen had been there twice over the years and Matt could not think of a better place to observe the action above a city of about 80,000 people. It was a forty minute drive from their home.

Jen asked "When were we there last? Not since ..."

"I read somewhere they re-did the lights on it and did some other improvements. I think it would be a great view of a fairly compact area of population. I want to see if there is angel activity visible over head. I think I'll be able to see angels fly."

"We can go but I don't want to leave Tommy and Erika here alone."

"Aw too bad, because I was hoping we could pull over and make out up there on Skyline Drive." Matt got up close behind her as she stood in front of the kitchen sink.

"Nice try big fella. You keep forgetting how old we are."

"But Jen, if we don't use these old parts we're gonna loose 'em."

"Maybe next time. This time the kids are coming with us and I wouldn't want to traumatize them with a wild display of parental affection."

"Good point. Therapy is expensive."

The four of them got into Jen's car, a red Ford Fusion sedan. It was much better on gas than Matt's truck and he had not driven her car for awhile. He often noticed things about the way her car handled or performed that Jen would never notice. She was not automechanically inclined. Matt liked to tell a story about how years ago Jen drove for some time with the check oil light lit on her dashboard. She thought the symbol of the can with the drip was a new type of reminder to get gas, but she could not understand why it did not go off after she filled up. She thought the light was defective and finally asked Matt about it.

It started to rain at about half way on the drive to Reading. "Oh well. I guess we won't be able to see much in the sky." Matt said.

Jen said "We may as well keep going. I want to see the Pagoda anyway and the kids were never there. They'll like it."

Erika could not quite grasp the concept of building a Japanese pagoda on top of a mountain in Pennsylvania 100 years ago. Matt had a hard time explaining why it was built. "Don't worry about why it's there. Just enjoy the fact that it is there. You'll really like it." She had Googled the Pagoda before they left home and found out that M. Knight Shyamalan had recently filmed part of a new movie there. Erika thought that was very cool.

It was still raining lightly when Matt parked the car at the Pagoda about 20 yards from the base of it. The parking spaces faced toward the city and the view. There was a long thick stone wall that kept visitors back from a steep drop to a pavement and an even steeper rock face drop off below that. The outlook was to the west and as they all stepped out of the car and stood against the wall. The rain stopped and the clouds along the horizon began to lift, revealing the last red glow of the setting sun. Within minutes the clouds had all moved off to present to them a clear sky with stars emerging slowly.

The Pagoda had been refurbished with new paint, gold lion head ornaments at the roof corners and red lights on every foot of all five stories of the roof lines. Thousands of feet of lights were visible to the horizon and beyond. Aircraft landing at the Reading airport use the Pagoda as a visual reference on their approach. Tommy and Erika walked all around the base of the building and explored an area at a lower level down a set of stairs. There were Japanese cherry trees blooming around the base and entry. It was after hours so they were not able to go inside the Pagoda and climb the steps to the top. Matt wanted to just look at the city and watch for angels. He was familiar with Reading and he had renovated three houses there. He pointed out to Jen the locations of the hospitals, larger roads and the two main shopping malls that were clearly visible. The grid of the city streets was easy to see with street and building lights and the movement of vehicles with their lights on. Matt remembered to bring binoculars along with them but surrendered them over to Tommy. Erika was taking photos with Matt's digital camera.

"What do you think you'll see?" Jen asked him.

"I believe the angels go back and forth from earth to heaven. I'm not sure where heaven is. Maybe it's another dimension. You know I'm no Einstein, but I know angels go somewhere and I know they travel fast. I'm hoping to see something like what I saw in the World Trade Center and the Challenger videos. I know I saw angels fly so..."

"OK. I'll just let you watch and I'll go see what the kids are doing. And I did like your idea about going parking." she said and she patted him on his rear end and walked away. Matt smiled at her and thought – Lord, thank you for her.

There were a few other people walking around and leaning on the stone wall to look out over the city. As the sun completely disappeared, the sky became black and even with the bright lights of the city, the stars all came out and were easy to see.

Matt thought the hospitals would be good places to watch. He watched in the direction of the closest one but did not notice anything unusual. He scanned all around and then thought about Jen and the kids. He turned to his left, toward the Pagoda to look for them. He saw an angel standing on top of the stone wall near the top of the stairs that lead down to the lowest level. His glowing white robe and tunic had the same soft blue tint that he saw in Erika's bedroom a few days ago. The angel looked at Matt and then rose straight into the air higher than the top of Pagoda and then streaked north looking like a brilliant white shooting star into the big dipper and out of sight.

Matt thought this was ten thousand times better than any meteorite he ever prayed to see. He was stunned and just started to laugh out loud to himself. People looked at him and he said out loud "Thank you Lord, thank you Jesus!" and he raised his hands over his head.

"Amen brother!" a woman said to him.

"God bless you friend!" a man said to him.

"Thank you. God bless you all!" Matt yelled to them. Jen heard Matt and she and the kids ran over to him.

"Matt did you see something?"

"Oh yeah Jen. Right here." Matt was still laughing and feeling the excitement. He told her what he saw and pointed in the direction the angel flew.

"What are you pointing at Dad?" Erika asked him.

"Angels baby. Right here. I saw one."

"Dad. Get a grip."

Jen said "Matt should you really..."

"Oh yee of little faith. You don't believe me? You believe angels are real don't you?"

Erika said "Yeah but..."

"I believe in angels Dad." Tommy said.

"Did you ever see one Tom?" Matt asked him.

"Not a for real one... I don't think."

"Well let me tell you all something. I know angels are real. I have seen them and I know that God loves us." They all stood close together by the stone wall.

Jen did not know what Matt was to going to say. She held her breath and did not say anything, but she did say a quick prayer – Lord, give Matt wisdom to say what you want him to say.

Matt went on to tell Tommy and Erika about the time long ago when he was saved from drowning at the beach by what he knew to be an angel. He also told them about the time God used his mother's voice to wake him when he fell asleep driving. "I know there are angels around and near us a lot of the time. We only see them if God wants us to. If it serves His purpose. Sometimes they look like regular guys. Regular big strong guys. But I'll tell you that with every cell of my body I know angels are real and I know that God knows each one of us and Abby."

Matt controlled his enthusiasm and did not take his story any further. He would have loved to tell everyone in the world what he knew about angels but he knew he could not. He prayed that one day he might be able to share this with his children at least, but for now he was grateful he did have Jen to talk to about all of this. Erika and Tommy went back to the car and looked at the photos in the camera she had just taken. Jen said "I know it's like holding a wonderful secret that you want to tell everyone about, but thanks for not telling the kids. Not yet anyway."

"Sometimes I want to burst and shout to the world, but I know I have to just wait and follow. It won't be long before something happens. The Lord knows I can't be trusted to keep my mouth shut much longer."

"Yeah, you sure can put the blabber on if you want to. You should go into politics."

"Can you see me elected to anything? Me and my flamethrower sent to Congress."

"Come here you crazy right-winger you." Jen kissed him and Matt put his arm over her shoulder and pulled her close.

They stayed at the Pagoda for a while longer. Jen and Matt stood and watched over the city. Matt saw a bright white streak of light take off from street level. He could not tell exactly where it came from but it looked like it rose as high as where they stood on the mountain and then accelerated out of sight. Soon afterward he saw two more streaks of light, one pinkish and the other yellow, go toward the hospital. He watched and saw the same two leave and fly away about fifteen seconds later. He saw other angels of different tints of color. Light blue, pink, white, greenish, and yellow. The longer they stayed the more activity there seemed to be. The angels flying with the black night background made him think that maybe many UFO sightings were really angels. He told this to Jen, and the more he saw the more he could imagine the confusion. "Maybe other of people can see angels but they don't recognize them. Maybe they're sensitive to spiritual things but don't know or don't believe."

He described everything to Jen as he saw it happen. She never got tired of Matt telling her about what he saw. This experience was drawing them closer than they ever were. They watched for angels until the kids started to complain and wanted to leave. Jen leaned into Matt and said "We have to go home."

"Yeah. I guess next time we need to bring folding chairs and a cooler."

THURSDAY AT HOME DEPOT

Two men from Arish-Asad followed Matt. They picked up Matt's trail at the usual spot, the GasQuick where he stopped almost every morning. They parked their car there and waited for Matt because they knew he either stopped there or drove by every day. They trailed him to a project house where Matt met with an electrician to discuss replacing the old electric panel box and taking some new wiring to the new kitchen Matt was having installed. After meeting with the electrician they watched him sit in his car making a cell phone call for ten minutes until he pulled out and headed away and up the highway. The men followed at an inconspicuous distance.

To Matt it seemed like he was at Home Depot every day, especially during a house renovation. There was always another bucket of spackle to get or another roll of insulation to buy, get a key made or pick up something. Always something else to buy. This time he needed a three-way switch for a light above a stairway. Several of the employees in the store recognized Matt and they always exchanged greetings. He knew the store so well that he thought he could always get a job there if things with his business went belly up. Matt walked right to the electrical aisle to find the switch he needed.

One of the Arish-Asad men followed Matt into the store. The driver waited in their small white Toyota that he parked close to the store in a handicapped space. He waited with the car engine running. The man who followed Matt was the boss who killed the sniper in the house in north Philly. He wore a black leather jacket, white collared shirt, dark brown pants, black shoes and black sunglasses.

There were no other people in the aisle where Matt was choosing a light switch. The boss walked toward Matt quickly. His right hand was inside his jacket over his left chest with his finger on the trigger of a Beretta handgun with a four inch silencer. He walked directly at Matt from Matt's left side. His plan was to bump into Matt and grab him while firing four shots into him at close range. He was two feet from him as the boss began to pull out the gun when two invisible angels grabbed the boss from two sides. One angel took the boss's left hand and at the same time he placed his other hand over the boss's mouth. The second angel grabbed the gun and the boss's right hand and placed his other hand on the boss's right shoulder. The angels slammed him down backward hard, and bounced his head off the concrete floor. Matt saw the boss approach out of his peripheral vision and he turned only fast enough to see the boss look as if he was having a seizure or spasm, and fall on his back and strike his head hard against floor. Matt did not see the angels. The boss was unconscious and his gun was in his right hand, still inside his jacket.

Matt yelled right away for help for the unconscious man. He immediately pulled out his cell phone and called 911 and asked for an ambulance right away. Store employees as well as customers came running to help. An older employee discovered the gun in his hand. He recognized it and knew that silencers, even on licensed concealed firearms in Pennsylvania were illegal. He shouted to a co-worked "Bobby! Call the cops! This guy's got a gun!" while at the same time he took the gun, released the magazine and cleared the chamber of one round. He was a US Army veteran and knew what he was doing. "Who is he? Check his ID!" someone said. "He looks like some kinda terrorist!" said another.

Outside, the driver of the white Toyota was getting impatient worrying about what was taking so long. He became very nervous when he heard the sound of sirens getting close. When he saw the red and blue flashing lights of an ambulance and police cars, he drove off leaving his boss behind.

Matt connected the dots and thought - I called the FBI about a Muslim senator, now this guy who looks like a Muslim, with a gun falls over at my feet! Oh crap. And I called 911. They'll know it was my phone, they'll know it was me who called. They're gonna think I did this to the guy. Matt turned away from the now growing crowd of people and left the store before the police arrived.

The police went with the boss to the hospital. They retrieved his gun, cell phone, a small bag of cacaine and $3,500 in cash in his pants pocket. He carried no ID or wallet. There would be a lot of questions for the boss. The store surveillance tape showed the boss arriving by car, the car parking, him entering the store and approaching Matt. The video showed the boss walking right up to Matt and having what all agreed, looked like a seizure and he fell backward hitting his head on the floor. Matt never touched him and never even looked at him until he started to spasm. Several employees recognized Matt on the video. They weren't sure of his name but said they saw him often. The video also showed the Toyota leaving the parking lot quickly, and Matt walking out and driving away in his truck.

It took police two days to enter the information from this incident into the Homeland Security database. The boss turned up on a watch list and the FBI was notified two days after that. Hannan was told that same day that this second attempt failed.

A few days later at FBI Headquarters in Washington, the Homeland Security Threat Monitor software matched the call Matt made on the tip line to the Home Depot incident. That match put Matt into a low level "unusual incident" category. This list was reviewed by agents every three days. No one at the FBI was looking for Matt. The only person at the FBI who knew about Matt was Rashid and since the first report of the tip line call, he had added Matt to his search list.

When Matt left the Home Depot he needed to go somewhere and think and pray. He knew he was now in trouble and someone bad knew about him. He also thought that there might be someone trailing him from Home Depot, so he drove around for 20 minutes until he was convinced no one followed.

The only thing that linked him to Senator Hannan was the FBI. He figured that Hannan might have someone in the FBI that informs her when anyone is asking questions about her. He thought - But what real threat am I? And why would they want me dead over a stupid phone call I made. They couldn't possibly know what I know about the demon activity. These people are seriously paranoid or really up to something bad. Matt was right about both.

Matt was not going to make another mistake like he did calling the FBI. He thought that if he called the FBI again, how would he know that the bad guys would not get tipped off and get to him first. He was going to only move forward with prayer and God's help. Matt drove to a quiet park where he liked to stop to make phone calls, eat his lunch or just take a break. The park had a playground area with swings and all the usual play equipment for children. There were picnic tables spaced evenly all around. He got out of his truck and walked to a table and sat on top of it with his feet on the bench. It was a beautiful day, sunny and breezy. He was the only person there. No other people or cars were in sight.

Matt sat and prayed. Head lowered, eyes closed. The sun felt good to him and the act of praying helped release his tension. Matt asked God for help, wisdom, clarity, and protection for him and his family. He had so many questions about what this was all about. He asked God to hear his prayers. He prayed to have his questions answered. He prayed to hear from God.

He meditated for a while. Being still and feeling the sun and breeze calmed him down. He noticed the air became still and everything became silent. No car noises or birds and the sound of the wind stopped. Through his closed eyes it seemed that this sunny day was now brighter. Matt opened his eyes and before him was a brilliantly shining angel. Beautiful with radiant colors like millions of diamonds glistening in the sun. The angel was almost too much for him to take in.

"I was sent to speak to you." The angel's voice was perfect.

Matt tried to see as much of the angel as he could. The radiance and color caused him to squint his eyes. He made himself look at this glorious figure. After a moment Matt found his voice and said "Why are these things being revealed to me?"

"You have found favor with God." The angel's voice was not loud but Matt felt every word.

"Will my family be safe?"

"Do not be afraid." With those four words Matt felt peace and comfort. Emotion filled Matt and his own voice was reduced to a whisper.

"I can see dark figures. Are they demons or devils? Why do they have no form?"

"They are with Satan. They are princes of the air. They have the faces of sin and death. The Father has revealed to you only what you can bear."

"I see what look like fights between angels and demons. Is that what I am seeing?"

"We battle against principalities of the dark on earth and in the unseen worlds."

"What am I supposed to do?"

"It will be given to you." Matt kept his eyes locked on the angel's eyes. Then the angel left him.

Matt felt the weight of worry lift from him. He fully trusted God for his own safety and that of his family. He gave all of that over to God. In recent days he had been so caught up in observing the angels and watching and looking for purpose in all of this that he had not given in to worrying about his business. He now knew the peace beyond all understanding. All Matt could do was, be faithful with what he was given, and look to where God was at work and follow Him. He would leave the rest to God.

***

At home that evening, Jen asked Matt about what he saw today. "Let's go outside and walk around the yard and I'll tell you."

They went out the sliding glass kitchen door onto the patio. They looked at the last of the daffodils and the tulips still holding their color and shape. Jen said, "I'd love to plant a few hundred more of each of those."

"Yeah and I'd like to plant more daylilies for summer. Let's just do it. Tommy likes dirt. That boy can dig holes. You've seen him at the beach. I've got to work him harder."

"Matt, you and Tommy are so alike. Sometimes you get the exact same excited look on your faces. He even walks like you, a little heavy on your right foot."

"Really?"

"Yes. And you walk like your father." They stepped onto the grass and walked across the yard. "Well what did you see today?" Jen asked.

"Well, I was pretty stressed most of the day. Something dumb happened with George the electrician over at the Maple Street house and I got a text message about the cell phone bill."

"Yeah, I got it too. Do you want me to pay it?"

"No. I'll take care of it." Matt said wondering where he would get that money from. They kept walking. "I had a little problem today at Home Depot." Matt stopped and put his hands around the trunk of a pin oak tree he planted six years ago. "Look how much this tree has grown. Remember that ice storm and how bent over it was?"

"What kind of problem?" Jen directed him back to the subject.

"I went over there to get a 3 way light switch. I was standing in the aisle looking at the switches and some guy falls over practically at my feet. Spazzed out, passed out or something. He cracked the back of his head on the concrete floor. I called 911 and an ambulance came for him. Well it kinda freaked me out and I had to go pray."

"Well that's good. I mean the ambulance and the praying part, not the guy cracking his head part."

Before he got home, Matt had decided he was not going to tell Jen he thought his 911 call today and his call to the FBI tip line about Senator Hannan were connected. She did not need that worry and Matt was renewed by the angel in the park. He was confident in his family's safety.

"After that I went to the park over on Township Road to get away from all that and think and pray. There was no one around and I sat on one of the picnic tables and Jen, the most wonderful thing happened." Jen took his hand and Matt told her "An awesome angel appeared to me. More radiant, more everything. He spoke to me and answered my questions. His voice filled me and went through me." Matt put her hand flat on the middle of his chest. "It was amazing. I prayed for it to happen and God sent him." Matt continued and gave her every detail.

Jen said "I think he was an archangel. Gabriel or Michael. You said he was more radiant than the others."

"Maybe. I'm not going to even think about it." Matt paused and then he did think about that. "But you're right. Just imagine if the same angel who told Mary she would be mother of the Christ child…. also spoke to me." His eyes welled up with tears. "Jen, don't be afraid about any of this. Everything I've told you is true. No matter what happens I know we will all be safe." They stood in the middle of their front yard and held on to each other.

Abby and Erika looked out the window and saw their parents in each other's arms. Abby asked her "Do you realize how lucky we are?"

"Yeah I do. That's what I want some day."

THE NEXT PHASE

One of the goals of militant Islam and the Iranian leadership was to penetrate the highest levels of the American government. Anika Hannan was the successful result of their effort to do so. Hannan's mission was to go as far in the national government of the United States as possible with the ultimate goal of her becoming President of The United States.

The operation to plant women close to the key figures was about to bear fruit. Now having one of Victoria Renard's women close to the vice president and two near the president created the opportunity they had worked toward for years. Tehran sent the message to the Arish-Asad commander in Washington to initiate the next phase.

***

Senator Hannan received a package delivered by UPS to her office in the Russell Senate Office Building in Washington. It was addressed to her personally. The sender was an administrator at the Canadian Supreme Court in Ottawa. Packages from other friendly governments were still never screened for anything other than explosives and illegal drugs. The Canadian was a career administrator at the court with an impeccable reputation. He was also sympathetic to Al-Qaida and was paid by them to function as a procurer and transporter of special items all over the world.

Hannan's staff was used to her receiving private letters and packages and she insisted on opening them herself. The package from Canada was inside a plastic UPS envelope and to her staff it felt like an ordinary business size report binder. Inside the binder were eight adhesive flesh colored bandages, finger size, the type used for minor cuts and wounds. On the outside of the middle padded part of each bandage were hundreds of very sharp microscopic pointed edges. Sharp enough to penetrate skin. Also in the package was a flat reseal-able tube of a meningitis bacteria that had been modified over several years in Saddam Hussein's laboratories in Iraq. It was shipped out of Iraq to Syria at the start of the Iraq War in 2003. The bacteria had been modified to show the typical symptoms of meningitis such as head ache, stiff neck and fever in a reverse order. The bacteria would travel quickly through the body to cause swelling of the fluid of the brain and spinal cord before the normal symptoms develop. With the brain swelling first, the fatal damage would be underway before the other symptoms are known. With the proper amount of bacteria introduced into the blood, death should occur within 24 hours and would be diagnosed simply as a tragic but fast moving case of bacterial meningitis. This bacteria was not breathable and only transferred by blood. The delivery process to the victim was to apply the bacteria to the sharp edges on the outside of the bandage, put the bandage on the right index finger and simply shake hands with the victim while giving a firm rub of the bandaged finger on to the victim's wrist. The scratch was barely noticeable to the victim.

Hannan and Omar were instructed to test the process and the bacteria. Since the election in November, Omar had been sure to hire a new staff person who was approximately the same height and weight as the President of the United States. Hannan told her secretary that she wanted to see Isaac Parker in her office to meet him and congratulate him on doing a fine job as part of her office team.

Parker had become a popular member of the Hannan's staff. He was eager to please and never complained about any task or assignment he was given. When Parker arrived to meet Hannan, she had him wait outside her office until she had time to put the bandage on her finger and apply the bacteria. When she was ready she told her secretary to send him in to her. She was standing in front of her desk when he entered. Hannan walked toward him with her hand outstretched to shake his hand. She gave him a solid handshake and tried to get a good grip on him to rub her finger on his wrist. He did not react in any way so she relaxed and the senator asked him to have a seat next to her desk. She wanted to watch him closely during their few minutes of small talk. She was like a spider that bit her victim and now waited for the venom to work.

"Isaac, thank you for coming. I wanted to meet you and thank you for your hard work and sacrifice." The senator said as they both sat down. She carefully pulled the bandage off of her finger and casually said, "I really don't think I need this any longer." and dropped it in her trash can.

"Ma'am, it is a privilege to work here. I appreciate this opportunity and want to do my best for you. I admire you and what you do for our country. I'm trying to model my career after yours. I've been accepted at Stanford Law for next year."

"Excellent. But that means you will be leaving us then. We will miss you."

"Well, I'll be here until next fall."

112

They chatted for five minutes. She watched him closely hoping to see some signs of discomfort but soon got bored with him and she gave up, knowing that the bacteria would not work that fast.

"Would you like if we took a photo together?" she asked.

"Yes, I was really hoping to. My parents would love it."

Hannan called her secretary who came in with a digital camera. The secretary took three shots. Hannan awkwardly avoided shaking his hand again in the photos. "Linda will email the photos to you and you can do whatever you like with them. Put them on your Facebook page. Maybe you can get a few votes for me!"

She turned him toward the door with her hand on his shoulder. "Thank you Isaac. I'm sure you will be moving along very quickly in your career." Isaac left her office beaming and feeling great about his future.

Late the next day, in the office men's room, Isaac passed out in a toilet stall. He was discovered by a coworker and rushed to a hospital. He remained there in a coma for three weeks until he eventually died. The autopsy would report the cause of death as bacterial meningitis.

Amy Daly and some of the others in the office, who had come to know Isaac well, were crying when Hannan arrived the next morning. Amy told Hannan what happened to him. Hannan had her secretary send flowers to his hospital room. Outwardly, Senator Hannan was shocked and saddened by the news of this nice young man being taken so seriously ill. Inside she was in an angry rage. Later that afternoon, Omar came into her office. She was seated behind her desk when he came in. He closed and locked the door behind him as he always did when they did not want to be disturbed. She stood up and walked in front of her desk and they stood face to face. "Why didn't this work!?! We can't have the president in a coma. We need a dead president! We cannot wait days for him to linger around and maybe not even die!" she said with her teeth clenched.

Omar stood there and let her rant without saying a word. She finally turned to her left to return to her seat at her desk. As she turned away from him, she heard a familiar three fast metal clicks but it was too late. Omar struck her hard from right shoulder across to her mid back with an extendable metal rod that he carried with him. She winced and the pain made her knees buckled as she caught herself on the corner of her desk.

"You will remember your place! This is your fault he is not dead! You failed such a simple thing. You are a worthless whore! I pity your father the shame you have brought to him. You have this chance to redeem your life and you cannot do as you are told?! How will you accomplish the real mission when you cannot do this one thing?"

She was leaning on her desk facing away from him. She supported herself with two hands and felt the burning sting of his lash. Her eyes filled with tears but she did not speak or look at him. She could feel the welt rising. He had struck her over her suit jacket. He knew how to punish her and not draw blood or leave visible marks that anyone would ever see.

"You must do this again. Try again on another man. I will send another to this office tomorrow." Omar said. He walked out of the room and turned back to her and said loud enough to be over heard by the rest of the staff, "I will check with the Finance Chairman as you asked." He closed her door and smiled to the others and went to his office.

***

It was 11:30PM that same night when Anika Hannan stood in her apartment bedroom and removed her suit jacket and skirt. She placed both neatly on a hanger and hung it in her closet. She walked to her bathroom wearing her blouse, slip and underwear. She looked at herself in the tall and wide dressing mirror over her sink and vanity. She thought her eyes looked tired. She covered her face with both hands as she began to cry softly. Anika's eyes filled with tears. A full sobbing cry escaped her for a moment and then she wiped her eyes with a tissue she took from the box on the vanity in front of her. She removed her blouse while turning to look at her back over her right shoulder in the mirror. The fresh mark of Omar's lash was a red pink 14 inch stripe that would throb for days. Her bare skin revealed five old scars of similar length. Cutting punishment that left marks to remind her of whose authority she was under.

***

Samir Omar had arranged for a computer technician from the senate building IT support division to come to Senator Hannan's office the next day. He instructed them that the senator preferred to work with men regarding computer issues and told them he must be in her office at 8AM.

Sam the computer technician left his home in Frederick, Maryland early that morning to be sure he was not late to her office. Hannan was late and made Sam wait 45 minutes until she arrived. He had to wait another fifteen minutes until she was ready for him at her desk.

The senator opened her office door and greeted him graciously and apologized for her delay. She shook his hand with both of her hands being careful not to touch her own left hand with her bandaged right finger. She had applied more of the bacteria than she did with Isaac and she did not remove the bandage right away.

Hannan had Sam add some icon shortcuts on her desk top computer and check a printer. She apologized that the problems seemed minor but she told him she could not take care of these things herself. Sam was very patient and told her it was all part of his job no matter how small or large the problem. Hannan was very kind to him and asked if he would like to pose for a few pictures with her. He was very happy for the opportunity and she shook his hand in every photo. Sam said "My wife and kids and gonna love this! I've worked in this building for eight years and you are the first senator that ever offered to take a picture with me!" He thanked her several times and he gave her his cell phone number in case she needed any more help. "I'm in this building everyday so I can be here pretty much as fast as you need me."

Sam had a bad headache by the time he got home that night and he took three Tylenol as soon as he got in the door. He told his wife and three young school age children about how nice Senator Hannan was to him today and they all looked at the photos her secretary had emailed to Sam's home. He fell asleep on his couch watching TV and his wife tried to get him to go to bed, but he said his head hurt too much and he would sleep there on the couch.

In the morning his eleven year old daughter went downstairs to wake him. She spoke to him and he did not respond. She shook him softly and then harder and harder. She got scared and began to cry. She yelled for her mother who came running. Sam was dead at age 39.

***

Erika was worried about Tommy because his bus was late coming home from school. She always arrived home an hour before he did and he was usually bursting through the door by now. She walked to the bus stop where some parents usually waited for the other three children who also took the same school bus. They were all concerned and one mom use her cell phone to call her friend whose child was on the same bus two stops before theirs. Her friend told her that her daughter said there was an accident. A little boy was hit by a truck, but it was not one of the boys from their bus.

Tommy's bus arrived 20 minutes late and when it stopped he came running off of it and told Erika what had happened. That evening when Matt and Jen were at home, Tommy retold the story to them about everything he saw.

When the school bus approached the stop to drop off third grader Kelly Springer, her mother and three year old brother were waiting for her by the side of the road. When the little boy saw the bus approaching from their right with the yellow flashing lights, but still at a distance, the boy ran from his mother straight toward the bus onto the road in front of an eight wheel dump truck. The truck was coming toward them from their left and had time to pass the bus before the red bus lights began to flash and all vehicles had to stop.

The boy's mother could not catch him and he was struck by the center of the truck bumper and the truck continued over the boy and completely past him before it stopped. The truck driver felt a thump against the bumper and he felt the entire truck rise and fall for an instant. The truck driver had looked at his side mirror to see if vehicles behind him were slowing, and in that instant the boy ran in front of him. The driver never saw him from his high truck cab.

The boy lay on the road motionless. His mother screamed and ran to him. The school bus driver immediately stopped and called on the bus radio for help. Tommy saw everything from his seat on the left side of the bus two rows behind the driver. Some of the children on the bus began to scream and cry.

The little boy lay on his back. He had a red mark and a quickly growing bruise on the left side of his forehead. The truck driver ran to the child. "I never saw him, I never saw him! Oh my God I am so sorry!"

The mother was on her knees bent over him. "Jeffery! Jeffery! Wake up honey its Mommy. Please wake up!"

116

Other vehicles stopped in the road and people gathered around the boy and his mother. The bus driver walked the little boy's crying sister off the bus and over to her mother. He told the mother the ambulance and police were on their way. She continued to talk to the boy and she touched his face and hands. She thanked God that he was breathing. She knew not to move him. All those gathered on the road soon heard the sound of sirens. Just then the boy's face took on a sleepy look, the tender look of a child just waking up. "Oh Jeffery honey, are you hurt?" His eyes opened and got big. He looked around to see where he was and then he looked at her and said, "Mommy, I saw big angels."

No one was able to see the invisible angel, who stepped in front of the boy and cushioned the blow of the truck. The angel protected him by laying him down on the road and covering the boy's body with his own while the truck passed over them both. Two more angels came and stood praying over the boy until he opened his eyes.

OPPORTUNITY

Omar waved to Hannan to catch her attention as she was ending a meeting in her office with a small group of United Auto Workers representatives. They were working every Democrat on Capitol Hill as hard as they could, to do whatever they could to get more government money to save their union jobs. "You know that I will do whatever I can. We are all in this together." Hannan told them as she shook their hands and escorted them out of her office.

"Senator may I speak with you a moment?" Omar said as he pulled her by the crook of her arm and directed her back into her office. He closed and locked the door behind him. They stood facing each other. "The president's office called and wants you with him tomorrow for a trip to New Hampshire. You will go with him on Air Force One. You will be picked up here at 9:45AM. This is the opportunity we have waited for. His office on the plane is an excellent place for you to speak with him. You must arrange it. You must be at your best." Omar took a copy of an email out of a folder and gave it to her. The email was from the White House and it included tomorrow's itinerary. He was as excited as she had ever seen him.

"Yes. This is what we have waited for. I will be ready."

Then Omar told her "The man in Pennsylvania is still a problem for us. There was a mishap when our men went to deal with him."

"Why do you tell me this? Why now? Why at this moment? I have enough on my mind especially after you tell me I will be with the president tomorrow." Omar pulled a photo of Matt out of his folder and gave it to her. She looked at it and gave it back to him. "Why do I need to see this?" she was frustrated and tense.

"You must know what we know. You will be as involved as all of us are at all times. You are accountable to us. If it is important for you to know, I will tell you. You ask no questions." Omar told her in his lecturing voice. He wanted to keep her on edge. He had known her for thirteen years and knew she was extremely focused under pressure.

"Yes. I understand. Now will you please leave me? I must read this email and do some work for tomorrow."

He nodded to her and turned to leave her office. "Please close the door after you."

She went behind her desk and sat down at her computer. She took some deep breaths and turned and stretched her neck and shoulders to work out the tension. Hannan did feel the pressure and she knew that if she failed this opportunity, she would rather be dead.

She used the Internet to find the floor plan of Air Force One.

AIR FORCE ONE

The President of the United States loved to campaign. It was something he was good at. His administration was eager to jump on any occasion to claim progress on the economic front. At the Segway plant in Bedford, New Hampshire where they manufactured the two wheeled personal transporter, Segway Inc. and General Motors and were announcing their joint venture to build a two person electric vehicle called the PUMA – Personal Urban Mobility and Accessibility. The president wanted to be there to help them make the announcement and to claim that jobs would be created and that this type of green technology was the future of the American automotive industry.

The event came together quickly and Senator Hannan and some other Democrat leaders were invited to make the one day trip. The president was getting use to depending on Hannan for her ability to articulate his plan on the TV news shows. The appearance with the president was to her benefit also because she faced re-election in 2010 and every good media opportunity was valuable. This was especially true since she was from the Detroit area that was so hard hit with the down turn of the "Big Three" auto makers. Hannan was included in every meeting regarding the auto industry and union bailout plans.

After the event and before they took off to head back to Washington aboard Air Force One, Senator Hannan asked the president's Chief of Staff Dwight Boreland if she could speak to the president privately. Her request was granted and 10 minutes after take-off Hannan met with the president in his executive suite toward the nose of the plane.

"Thank you for seeing me privately." Senator Anika Hannan said.

"Welcome to the Oval Office, elevation 35,000. That really was a great event and you'll get a lot of good press from it." The president sat down at his desk and lit a cigarette. "Don't tell anyone about this OK?" pointing to his smoke.

"Mr. President is this office secure. May I speak to you confidentially?"

"They tell me it's as private as it can be. Have a seat." he said pointing to a window seat near his desk. Hannan knew his office was the only place on the plane that was free of recording devices, but she also had her own white noise device that was built into her cell phone and she carried it inside her suit coat pocket. It was able to mask conversational speech from being recorded. It was designed for a space like his office.

That and the jet noise made her confident that their conversation could not be recorded.

She remained standing as she began to speak. "Mr. President I'll get right to my purpose. Sir, I have terrible information regarding the vice president. Scandalous, embarrassing information that will do you great damage. The information is true and reliable."

"Excuse me Senator, but what kind of bullshit is this?" He was angry and leaned toward her while still seated behind the desk.

"Mr. President, I have materials proving Vice President Peterson has had an affair with a woman. High resolution photographs, we have video, audio, DNA, hotel receipts, cell phone logs and a signed statement from the woman who has known and worked for him for ten years. She works for him still." Hannan opened the file folder she was holding and pulled out what looked like a 8.5 x 11" typed letter. The letter was actually a thin dry laminate that she peeled off of a photograph of the same size. The laminate covered the photo until she wanted to reveal it. She handed the photo to the president. The photo was of a nude woman and the half dressed vice president. He took a deep drag of his cigarette and exhaled smoke all over his desk.

"Why do you have this? Who else knows about this?"

"We do not want to release this information. We want the vice president to resign for health reasons and you to nominate me to replace him. That is all."

He stood up and glared at her. "That's all? Who the hell do you think you are? I am the President of the United States. You can't blackmail me. You're going to prison." As angry as he was, he kept his voice calm so he would not cause any alarm from anyone outside his office. He was smart enough to think that she had probably not played all her cards yet.

"Mr. President we have similar information about you. We have digital photos encrypted and alterations are undetectable. We can prove you had an affair with Stephanie Jackson, your staffer from Chicago, who also worked for you in Washington until last October."

"I barely know her. She's married and I think she has a baby."

"She has given us a statement that her baby is yours. We have DNA proof."

"That's impossible. You're insane."

"No sir. We have considerable resources at our disposal. We matched your DNA from samples we have collected from you over the last four years. The baby will pass any paternity challenge. I can give

122

you a tissue sample of the child to test if you like." She pulled a lapel pin off her suit and showed it to him. On the back of an American flag shaped pin was a small clear glass circle of fluid and a pink tissue sample within it.

"Keep your damn pin. You're sick." He sat back down and put out his cigarette.

"I'll have you in handcuffs in ten seconds..." and he reached for the phone.

"Think clearly Mr. President. You cannot afford to have this information made public. If we release it, your presidency will be ruined. Do you want the world to see you as the betrayer of your beautiful wife and children? Do you want to spend the next three years fighting off this scandal? We have more information than the press could digest in five years and we have other women willing to say the same thing. The world will see all of it unless the vice president resigns in 24 hours. You will nominate me as your vice president two days later. No discussion."

The president felt like he was hit in the chest. His mind raced trying to see some way out, or at least think of something to say. He went blank. He was never fast on his feet and he had no internal resources to call on nor did he have enough political savvy to know how to handle this. Hardball was a game he imagined he was good at but he had never played.

"Gather yourself and escort me out of this office. We will shake hands and smile outside this door. Do not contact me until after the vice president has resigned on television. You will call me two days later to ask me to accept the vice presidency. Do not test me. You have 24 hours from now." It was 4:30PM.

They stepped outside his office and in the doorway a White House photographer captured them exchanging smiles as they posed. They were both good actors. Senator Hannan walked away from the president past the president's security team and some senior staff. She took a bottle of water from a waiter and stopped to speak for a few minutes with two senate colleagues who also made the trip. Then she calmly returned to her seat in the guest area. This play had gone just as she had rehearsed it a thousand times in her mind.

It took the president a long time to calm down. He sat at his desk smoking and trying to think of some way to stop this, but he was not a fighter. His phone buzzed, "Mr. President, are you ready to practice the G-20 speech?"

123

"No. Not now. Give me a couple of minutes. I'll call you."

Things always came too easy to the president and he never had to work hard at anything. It did not take him long to realize Vice President James Peterson was not worth the effort of saving and he felt Peterson never really brought anything to his administration anyway. He was chosen as the vice presidential candidate because he was supposed to bring gravitas to the ticket, but even his own campaign staff said there was "no gravitas, just pain-in–the-ass". Peterson had been in the US Senate since 1972 and had himself run for president four times never getting his party's nomination. The president was already tired of "Old Jim" shooting off at the mouth. He had a reputation as a blowhard and had a habit of free lancing and getting off message on a weekly basis. Critics on the other side called the vice president a "serial exaggerator".

The president was exhausted by Peterson always wanting to be included in every meeting and photo op. He sent the vice president to his first funeral as soon as he could. The Prime Minister of Luxembourg died three weeks after they took office and that was a great reason to send Old Jim out of the country. The White House arranged some other meaningless diplomatic visits for him on the same trip to keep him out of Washington for seven days.

With the president's approval rating falling and his administration looking weak and unorganized in the face of the housing bubble bursting - economic crisis - Wall Street in the tank – banking and credit mess – AIG – TARP - bailouts – his stimulus plan, Iraq, Afghanistan, Iran and the North Koreans testing nukes and intercontinental missiles - he knew he could not have anything to do with a sex scandal. He knew the easy route was to cut the vice president loose.

The president was rattled by Senator Hannan. She scared him. He had met and spoken to her dozens of times since he was elected to the US senate in 2005. She was always friendly, amiable and had a sense of peace about her and lately she was one of his best allies in the Senate, always supporting his economic plan. She was very attractive and looked younger than her age. Hannan appealed to women and minorities and she was the most effective member of the senate at selling his recovery agenda.

This new side of her stunned him. Now it was as if she were another person. She was cold and mechanical and her dark brown eyes drilled right through his. He felt evil and danger about her. He knew he had no control of this situation. He just could not deal with any kind of scandal at this moment in time. His plate was overflowing. He did not know

Senator Hannan's motives beyond becoming vice president and he was worried about who was with her.

The president had been in Washington such a short time before becoming president that he knew he had no one he could trust or turn to. He knew his political enemies from either side could use this situation against him. He had no loyal friends at CIA or the FBI. There was no one on his own staff that he was close to on a personal level. They were primarily inexperienced leftovers from the presidential campaign. Almost everyone else was new to him and the new hires were mostly recommended by other Democrats who needed someone on the inside. His own closest staff members were really just a collection of career political hacks and pollsters. None of them had real political skill or situational experience. None of them could handle this type of crisis. He knew there would be leaks if he told anyone. His staff would write and sell a book about this faster than he could finish a press conference. He had some older friends in Chicago but they were people he had sought out and used to his advantage there and would be no use to him now. His wife had been his confidant, but this was beyond her pay grade. He always thought he was the smartest guy in every room, so he resolved himself to tell no one and try to control it by himself. He thought he could gather information and wait. He could not let his friendly press corps ride to his rescue this time. He was isolated by his own ego. The president only had hope, and he hoped he would get lucky.

After some time the president stepped out of his office and waved to his Chief of Staff Dwight Boreland. Boreland was a recycled politico from the last Democrat administration.

Boreland walked toward the president and saw a different body language on him. The president slumped and leaned on the door as if he were exhausted.

"Where's the VP?" the president said in an unusually soft tone.

"Sir, are you OK?" He thought the President did not look good. He said, "The vice president is in San Francisco with the speaker of the house. They were traveling together today and they have a fundraising event for the speaker tonight."

"Call him right away. Talk to him personally and tell him I must see him tomorrow, 7AM in the Oval Office. Be certain that he knows it's very important."

"He's gonna complain."

"You have no idea." the president said.

***

Senator Hannan did not speak to anyone for the rest of the flight back to Washington. She sat with her eyes closed and everyone thought she was asleep. She was mentally replaying in her mind what had just happened with the president, and she was preparing for what would happen in the next few days.

***

Al-Qaeda and Arish-Asad were now one step closer to their goal of having Anika Hannan one heartbeat away from the presidency. With Hannan as Vice President of the United States, Tehran would be prepared to quickly offer a new chapter of cooperation with the United States and Israel. They would agree to back off of their nuclear weapons program and invite the International Atomic Energy Agency inspectors back into Iran. Most importantly Iran would call on Al-Qaeda to lay down their arms and Hamas would agree to a cease fire arrangement with Israel. Tehran hoped the American President would believe these gestures and begin his withdrawal of troops from Iraq and Afghanistan, withdraw trade restrictions and make other concessions to Iran. The Iranians knew the American liberal press would be overjoyed and shower the American President with praise for his skills as a peacemaker.

Tehran's ultimate goal was to have Anika Hannan as a controllable President of the United States. Hannan was prepared to kill the president by using the meningitis bacteria, at a moment that that best suited Tehran. The timing had to be right to strike him down when it would maximize the appearance of weakness and vulnerability of United States. The world would mourn the death of a beloved world leader and it would offer overwhelming support to the first woman Muslim American President. As president, Hannan could completely withdraw the United States military presence in the Middle East under the banner of peace and new cooperative spirit. Formal peace treaties could be made between Iran and Israel. In time, when they felt Israel's defenses were down, the false peace would ultimately make it easier for Iran to make a grab for all of Iraq, Kuwait and Saudi Arabia to enrich their treasury and control the region with the largest oil supply in the world. Then they would attack Israel. Iran could depend on a President Hannan not to confront their moves and Israel would stand alone. If nuclear war came as a result of it, so much the better because the extreme fundamentalist Muslims like Ahmadinejad believe the war and apocalyptic chaos that would kill all the infidels would usher in the Twelfth Imam – Mahdi, to bring peace to a world totally under Muslim control.

BRITTNEY'S HOUSE

It was late Friday night and Matt was ready for bed. He walked into the kitchen to turn off the lights when he heard Erika's cell phone on the counter vibrate and buzz. It was unusual for it to be there because she usually charged it overnight in her bedroom. Matt thought - Why would anyone be texting Erika so late? He looked and saw that it was a message from Abby. She knew Erika is always asleep by now. He sensed it was something different so he opened the message. "Dad come get me brittney house help". His adrenalin surged. He found his sneakers grabbed his truck keys and yelled to Jen in the family room, "I gotta go get Abby!" The door slammed and Matt was out of the house before Jen could ask "What's wrong?"

He jumped in his truck and took off fast. Brittney, Abby's friend from school lived three miles away. Matt knew her house well. He had dropped off and picked up Abby and Brittney at her house a hundred times since the two were little girls in the same dance class in fourth grade. Matt knew Brittney's parents to be great people and knew there must be a big problem if Abby sent the text. Matt drove fast. He prayed God would help him and send angels if he needed them. He went through two stop signs without stopping, rounded the last curve then saw Brittney's house. The house looked dark. There were three cars in the drive way. Abby's, Brittney's and the last car pulled in the drive was an SUV Matt did not recognize. He pulled in as close as he could behind the SUV and jumped out of his truck. He saw the patio lights on around the back of the house and then he heard male laughter and voices. Matt ran toward the sounds. Before he got to the end of the driveway he saw one demon fly straight up from the direction of the voices. It flew fast into the air and out of sight. He thought - That's no good. If anyone lays a finger on these girls I'm gonna break some bones. He got angry and his heart was pounding. As he ran he also looked for something lying around the yard that he could use, like a baseball bat.

He rounded the corner and ran up to the patio. "Who the hell are you?" said a startled male who looked to be about 20 years old. He had dyed blonde hair and was same size as Matt's but 30 pounds lighter.

"Where is Abby? I'm her Dad."

"Hi Dad. Wanna beer?" a second one said and took a swallow from his own beer can. This guy was the same size as the other but with a younger face and a scroungy teenage looking beard.

"Look smart ass, where is Abby?"

"Which one is she? The hot one or the slutty one?" the dyed blonde said as he moved to get between Matt and the door to the house.

"Get out of my way" Matt said as he headed for the back door of the house.

As Matt stepped up onto the deck which led into the kitchen, a third male, shorter than the others but solidly built, came out of the house. No lights were on inside and it was completely dark. "You're not commin' in." he said to Matt while blocking the door. Matt sized all of the guys up fast. He thought he could take two of them at the same time, but three would be pushing it.

"Move!" said Matt as he stepped forward and he landed his right elbow under the third guy's chin knocking his head back and driving him into the doorway behind him landing on his rear end inside on the kitchen floor. He bit the tip of his tongue off when Matt hit him and he spit out blood. The other two ran at Matt and jumped on his back. Matt was able to spin the two around and onto the deck floor.

"Get off of him!" a loud voice said. They all looked up to see six huge men who seemed to appear out of nowhere. The men were dressed in regular street clothes, khaki pants, and golf and dress shirts. Two of them had neatly trimmed beards and they all had short hair cuts. Matt thought they looked like they just walked off a golf course at a country club.

"Oh crap!" the scroungy beard said. "Who are you guys?" The six men were angels. One of the angels grabbed the scroungy one by the belt of his pants and flung him backward off the deck and onto the grass where he landed 20 feet away. He tried to get up but instantly an angel put a foot on his back and pinned him tightly to the ground.

Dyed blonde was picked up and pressed against the vinyl siding of the outside wall of the house. His feet were two feet off the ground. The one with the short tongue was picked up by a third angel and also pressed against the same outside wall, feet dangling. Dyed blonde started to say something, "Silence!" an angel boomed at them. They felt his voice press on their chests like the concussion of thunder up close.

Matt and the three other angels went inside the kitchen and every light in the house came on at once. "Dad, is that you? We're up here!" Abby yelled from the second floor. In a white flash of light speed Matt and his team were inside the master bedroom where they found two other males. One was quickly pulling his sweatshirt on and his partner was trying to pull up his baggy pants and buckle his belt. Brittney, wearing jeans and just a bra was on the bed covering herself with a pillow. Abby was on the floor trying to get to her feet. Her hands were tied behind her back with a belt.

Baggy pants pulled a knife from his pocket and took a swipe at Matt. An angel grabbed him by the neck and belt, lifted him and pressed him against the ceiling, then slammed him into the bedroom wall so hard that the drywall was broken and dented with the shape of his body between the studs in the wall. He crumbled to the floor unconscious. The sweatshirt guy wound up to take a swing at Matt. Matt saw it coming and stepped out of the way and returned his own right cross that hit sweatshirt guy hard across the jaw. As his head snapped to his right, an angel gave him some extra momentum and drove him into a wall where he cracked a big hole in the drywall with his face. He also was knocked cold.

Both girls were crying. Matt untied Abby's hands and she hugged him. She then handed Brittney her top from off the floor and comforted her. "Oh Daddy you saved us. Thank you, thank God you came."

Matt saw a digital camera on the bed. He pointed to it and Abby said the guys were forcing them to take pictures. Matt deleted six pictures and said "No one needs to see them."

"You crushed those guys." Brittney said, still shocked and shaking from what just happened.

"Well, I had some help."

"Who? Is someone outside? Are the police here?" Abby asked.

The angels were gone. "Just now, you didn't see anyone else?" asked Matt.

"Of course not it was just you. Dad... wow I didn't know you could do that! I can't believe it. It was like in a movie!" Abby said trembling.

"I'm just glad I got your text message."

"Daddy, I couldn't use the phone. They would have heard me talking. I had to text fast and I knew your phone would be turned off so I sent it to Erika's."

"Thank God you're both safe. I have to call the police. No, you call 911, tell them to get here right now. Then call your Mom, both of you. I have to check the other clowns outside. If these two jerks wake up, drop that TV on their heads." He said pointing to the heaviest object in the room.

He ran down stairs to the kitchen and outside. All the angels were gone and the other three bad guys were asleep in chairs on the patio. Matt thought - How am I going to explain this? Yes officer these three

129

just fell asleep while waiting for you to get here. OK, if I just delete the angels from this story will that make me or these jerks look crazy? The police aren't gonna go for the angel theory so I guess I'm it. And that's how it went. Matt did not mention the angels, the jerks did not remember the angels and Abby and Brittney never saw the angels. The Police arrived quickly and took all five away for booking. They were facing serious charges.

"Did you guys see the hole in the wall where that kid put his face?" one police officer asked two others.

"Nice work Mr. Davidson. Care to do a demonstration for some of our officers sometime?" the police sergeant asked Matt.

"Hey no. Not me. This was just a lot of adrenalin, nothing fancy, well... I used to play football." Matt smiled feeling pretty embarrassed by it all and hoping the angels we not listening.

Abby, Matt and Brittney gave statements that night to the police. Matt took the girls back to his house until Brittney's parents arrived there at 2:30AM. They rushed home as soon as they could from what they hoped would be a relaxing overnight trip to Atlantic City for just the two of them.

The trouble started that evening while Brittney and Abby were at the mall. There they saw one of the guys who Brittney knew from school. He pestered them and followed them around while they shopped. Brittney made the mistake of mentioning that her parents were out of town. When they finally told him to get lost, he got mad, called his buddies and they all followed the girls to Brittney's house without the girls knowing. They forced their way into her house and it all got worse from there.

Standing in Matt's kitchen, Brittney's parents thanked him over and over again. Her mother said "God bless you Matt. You saved our daughter...our daughters."

"Well we can all thank God. You three should go home now and get some sleep. We can talk about this some more tomorrow if you want. Oh, and I can fix the drywall in your bedroom for you." Matt said. Brittney's parents looked at each other wondering what he meant by that.

Brittney said to her own father "Dad, wait till you see what Mr. Davidson did. Totally, totally awesome." She looked at Matt and said "Mr. Davidson, do you have any really young brothers like you that you could introduce me to?" Jen and Abby laughed and Matt blushed.

The next morning, Matt was sitting at his desk thinking about what happened at Brittney's house. He decided to write some notes for himself because he knew it was likely he would eventually need to retell this story in court. He could recall everything. He remembered what happened and who said what, but he could not remember running through the house and up the stairs to the bedroom where Abby and Brittney were. It did not take him very long to realize that he was moved or carried by the angels faster than he could understand. He believed angels traveled between heaven and earth at the speed of light or faster, and now he knew he had done the same...with their help.

SATURDAY – THE WHITE HOUSE

On Saturday morning, the President went to the Oval Office at 6:30AM after staying up late thinking about what he had to do. He was seated at his desk when at 6:50 Dwight Boreland came in to speak to him. "Mr. President, is there anything I should know about your meeting with the vice president this morning?

"You'll find out soon enough. The VP has something to tell me privately so it will be just me and him and make sure we are not disturbed." The president said without looking up at him.

"Yes sir. He should be here soon."

At that moment the president's secretary, Nancy Kline buzzed his phone. "Mr. President, the vice president is here to see you sir."

"Thanks Nancy, tell him to come in."

Boreland turned and took a few steps toward the door to leave as the vice president entered the room. "Hey Dwight, how ya doin pal?"

"Mr. Vice President." Boreland said as they shook hands quickly. Boreland then continued on his way out of the office.

Vice President James Peterson walked toward the president and reached out to shake his hand. The president rose from behind his desk, picked up a folder with his right hand and walked past the vice president without shaking hands. "Jim, let's take a walk." and he led the way out the door to the West Colonnade between the Oval Office and the White House Residence. It was a cool and crisp morning and the sun was rising over the trees in the east. The two walked side by side along the row of white columns without speaking. The vice president felt the mood of the president and he let him lead the conversation. There was a Marine honor guard standing at attention in his dress blues. When the president thought he was far enough away from him to be sure the Marine could not over hear them, the president stopped, turned and stepped in front of the vice president to face him and said "Jim, I want you to resign."

"Resign what?"

"You will resign the vice presidency today by noon."

"Are you out of your freaking mind? I will not! I got you elected you…"

"I was elected despite you, you pompous fossil."

"What the… Look, I've been in this town a lot longer than you pal." The vice president pointed his finger in the face of the president and he raised his voice. "Nobody messes with me. I'm one of the big boys…"

133

"Jim, shut up and keep your voice down. You're out. You'll resign today by noon in the White House press room because of your heart condition." He looked right past him as he said this. The president had a hard time looking the vice president in the eye.

"I don't have any damn heart condition!"

"You do now. And we're gonna have your medical history figured out by noon."

"What did I do? Why are you doing this?"

The President gave him a file folder that had the photo of him and the nude woman.

"I know her. Lindsay... something. Starts with an H. She works for me. That's at the Palomar Hotel. Who gave you this?"

Surprised by his reaction the president said, "Is this real?"

"Yeah, but I only nailed her a couple of times." He paused for a moment then said "We can fight this."

"You ass. This isn't the only photo. There's video, audio, DNA. There is a pile of information and she's ready to talk. You will not complicate my agenda and you will not take this presidency down into some sort of Clinton crap hole that I'll have to deal with every day for who knows how long. Look, the timing couldn't be worse. I'm up to my neck in this economy bullcrap, the banks and the GM thing. If this get's out I'm not gonna get anything done and you know I have even bigger things I want to do. I have Cap and Trade to push through and I owe the unions the Card Check bill. I've got to expand healthcare and get the Value Added Tax... I just don't need this problem or your crap."

Peterson's attitude changed. He knew he did not have much of a case to plead and he knew the president was serious. "Please don't do this to me. I'll be a great VP. I'll keep my mouth shut. I'll do anything you want. Can we pay her off? I had to pay off some girl about twenty years ago. How about you? Do you want money, cash? I know guys who..."

"Just shut up. This is all your fault. If you weren't such a jerk to work for... the woman hates your guts and she wants you out. This will all stay quiet if you resign. You don't want to drag your wife and family through this."

"Can't we take her out? You know... "

"You idiot. She isn't alone." The president said exasperated and not believing how stupid he was. "She's got lawyers negotiating this with us." He lied to Peterson to build his own case for getting him to resign.

The vice president took a long look at the photo. "I'm screwed."

"Yeah." the president said. They were both silent for a long moment. He could not look at the vice president. He stared off across the Rose Garden looking at the blooming cherry blossoms. He thought about what other good news spring would bring to his presidency.

"We've got work to do. We have to figure out the history of your heart problems and you have to write a resignation letter and something for the press. I already wrote my statement last night. Dwight Boreland will help you and we need to talk to your doctor right away."

The president called Boreland into his office and explained to him that the vice president would resign today because of his heart condition. Boreland helped with the statements and called the press secretary to the Oval Office and briefed him.

They announced to the world that the vice president was being treated privately by his family doctor for the last nine months for an irregular heart beat and angina. They said his trouble started last August during the presidential campaign. They told the story that yesterday in San Francisco he had chest pain that he did not report to anyone because he did not want to disrupt the speaker of the house's trip. He saw his doctor last night when he got back to Washington and had an EKG test done at his doctor's office. All of this explained and gave cover for his unexpected return to DC. They explained that the vice president decided this morning with his wife that he needed to resign because he could not make a 100 percent effort to his work toward revitalizing the ailing economy and he needed to eliminate the physical stress of the constant work he was doing. The vice president said he had full confidence in the president to find the best nominee to replace him. At 1PM they had their press conference and by 2PM the former vice president was home explaining it all to his hysterical wife.

***

There were now a hundred things running through the president's mind. He worried about how much further Senator Hannan would press him. Would she use the same blackmail threat to force him to resign after she became vice president? He hoped he would have time to intercept her plan somehow and keep it from getting that far. The president also worried that Jim Peterson would not be able to keep his mouth shut.

The president's staff hoped they could delay the nomination process as long as possible in order to distract the public from the stream of bad economic news every day. Most of Washington was glad to see Peterson gone. The press did not care about him but they were thrilled that now they had a new story. Who would the president nominate to replace Old Jim? Within minutes of the resignation, the talking heads on the news networks had names flying everywhere. Most of the names were the same old players but there were a few new ones. Senator Anika Hannan was on several lists.

***

At 1PM Saturday, Jen, Matt and Tommy were inside Sam's Club buying a jumbo pack of toilet paper, a big pack of napkins, a giant bottle of dishwasher liquid, and a big box of frozen quesadillas. Matt loved anything in bulk. He wished he could buy his favorite brand of underwear at Sam's in 30 packs, but so far the Fruit of the Loom Company had not taken up his suggestion to package them in bulk. Matt liked anything that saved money and roaming around the big store relaxed him. He and Jen liked to people watch, and this store on a busy afternoon was a goldmine.

Matt watched some gasbags cruising about the store, but there seemed fewer than usual. He saw one angel standing close by a shopping cart where an unattended three year old boy was standing in the middle of it. The parents were several feet away not paying attention. The angel looked at Matt and then turned his head to look at the parents. "I can't believe these people." Matt said out loud to himself and walked directly to them. The parents saw him coming. "You can't leave your baby alone like that. He has to be in the seat strapped in."

"Who are you?" the mother asked.

"I'm Mr. Commonsense. Pay attention to your boy before he falls out of the cart and breaks his neck."

The mother yelled at the boy "Reggie, sit down!" then she did as Matt told them to do and placed him properly in the child seat.

Matt looked at the angel who nodded to Matt and vanished. Matt told Jen what had just happened and he said "I hope the angels don't have to do this kind of babysitting all day long."

"It's amazing. Some people are so carelessly, ignorantly stumbling through life only kept from harming themselves by the grace of God."

"Amen sister." Matt said, and they shared a frustrated laughed.

They paid for their things and carted them to Jen's car and loaded the trunk. As they drove away, Jen turned on the Philadelphia news radio station. They heard the announcement that Vice President Peterson had resigned and they looked at each other in disbelief. "Matt, if Hannan gets the vice president job we'll know for sure she's the reason for you seeing all the ... stuff." Jen stopped herself from saying angels when she remembered Tommy in the back seat. Tommy was not really listening to them. He was playing with his Game Boy.

Matt said, "Ya know, I feel like I'm standing in the middle of a circus. There's clowns all over the place, jugglers throwing knives up in the air, acrobats tumbling and flip flopping, and high wire walkers teetering between chaos and what used to be ordinary. I'm just waiting for the wild animals to break out of their cages and tear everything apart. I see all these things in motion. Nothing is normal. This president practically came out of thin air, now the vice president resigns, Hannan is a media superstar with those things swarming all over her. This economy is free falling, and the president is taking over corporations. We're in Alice's Wonderland. All logic is gone. Who is the ringmaster at this circus?"

Jen let out a sigh and said "I just want to go home and get on the couch and cover up with a blanket. But I know we have to keep watching. There is purpose in all of this. Maybe we should be talking to someone at church."

"I don't know. If the shoe was on the other foot, would you believe my story? – Hey Matt, you see angels huh? Well good luck with that. Gotta go! I've been praying that if God wants someone else to know about the angels, He will bring them to us. I'm not going to worry about it. If it's just you and me for however long, so be it."

"Dad, what about angels? Are you talking about angels again?" Tommy asked.

"Yeah Buddy. Mom and I just love to talk about angels."

"Well could you talk about them while we are in the McDonald's drive through?"

Just then Matt's cell phone rang. It was a tenant calling about her heat not working. Matt knew her second floor apartment thermostat might fail soon, so he told her he thought he knew what the problem was and he would be over later that afternoon to take care of it. They stopped at McDonald's and then drove home and unloaded their goods. Matt went by himself to go to his other favorite store.

***

The parking lot at Home Depot was unusually busy and Matt found a parking spot about fifteen 15 rows from the front of the store. As he walked to the entrance, a Jaguar XKR open convertible in Salsa Red zipped into a handicapped parking spot right in front. A young man in his thirties got out and ran into the store. Matt thought – That guy better be handicapped or he will be after I kick his... Oh Lord, forgive me. I'm sorry for thinking that way. Matt walked by the car and looked and there was no handicapped license plate or handicapped parking tag hanging off the rear view mirror. Matt sent up a quick prayer "Lord I pray that young man has some urgent mission that requires him to take the parking space from someone who may truly need it. But if he is indeed healthy, and has parked in a selfish manor, please send a flock of birds to smite the lovely leather upholstery of his fine $80,000 British automobile. Amen."

SUNDAY AFTERNOON

The president had cancelled all of his appointments Saturday so he would appear to be thinking about what to do regarding the Peterson resignation. He still saw no options. He told no one about what happened with Hannan and he came up with no plan for what to do. He knew he needed to keep to her deadline so he arranged a meeting with a group of assistants and advisors at the White House to discuss who should be the nominee for the vice presidency. The meeting included Dwight Boreland, Press Secretary Albert Jones, the president' former campaign advisor Dennis Anckel, the Democrat Senate Majority Leader, the Chairman of the DNC, and the editor of the New York Times, Arthur Sulzberger Jr. The president went into the meeting knowing what the outcome would be.

They all arrived at the White House after the Sunday morning news shows. Everyone at this meeting except the president had made the rounds at the news networks early and did interviews and speculated with all the other experts and pundits. Every news program was focused on who would be nominated. The meeting was held in the Cabinet Room in the West Wing. They all sat at the middle of the long conference table. The president, Boreland and Jones sat on one side and the five others sat across the table. Former Vice President Peterson asked to be in the meeting but Boreland was told to make it clear to him to stay home.

"You guys know I don't like to go slow on anything. I need to make this VP pick and keep moving ahead. I have my own list of names and I'd like to hear any suggestions of others and your rationale." the president said.

Boreland asked "Mr. President, would you prefer to tell us who is on your list and then we can add to it, so as not to be redundant?"

"No. You guys let me know who you think could work." He said this because he wanted to know what they were thinking before he gave up his names, just in case he forgot a good choice. He was committed to playing out this charade so he put himself into the game of working through the process. "I want to scrap the list from last time when we picked Jim Peterson."

Two of the men took their pens and crossed out names on their lists.

Boreland said "Sir, there are no 100 percent obvious choices. May we just start naming names and discuss each as we go?"

"Good idea. OK, who do you have?"

The majority leader said "Well, I'll point to the elephant in the room. Hillary Clinton."

"How many times do I have to tell you guys? No freakin way. I have her right where I want her and it cost me a lot to put her there. She gave me nothing but crap during the primaries and then I had to kiss her rear and make up. We've all been dealing with the Clintons since '92. Listen to me. No. Got it?" the president could not believe that he could not get out from under her shadow.

The majority leader said "Sir, would you consider Bill Clinton? He'd do well for you internationally, his fundraising pull is down but he can sell anything."

"Harry ... guys." The president said shaking his head "This is not a good way to start our meeting. Let's just get past them please."

"Sorry Mr. President." Harry said.

The DNC Chairman said "Sir, John Kerry is extremely available. He has fallen so far off the radar since 2004 he would not be controversial. He is bored in the Senate and would love the vice president job."

"Kerry? I wouldn't have thought of him in a million years. Did he ask you to bring up his name?" the President asked.

"Sir... Senator Kerry has always polled fairly well nationally and ..."

"Yeah but he couldn't even beat Bush. Next."

"Ron Paul." Albert Jones said. "You'd pick up a lot of independents, tea baggers, and libertarians."

"What the ... are you serious? He's old, goofy and ...no. Just no."

Boreland spoke up next. "Governor Schwarzenegger, sir? I know he would accept a nomination and he is desperate to get out of the mess in California. Plus he's virtually a Kennedy."

"What about being foreign born? Those wack jobs are still dogging me on that one."

"Well sir," Boreland continued "there is similar a case in France where a Belgian was elected to the Assemblee Nationale, contrary to the French constitution. We think there may be an international precedent....."

"Come on, even so, Arnold campaigned for McCain. I'm not liking the trend here, who else do you guys have?"

Anckel threw a name into the ring. "Bill Richardson. He's dying to get back in the game."

"Possible. He supported me against Hillary and we did give him about ten seconds of consideration last time. Put him back on the list.

No, wait. What's wrong with you Dennis? Don't you remember we just went through this with him and he had to bail out from the Commerce Secretary job I nominated him to because of some investigation about him exchanging state contracts with somebody for contributions. Nope. Sorry Bill, see ya next lifetime."

"Look you guys are 0 for 6. I'm getting pretty pissed. Is this it?" the president said. He enjoyed acting like he was angry.

"Mr. President, I have not spoken to him or his people directly but would you consider Vice President Al Gore as a candidate?" the DNC Chairman asked.

"OK. Let me hear what you want to say." The President said as he stuck out his chin and looked at the ceiling.

"Al Gore could seal the deal for you regarding Cap and Trade, green technology, clean coal, you name it. He has the Nobel Prize, did the movie, he looks old and out of shape but…"

"Do any of you really think Al Gore would want to be a three time Vice President? He is too busy making money selling his global warming stuff. Did you know he was worth two million dollars when he left office and now he is worth 100 million dollars? He wants to be the first environmental billionaire. Is this really it? Is this the best you guys have? This is ridiculous." The President said this with his serious tone while inside he was laughing.

Boreland said "Colin Powell, Mr. President. He definitely has the gravitas factor and he has come a long way toward supporting most liberal views since he worked for the Bush's. He would be comfortable in the VP role, and he knows everybody in the world."

"OK. Now here we go. I will say that he is on my list, and he is a good man. He'd support me on military issues, Iraq, Afghanistan and I think he's on board with missile reduction. I'll tell ya, if he can go to the UN and make the case for the Iraq war and talk about uranium cake…"

"Yellowcake sir."

"…whatever, and look like a fool in front of the world for Bush, he'd do whatever I send him out to do. I am definitely considering him. We don't need any further comment about Powell."

Boreland was feeling confidant after throwing Powell's name on the table so he wanted to be the one to say "Mr. President, you must consider Anika Hannan. Sir, I don't have to tell you how active she has been…"

"You have no idea." The president said out loud to himself then he rubbed the back of his neck.

"…supporting you through the campaign and now articulating your economic agenda. She probably should have gotten the treasury secretary's job. She is a genius at speaking without notes…"

The president gave an annoyed cough to clear his throat.

'Sorry sir. Of course she would be an historic choice, first woman VP, she is a minority - Iranian American, she has a 69% overall approval ratings, all women seem to love her. All men think she is great to look at. We found out that she polls unusually high with gays because they hope she might be gay. She's from economically challenged Detroit, she's a lawyer, a PhD. Sir, Hannan was built for this. She's got the whole package. It's a shame she wasn't the pick first time around instead of Peterson."

"Yeah, Peterson. Look where that gravitas pick got me." Then he paused and asked the group. "What do you guys *really* think of her? What do you know *about* her? Does *anyone* really know her?"

Sulzberger Jr said "Mr. President I've been following her for years. Since she first ran for the Senate. I have never heard an ill word about her, not on our side at least."

"Sir, we all know she works like she's on a mission. I've never known of her to turn down any of our candidates for help. Everyone looks better when they are with her on camera or in person. She has some kind of natural credibility when she speaks." The DNC Chairman said.

The majority leader added "She runs a tight office, kinda private, not a lot of inner circle types but she has been consistent and always supports what we need. There is some level of mystery about her. It's probably because she is single and just works all the time. There seems to be no private, personal side to her."

"I'm certain she has a private side." the president said and he just stared at nothing as he spoke. "OK. She's on my list."

Jones asked "Mr. President, may we step outside the box for a moment?"

"Go for it." He was curious where this might lead and he was glad to move off Hannan as the subject.

"You… we could approach Bill Gates or Warren Buffet. Sir, their help, their stature on the economy would be…"

"No. Guys, come on. I don't need one of the two wealthiest men in the world trying to help me sell my brand of economic recovery. Anyway, they don't believe in it. I've talked to both of them privately.

Buffet especially doesn't buy into my stuff. He is polite to me but no, and Gates would be bored to death, he'd never say yes. What does that radio guy Limbaugh say? Couldn't afford the pay cut? Hey Jones, you aren't going to say Donald Trump next are you? He's peed on my leg quite a bit lately in the press."

"No sir. You're right."

The Leader spoke up again with a slightly timid tone. "If you don't mind Mr. President, I'd like to toss up one more. And please consider that I am under great pressure to do so." He smiled one of those - you know what I mean smiles. "Mr. President, please consider the speaker of the house. Sir, this could be an opportunity to get her more under control and she'd love it, another first for her career. It would be a great finishing touch for her legacy. "

The president smiled and said "Are you kidding? After all the water boarding CIA stuff. I can't trust her to tell me the right time of day. Did you guys see the video somebody did as a spoof of her at my state of the union speech? Her sitting aside of Jim Peterson. Remember when she was jumping up and down behind me every ten seconds applauding and clapping her hands like a wind up monkey. They turned video clips of her into a workout video. Check it out on YouTube. Really funny."

"Thank you sir. I did what I was asked to do." Harry said. The president gave him the OK sign with his hand.

"Well is that it? Have we forgotten anyone?" the president asked. They all just looked at each other and no one had anything else. "OK. When I decide, what do we do then?"

Boreland said "Pretty simple sir. Just give the nominee a call and then the White House Management Office will prepare the docs. All these people have been vetted before for various appointments or committees so that won't be a problem. Then we get him or her in here for the presser, the usual big announcement scenario here at the White House. We will write your nomination speech. After that we should send the nominee out for as many appearances as we can in between nomination and congressional approval. We can dominate the news for days, get people's attention off the economy for a while."

"Would you tell us your thoughts sir?"

"No. Let me consider it a little longer and then I'll call Boreland. Gentlemen, thank you for your input."

CHINESE FOOD

Matt and Jen were exhausted from trying to keep up with events. They both did their best at work to get things done all week. Jen would peek at news on the Internet at her office and was constantly listening to news radio in her car. Matt was trying to keep his projects going but found himself completely distracted. With the resignation of the vice president yesterday, the intensity level went up and they both felt a sense of urgency to watch Senator Hannan and find out how God was using the gift given to Matt.

They had been home most of the weekend and the kids were bored and cranky. This was a rare Sunday evening when they were all together so Matt decided they all needed to get out of the house. They gathered up all three kids and went to the mall to have dinner at their favorite Chinese buffet restaurant. It was 5PM when Matt pulled into the mall parking lot and found the spot closest to the entrance right next to the blue handicapped spaces.

"Primo parking... I feel like I won a contest."

Erika said "Dad you're the king of the parking thing."

"Dad when I grow up I want to be able to park a truck just like you." Tommy added with his nine year old sarcasm.

"Why thank you Son. Ya know, when I was a young man like you, I dreamed of the day when I would be able to park my truck in a spot just like this one surrounded by my family and loved ones. Sniff sniff. Today is a dream come true." Matt said while pretending to get choked up and wiping away a fake tear.

"Well let's go inside so you can accept your parking award." Jen said.

The family was followed to the mall by three Arish-Asad men in a van. They parked at the far edge of the parking lot where no other cars were. The driver of the van stopped with his passenger side facing the driver side of Matt's truck. The parking lot was flat and they were at the same elevation. Two men in back of the van opened the sliding door half way and readied their high powered rifles. One shooter was to target Matt's head and the other his chest.

Erika and Abby got out of the truck on opposite sides. Tommy followed Abby out of the right side. Matt waited a moment until Jen finished using the visor mirror to "put on her lips."

The shooters had clear lines of sight. They had Matt's door window in their cross hairs and were ready to fire their weapons. The shooter with the head shot would fire first.

A shining black Cadillac Escalade pulled up fast and stopped behind Matt's truck completely blocking the view of the shooters. Two seconds later, four more identical vehicles pulled up all around the truck and formed a shield of steel. A fifth vehicle pulled up in a position closer to the Arish-Asad van. It's roof popped open and a M134 Gatling gun on a swivel capable of firing 4,000 rounds per minute rose up and the gunner pointed it directly at them. The shooters saw four large men jump from each vehicle and surround the Davidson's. To the Arish-Asad, the men appeared to be Secret Service agents wearing dark suits and dark sun glasses and half of them holding weapons. They all looked directly toward the shooters. Matt and Jen got out of their truck and the whole family walked pleasantly into the mall surrounded by twenty angels.

One shooter slammed the van door closed and yelled "Let's go! Let's go! Get us out of here!" The driver took off as fast as he could, speeding through stop signs on their way.

Matt and the family had a great time together at dinner. They all ate too much. They enjoyed being with their kids and trying to keep their minds off their situation. Matt noticed that he did not see any angel or demon activity the entire time they were out. It was as if God knew he needed a break. Matt and his family were unaware of what had happened in the parking lot and they did not know that they had a legion of angels at the ready.

***

At the White House the president called Boreland on the phone to tell him he selected Senator Hannan for vice president. "Keep this quiet until I call her."

"When do you want to call her? I can set it up right now."

"No. I can't call her till tomorrow."

"Why not?"

"Look, just don't do anything or tell anyone till then, OK? What you can do is get the paperwork started, and absolutely no leaks. Be here early tomorrow. I'm gonna call her in the morning."

***

The Arish-Asad men in the van, who fled from the mall, drove for miles before stopping to calm themselves down and decide what to do. They had crossed the Benjamin Franklin Bridge and gone into New Jersey. They pulled along the side of a smaller two lane road outside a small town. They were not sure where they were and at the moment they did not care.

The van driver said "We must go back and tell what happened and tell what we saw."

"We did not complete our assignment." the first shooter replied.

"How could we? You saw all of them." the second shooter said. "You know what happened to Nazim!"

"He was a fool. Talking about demons. This was real. It must have been Secret Service. No one else has vehicles like that. How did they know about us? Who tipped them off? There must be a spy or a traitor with us. Who is this man that he has such protection?" the driver asked.

"I am not going back to tell them we failed. I am not going to die for this. You can do what you want. I am leaving. I quit!" the second shooter said and he got out of the van and started walking ahead of them along the side of the road.

"He cannot leave us." The driver said. The second shooter was already 100 feet in front of the van, walking fast and he had just pulled out his cell phone to make a call. The driver started the van and drove toward the second shooter and suddenly accelerated and drove over him and then stopped. "Get out! We must pick him up. Make sure we get his phone and anything else." They both got out and quickly lifted his injured and unconscious body into the back of the van and slammed the doors closed.

"We must take his things back with us, but I want to dump his body. Get back there and cut off his hands and head. We will throw them in the river on the way back. We will dump the rest of him somewhere else."

"I will not! He is not dead! You do it! Do you know what a mess that will be? I only have a pocket knife. You kill him, you do it. Why do you want to do this? No one knows him. He does not have a police record. He is not registered in this country."

"Forget it. We will dump him as he is in the river off the high bridge."

They found their way back to the Benjamin Franklin Bridge that crosses the Delaware River from Camden to Philadelphia. They waited until dark to cross. At the midpoint of the bridge, they stopped in the far right lane, turned on their hazard flashers and pulled their now groggy partner out the side door and dropped him 200 feet over the side into the cold water.

147

One hour later they met with their cell captain and reported what they saw and what happened. The information was relayed up the chain. Killing the quitter bought them some credibility and they lived to see the next day.

**

When the DC commander was told about Matt and his family at the mall, he immediately thought that either Matt was a set-up placed with Rashid at the FBI in order to draw the Arish-Asad out, or the president had told the Secret Service about the play Hannan had made on Air Force One and somehow Matt was connected. Either way, they could not stop the operation because they could not be sure if either of his theories was correct and they could not waste the opportunity that was already in motion. He contacted Tehran to keep them informed. They were much more upset than he was, but they agreed there was no way to stop at this point. They instructed the commander to make sure Hannan was aware of the possibility the president was talking to the Secret Service or another agency. The commander wanted to hear Rashid's side of the story.

**

Omar's cell phone rang at 12AM and the commander told him what happened with Matt and to prepare for the possibility that the president may have spoken to the Secret Service. Omar in turn, called Hannan immediately and relayed the information.

"Senator, it is possible the man Matthew Davidson is a FBI plant. Another attempt was made today to eliminate him and he had Secret Service protection that kept him alive. We do not know what connection there is between him and the president. The president may have told the Secret Service about your conversation with him."

"Why do you do this to me? You tell me this at the worst time. I am supposed to hear from the President at any moment and you give me more of this to burden me."

"We all follow orders. My orders are to keep you informed."

MONDAY – ROAD TRIP

Matt woke up early at 5AM. His first conscious thought was to pray. Jen was asleep facing him. She usually slept on her side with her hands together under her chin. He looked at her and thought how much he loved her and how much she still looked like the girl he fell in love with at college. He got out of bed as quietly as he could so as not to disturb her. He wanted her to sleep as long as possible before she had to get ready for work. He was careful to tuck his side of the blanket up against her so she would not feel any cool air or feel an empty space.

He walked down the hall to his office. He was wearing a t-shirt, pajama pants and slippers. He sat down at his desk in front of his blank computer screen. He disconnected Erika's iPod that was lying on the desk plugged into his computer charging. He put the stapler, Post-it-Notes and some pens and a pencil back in their places. His kids had a hard time putting things back where they found them.

Matt settled into his chair and he put the fingers of his hands together and leaned his head onto his hands on top of the desk. Matt prayed, "Lord Jesus, thank you for this day. Thank you for knowing me and my family. Thank you for always being faithful to us, providing for us. We have never been without. Jesus I seek wisdom and your guidance, and instructions for what to do with all I know and have seen. All these things make me believe that the senator is the focus of what you are showing me. Tell me Lord what to do. Please tell me what I can do to serve you. Who should I tell? I am not afraid. I will wait for you and I will not go forward without you. Lord please make it plain to me or speak to me through your Word or through your angels. I pray in the name of my Lord and Savior Jesus Christ."

Matt sat still and he listened. Answers to prayers came in many ways. Sometimes the answer was no or not now. Sometimes it took years to get an answer. Matt was learning patience and listening for God was hard and he struggled with it his entire Christian life.

"You will know my voice." came to him. It seemed like one of his own thoughts but he believed it. Yes, he would know God's voice and he prayed on that thought for a time.

"Seek her out." came to him as clear as if it was spoken to him. It was so real he could play it over in his head. He got goose bumps and he felt his heart swell up. Matt heard the Lord's voice. He got on his knees and prayed thanking Him.

Matt checked the Internet news websites to find out the latest about Hannan. She was getting the most talk from the media about her possible nomination. He discovered a story from the Detroit Free Press that reported she would be in Detroit tomorrow at an economic recovery rally.

Jen was still in bed. He went to her side of the bed and said "Jen, I'm going to see Hannan."

She was just starting to push back her blankets to get out of bed. "What are you saying?" she said as she sat up.

"Hannan's going to have some sort of stimulus, recovery slash big giant bank bailout party tomorrow in Detroit... where she's from. She's out selling the president's plan. It will take me about nine or ten hours to drive there. If I'm ever going to get to meet her it has to be soon because if she gets nominated for vice president, I'll never get near her. They'll beef up security around her and..."

"Wait. Why do you think you have to get near her?"

He sat down next to her "God told me to." He gave her his little boy smile.

"Ya know, if you had told me that a month ago I'd have locked you in the basement... what exactly did God tell you?"

"I was praying and he told me to "Seek her out." I heard his voice in my head as clear as you're speaking to me now. Jen, I know His voice. I heard it. I'll know it forever."

"Oh Matt, this is wonderful. Thank you Lord! But what are you supposed to do when you seek her out? What do you think that means?"

"Not sure. But I finally have some direction and I'm going. I'm not afraid. What the heck could happen?"

"Well remember what happened to John the Baptist? The apostle Peter was crucified upside down and Stephen was stoned to death and..."

"Aw gee honey, you're such a comedian. Really, I'm nervous but I'm not scared."

"When do you need to leave?"

"I'd like to be on the road by noon. Pack a bag and just go." He stood up and went to his closet to look for a travel bag.

"I can go with you." She said it but she did not mean it.

"Actually I was thinking about calling Pete to go with me. He likes when I drive fast."

"Great. Get killed driving fast on a mission from God".

He turned around and looked at her and said "It's 106 miles to Chicago, we got a full tank of gas, half a pack of cigarettes, its dark, and we're wearing sunglasses." Matt quoted his favorite line from The Blues Brothers movie. "I'll have to tell Pete to bring his sunglasses."

***

At 7AM Hannan was just about to leave her apartment. She lived east of Washington DC, between the U.S. National Arboretum and Fort DuPont Park near the Anacostia River. It was a beautiful area where she spent time walking for exercise. Her phone rang. WHITE HOUSE GOVT showed on her display. She pressed the green button and said "Senator Hannan here."

"Senator, please hold for the President of the United States." It was the president's secretary calling. Hannan waited about fifteen seconds and noticed herself standing straighter as if at attention.

"Senator, this is the President."

"Good morning sir."

"Senator I'm calling you to ask you to accept the nomination for Vice President of the United States. I would like to submit your name to Congress today. Will you accept?"

"Yes sir. It will be my privilege to do so."

"OK. We would like to do this today… this afternoon. Can you be at the White House by 11AM? There are some documents to take care of and we'd like to keep a lid on this till then so please use the special access. We don't want anyone to see you enter the building."

"Thank you sir." She said and hit the off button. She picked up her briefcase and headed to her office.

Dwight Boreland was with the President when he made the call. "Well Mr.President, that was pretty quick. Pretty business like. No congratulations, no slobbering thank you sir."

The president said "Don't you have things to take care of? Who is going to tell the press to get their asses in here before noon? I want to see a nomination speech on my desk pretty fast, so get moving."

***

Matt waited until 8AM to call Pete. The two of them had met three years ago at church and had become friends. They felt relaxed around each other and they realized right away that they shared a similar sense of humor. The first time they spent time together was when they worked

151

the griddle at a church pancake breakfast. Both of them loved pancakes, eating and making them. Matt prided himself on his home made pancake batter and Pete had a home recipe of his own. They had fun discussing techniques for folding the egg whites into the batter as the last key step to fluffiness. "It really is more art than mere cooking. Batter is my medium." Pete said.

"I think of each pancake as unique and beautiful, like snowflakes really. I wish I could take a photo of each one." Matt said. Both of them signed up right away to make pancakes because they wanted to work the big professional griddle in the church kitchen. Matt always wanted to someday have access to a large griddle where he could make dozens of pancakes at the same time.

"I have got to get one of these." Pete said. "I could make room for it. I don't really need a kitchen sink."

Matt told Pete "I almost got a job at McDonald's when I was a kid, just so I could work the breakfast shift and make pancakes."

Pete said "Maybe my wife would go for one of those Japanese hibachi things. I could put it right there in the dining room and throw out the dining room table. I could make a three foot diameter pancake. I'd need one of those long handle pizza lifter things for it."

"Hey Pete, ya know, workin' this griddle, I feel like I went to fantasy pancake camp and I'm getting to play on a professional field. I'd pay to do this." Matt also told Pete "Just for one game I'd love to sell popcorn or cotton candy at a professional baseball game. That way I could honestly say I once worked in professional sports."

Pete and his wife Debbie had been to Matt and Jen's house for dinner a few times so they were all well aquatinted and liked each other. Pete was an information technology employee at a large pharmaceutical company until he was laid off three weeks ago. Pete joked with Matt and said that since the economy was bad, people could not afford their recreational drugs. The company he had worked for made Viagra, so he was now out of work. Pete was a large man. At 6' 3" he was three inches taller than Matt. He had a big chest, thick neck and big arms. Pete was a heavyweight wrestler in college and kept himself in good condition. Matt was always amused by watching how other men looked at Pete. They always gave Pete plenty of room when he entered a space. With Pete's black hair and short thick black beard, he reminded Matt of the character "Bluto" in the old Popeye cartoons. Matt always wanted to call him Bluto, but he never did.

"Pete, its Matt. What are you doing today and tomorrow?"

"Hey Buddy! What am I doin? Well I'm lookin' at five job offers right now and more offers are pourin' in. Just considering who best fits my needs. It's a regular bidding war for my awesome IT talents." Pete said. Matt could hear the sarcastic humor in Pete's voice.

"Hey great, well I guess you're busy then."

"Dude, no. Seriously…other than Oprah on at four o'clock, I'm kinda wide open."

"Good. Then you can come with me to Detroit. I've got to drive out and look at two houses I might buy."

"Detroit huh? I bet you can pick stuff up there cheap."

"Yeah but this will be… I mean yeah they are pretty interesting. Wanna go? Just one overnight."

"Why not? I'll call Debbie at work and tell her the good news…she can sleep in the middle of the bed tonight!"

"Alright, I'll pick you up at 11:00?"

"I'll be ready. We can stop for supplies on the way. Coffee, Gatorade, beef jerky, pork rinds, Cheez Doodles, Yodels, Ring Dings, Twinkies and a case of Spam."

"Bring a pair of sunglasses." Matt said and he hung up.

Jen walked into the office just as Matt was ending the phone call and she overheard the last part of the conversation because he had it on speaker while he looked at Internet news.

Jen said "God's got some sense of humor to get involved with a guy like you."

Matt got up from his desk chair and went to her. "You've got some sense of humor to be involved with a guy like me."

"It's been fun and you can always make me laugh." Then she gave him her serious look. "I want you to be careful, drive nice, no speeding. Let Pete drive too."

"OK. I will be careful." He paused for a moment and said "I've got to do this."

"I know. I know you do. I'll be praying for you. Call me, text me whatever but I need to hear from you."

"Don't worry, I'll call." Matt pulled Jen to him. "Thanks for believing me. I know I haven't given you any proof but it's all true."

"I do believe you. Go do what God is calling you to do and then come back home to me."

Matt made up the story about looking at two houses because he knew Pete would not be interested in driving all the way to Detroit for a political event. He also knew that Matt would never drive 569 miles to see a liberal like Hannan. He promised God that he would look at two houses in the Detroit area. He just did not know which two.

***

Matt pulled up at Pete's house at 11AM exactly. Pete came right out carrying a travel bag, a GPS car navigation system, a cooler and a sleeping bag.

"What's with the sleeping bag?"

"A good Scout is always prepared." Pete said.

"Man, I've got plans for you... ever hear of the Burnt Mattress Motel?"

"No. Did you ever hear the story about the cranky passenger who was forced to stay at a cheap motel and then wound up killing the driver of the truck he was riding in?"

"No. You'll have to tell me sometime. Sounds nice."

Pete put his gear on the seat in the crew cab of Matt's truck where Matt also had his things. He got in the passenger seat, buckled up and they both put on their sunglasses.

Matt said, "Let's roll."

There was an entrance to the Pennsylvania Turnpike in Valley Forge close to where Matt lived. The turnpike would take them straight across Pennsylvania to the Ohio state line, then to Cleveland, Toledo and north around Lake Erie to Detroit.

***

At the same time Matt and Pete crossed the Susquehanna River west of Harrisburg, the Arish-Asad completed the procedure to tap into Matt's cell phone. They used one of the services found on the Internet that offers to allow anyone to listen to anyone else's cell phone calls. It also sent a copy of the tapped person's text messages to another phone and could trace a cell phone location by GPS signal. Now they would know where Matt was and who he was talking and texting with. They could also activate the microphone of Matt's phone and listen to him and anyone else who was close by.

***

They had been on the road for a few miles and Matt got into the pace of the turnpike traffic. He liked to drive a little faster than the speed limit, but never fast enough to stick out of the pack and get picked off by police. Conservatively assertive – is how he once described his highway driving to Jen. As they were moving along, Matt was in the right lane following a car as a semi-trailer truck was passing them both from the left lane. As the semi passed and cleared Matt's truck, Matt went into the left lane to follow the truck and pass the car also. The truck had not completely passed the car before it began to drift to the right.

Pete had just finished entering their destination into his GPS device when he looked up from it. "Matt, watch out! He's gonna clip that car."

"Yeah, I see it." Matt said as he tapped his brakes to get some distance from the truck. At the same time Matt saw an angel appear on the driver side of the semi-trailer truck cab. The angel stood on the top step of the cab holding the chrome handrail in his right hand as he leaned back, seemingly pulling the semi to the left and away from the car, preventing the collision. With his left hand the angel also banged on the cabin door of the truck one time and then vanished. "Wow!" Matt said.

"Wow is right." Pete said "That was close. That guy got lucky."

"That wasn't luck."

"Divine intervention?" Pete asked.

"It sure was." Matt laughed to himself knowing that Pete recognized what he could not see. He thought about how probably millions of times a day, fragile humans are kept from danger and harm by the protection of unseen angels.

***

It had been over two hours of driving and listening to syndicated radio news talk shows when Pete said "Do you really listen to news radio all day? I didn't know you were such a news junkie."

"Yeah I do. More than ever lately. I can't seem to get enough news, especially on TV. I'm getting worse by the minute."

"I get most of my news on TV and the Internet but I feel like I need music in the car though. Do you have any CD's in here?" Pete said and he opened Matt's glove box.

"No. Well I think there might be an old Jessica Simpson disc, pre-Tony Romo. One of Abby's."

"How about we turn on a little music?" Pete asked as he reached for the radio dial.

"Honest Pete, I really need to hear what's going on in the news, especially now. This thing with the vice president resigning is a little hard for me to believe. That guy Peterson is as hard core a politician as they come. Guys like that just don't resign the vice presidency over some chest pains. He'd have to be coughing up his lungs before he would quit."

On the radio, they announced there would be a special press conference at the White House at 1:30PM that would be covered live. Matt said "This means the president has picked his new vice president. I can't wait to hear who this is gonna be."

"That didn't take long for him to decide huh? What, four days?"

"Three. Closer to 48 hours. This president works really fast."

At 1:30PM the radio reporter said "Live from the East Room of the White House the President is about to make known Senator Anika Hannan as his choice to replace James Peterson who resigned three days ago."

"Oh no. This can't be." Matt said and he drifted his truck off the right edge of the highway across the rumble strips. He pulled back right away. "Sorry about that!"

"That's OK man. Keep 'er straight." Pete said and looked at him with surprise.

The reporter said "The senator is standing to the president's right. The President of the United States is at the podium. He is about to begin."

The president started his announcement - "Good afternoon. The individual who serves as Vice President of the United States of America must be qualified to be president. That individual must also be one who shares and will support the views of the president. Today we have many serious challenges before us and we have objectives we must achieve. We will continue to work on our economy and our plan to revitalize it. We must reform healthcare in America. We have our partnering role in reshaping our new global economy. Our new energy policies, and Cap and Trade legislation that will protect our environment and reduce climate change. The work we have begun on education and our commitment to the civil rights of every minority, the elderly, the unemployed, the disabled, the foreign born, the homeless and gay and lesbian Americans. We have begun to reach out to all our neighbors across the world, to engage old foes and old friends and we will continue our overseas contingency operations in Iraq and Afghanistan. It is important the next vice president be someone who the American people can trust and she must be able to work with both parties in the congress to move our agenda forward. Over the past two days I have considered the needs of our nation and the need to have the best and most capable person by my side to meet these challenges. The person I have chosen fits the model of a great American leader and she will help us to a bright new American future. My fellow Americans, I present to you the woman whose name I will submit to the Congress of the United States for confirmation as Vice President, the Senator from the great state of Michigan, Anika Hannan."

They could hear loud applause that went on for thirty seconds. The radio reporter said "This is an historic occasion here in the East Room of the White House. Senator Anika Hannan has been nominated to be the first woman vice president of the United States. She is the junior Democrat senator from Michigan and she has been in the senate since 1998. She is the daughter of Iranian immigrants and she was the first Iranian American elected to the United States Senate. She is approaching the microphone and is about to speak."

"Mr. President, I thank you for this great honor. If I am confirmed by the Congress, I will dedicate myself to bringing real change to the United States of America."

The press corps was caught up in the moment and left objectivity behind. Wolf Blitzer said "Well it didn't take the president long to make the right choice this time around the VP block."

Chris Matthews said "I know I said the president gave me a thrill up my leg, well Anika Hannan gives me a bigger thrill up the other leg."

Keith Olberman commented "As much as I hate to enjoy saying this, today is all the fault of George W. Bush. While Bush was in the White House, Jim Peterson lectured him on his lack of leadership and the stress of Peterson's concern about President Bush's direction for our nation was so great it led to Peterson's heart trouble and his recent resignation from the office of vice president hence opening the door to the brilliant choice of nominee Senator Anika Hanna from the US auto maker state of Michigan. So yes, it really is Bush's fault."

The liberal media was gushing. They all said Hannan should have been the choice for vice president the first time instead of Jim Peterson. She was the Democrat answer to Sarah Palin. Good looks, intelligence, popular in all polling and of course a history making first woman and a minority as well. They speculated about what would be the reaction from Tehran and the other Muslim nations to the first Iranian American Vice

President. The media thought this fresh intelligent multi-lingual vice president would be loved internationally, and especially in the Middle East. They said Hannan would be able to energize the Israeli and Palestinian peace talks. They assumed that Hannan could personally charm Iranian President Ahmadinejad into slowing or stopping his nuclear weapons program. The media hoped that somehow just by being from Detroit she would be able to save the American auto industry because she "understands what it's like".

"Oh man this is bad, really bad." Matt told Pete.

"Why? Just because it's her? So what, they're all the same. One is a lame as the other."

"No, that woman has problems, serious stuff."

"How do you know? What do you know about her?"

"I've been watching her for a while on TV. I even started TiVo-ing her."

"You're kidding. Why? Because she's good looking? Are you some kind of political groupie?"

"No it's …it's hard to explain. Forget it." He did not want to tell Pete about the angels and everything that was happening with him. It was too hard and too deep. Matt did not know where to begin to even try to explain it all. "I just have a gut feeling about her and it's not good." Matt was rubbing his forehead and felt his headache growing.

"OK. Speaking of gut feelings, how about stopping to eat?"

Matt's mood had stayed somber after learning about Hannan's nomination. He felt the pressure of all these events and he knew what God was showing him. All he could do was "Seek her out."

His phone rang; it was Jen, "Matt did you hear the news about Hannan?"

"Yeah we heard on the radio. I have a headache and I feel sick in my stomach. This stuff is killing me. We're gonna stop soon and eat something. I'll force myself to eat."

Jen was calling from her cell phone standing outside her work office. "Me too. I feel like I need to cry. Well I'm sure you can't say much with Pete there but I wanted to make sure you knew and I wanted to tell you I love you and I'm praying for you both."

"Thanks Jen. I love you." He looked at the clock on his dashboard, "It's almost 2:30, I'll call you later."

***

The Arish-Asad in Washington, listened to Matt's phone call. They did not think he sounded like a threat and they knew he was still in Pennsylvania.

***

As they kept driving, Matt and Pete listened to everything about Hannan they could find on the radio. They listened to the media gush over her. Quickly the liberal media had their key talking point descriptors of Hannan. Almost all of them said she was a brilliant choice. Several used the word serendipity and they called it - serendipitous good fortune - for the president to find such an outstanding and capable replacement for the resigned vice president.

They kept driving until they got off the turnpike at an exit in Somerset County, Pennsylvania. Matt usually stopped there when he headed west to Pittsburgh or Ohio. He would get gas and there was an all you can eat restaurant there that he knew Pete would enjoy getting his money's worth.

159

RASHID

Rashid drove out of the FBI parking lot at 5:15PM. A car with four Arish-Asad men followed him in an older Lincoln Towncar. The highway was filled with after work traffic and when they came to a straight stretch of stop and go with several intersections and traffic lights, the men following him, rear ended Rashid's BMW Z3 Roadster. Rashid's head snapped back into his headrest. He immediately got angry and looked in his rear view mirror. He saw the driver wave to him to pull over out of traffic. The driver followed Rashid off the road into a strip mall parking lot. Rashid got out of his car and slammed the door. He looked at the scratches and dent on his back bumper and trunk. All four of the Arish-Asad men got out of their car. In Arabic one of them said "Rashid, you come with us." Two of them took him by the arms and put him in the back seat of their car. One of the men got into Rashid's car and followed them to an empty beat up house near Washington Dulles International Airport.

Inside the house, they searched Rashid and forced him to strip. They tied him naked to a kitchen chair with his arms behind him. They also tied his feet to the legs of the chair stretched behind him, soles up. There was a table in the room and on it was a hand held soldering torch with a blue propane fuel tank. One of the men picked up the torch and ignited it with a spark from a friction striker. He adjusted the flame to a beautiful blue pointed tear shape. He showed it to Rashid. "If you lie to me I will burn your eyes out and deliver you blind and naked to the home of your mother and father in Baltimore."

Rashid gasped with panic and said, "I'll tell you anything you want. Anything! Please don't burn me!"

"I do not want anything. I want the truth." He brought the flame of the torch close to his face. "What have you told the FBI or Secret Service about Arish-Asad?"

"I have never said anything. Never! I swear to Allah."

"I do not believe you." said the man with the torch. He motioned to the two men standing at the sides of Rashid and they took hold of his head and arms. Rashid struggled against them. The man burned one of Rashid's eyebrows off leaving bright red skin and small blisters. Rashid screamed and cried.

"Please don't do this. I'm telling the truth!"

"The man you gave us, Matthew Davidson has been protected by the Secret Service. How can this be?"

161

"I don't know. Please I don't know!"

The man took the torch and burned the eye lashes off the same eye where the eyebrow used to be. His eye lid became red and swelled with blisters. Rashid screamed and tears and snot poured from his face.

"We believe the man Davidson, was planted in an attempt to draw us out. Is this true?"

"No. Absolutely not. I checked him out every way possible. He is no one. Not even military. He is no one special. Please don't do this! Please I beg you!"

"I do not believe you." The man stepped behind him and the other men adjusted their grip on Rashid and held his right leg. The man kneeled down and burned a one inch wide hole deep into the ball of Rashid's left foot leaving it bright red and singed black. The raw wound was weeping clear fluid. Rashid screamed and urinated. His body convulsed from the pain. There was smoke from his burned flesh.

"Are you being monitored by the FBI?"

Rashid was drenched with sweat and he was shivering uncontrollably. "No. No please no. I check everything every day." Rashid could barely catch his breath. "I have never seen anything that looks like I'm being watched. Please stop. I have never given bad information. I am careful. Please stop. Please let me go." He begged, crying in agony.

"Alright. We are finished. Cut him loose." The man put his torch away and threw Rashid's car keys at him. "You should put something on that eye. You look ridiculous." They all left the house leaving Rashid behind.

***

The reaction to Hannan's Vice Presidential nomination in Tehran and in all of the Muslim countries of the Middle East was joyous. People celebrated in the streets. The feeling was that America was finally becoming more like the Muslim world, not America forcing them to Americanize. The Al-Qaeda leadership and the Iranian Ruling Council were pleased, but they kept quiet. They knew their mission was far from accomplished.

***

Over the next few hours, Matt and Pete exchanged a few cell phone calls and four text messages with their wives, but the conversation and messages were mostly – yes we are OK and where they were at. The only information Arish-Asad gained was their GPS location. At 9:50PM,

they drove under the "You are now entering the City of Detroit" sign.
"Welcome to Mo-Town." Matt said.

"Maybe we could see the Capitol Records building. The cool round one that looks like a corn cob?"

"Corn cob? I think it's supposed to look like a stack of records and I'm pretty sure that it's in Hollywood. Capitol and Mo-town were two different record companies." Matt said while he was watching the traffic signs looking for their exit.

"How do you know that?"

"I saw the record building fall over in that old movie with Charlton Heston, Earthquake. I remember lots of useless stuff."

Pete started to sing "Ain't no mountain high enough, ain't no river wet enough, ain't no sumthin', sumthin' enough to keep me from gettin' to you babe!"

"You belong on American Idol."

"I thought about trying out."

"What stopped you?"

"Groupies. I knew the wife would have a problem with groupies."

Pete found a Holiday Inn located off I-94 near Dearborn by using his GPS device. He had called ahead and reserved a room with two double beds. As they pulled into the parking lot Matt saw three gasbags hovering near a van parked to the side of the lot in a dark spot away from the parking lot lights. He watched the van while they got their bags and Pete's cooler out of the truck.

"See that van? Let's go check it out."

"What for?"

"Just come with me. Leave the stuff here."

They put their things on the sidewalk in front of the truck. The van was 40 yards away from where they parked and as they walked up to it they could hear sounds of a struggle from inside. The van had dark tinted side windows but they could see through the windshield. A thirty something man was all over a twentyish woman who was resisting him.

Matt banged on the window and yelled "Hey! What's goin on in there? Are you OK?"

"Who are you? Take off before I kick your ass!" the man inside the van yelled to Matt. They could see the woman was in trouble and trying to get away from him.

Matt said "Open the door and let her out or I'll break the windows and pull you out." He was angry and so was Pete.

"Let's be careful in case he has a gun." Pete said calmly to Matt.

"I know. I'm watching his hands."

"Open the door!" Pete said as he banged on the opposite side door. The man unlocked the side door toward Matt and pulled it open fast. The man was 5-10" and about 30 pounds overweight. He came out and had a hammer in his hand. "Who the hell do you think you are?" he said. At the same time the woman unlocked her side door and got out. Pete went around to the other side of the van and now the man was between Matt and him.

"Look genius, just get back in your van and go home. She's away from you and that's all she wanted. Do it now or I'll call the police." Matt said.

The man took a wild swing at Matt with the hammer. Matt avoided it and then stepped toward him and gave him a forearm shot to the chest that knocked him back and he bounced off the side of the van dropping his hammer. Pete grabbed him and spun him around. He put his big left arm around the man's neck in a choke hold and he twisted the man's right arm behind his back. Pete pressed the man's face into the van.

Matt went to the woman who was now standing about twenty feet away crying. "He is such a turd. I can't believe I ever went out with him."

"Do you want us to call the police? Will you be OK?"

"I'm alright. He tore my blouse. The jerk. Don't call anyone. It'll just get worse if the cops get involved. I just want to go home."

"OK. If you're sure. I'm gonna tell this guy to take off." Matt noticed that the gasbags were gone and he did not see any angels around.

Matt went back over to the van. Pete was still holding the man and said to him "Look, just stop talking or I'll crush your trachea and you'll never talk again... much less breathe."

"What's a trachea?" the man strained to ask.

"It's your wind pipe dummy. Where air goes into your lungs."

"Hey, hammer boy." Matt said to the man. "She doesn't want to ever see you again. If you so much as look at her she will call the police and then she will call us and we will do this all over again. Do you understand?"

Pete nodded his head for him.

"Any questions?"

Pete moved his head side to side. "Good. Now take your hammer and go home."

The man left in a hurry and they took the woman into the lobby of the hotel and called a cab for her. They waited with her until she was picked up. Pete looked at Matt and said. "That was fun. Want to go meet some more people?"

***

The two checked in and when they got in their room, Matt tossed his bag onto the bed closest to the door and he found the TV remote. He turned it on and all the news networks were going wall to wall with the Hannan nomination. He sat on the edge of the bed close to the TV.

"Hey before you get all cozy with the TV, we better call home one more time and tell the girls we made it." Pete said.

"You're right." Matt said, and he took his cell phone outside and made his call to Jen, Pete called from the room. They told their wives where they were staying and made plans to call the next day and said good night. The Arish-Asad now had an exact location for them. The men monitoring Matt's phone reported what they had learned to the DC commander. The commander contacted the Detroit Arish-Asad leadership and ordered them to launch a raid on Matt's hotel room and kill him and anyone with him. He provided the address of the hotel and descriptions of Matt and his truck.

***

Pete stretched out on his bed for a few minutes then decided to take a walk to loosen up after their long drive. He was hungry and energized by their encounter with the couple in the van. Pete was a very physical man and he worked out with weights and played basketball in a YMCA over 30 men's league to stay in shape. "I'm gonna take a little walk and find something to eat. Maybe talk to some more nice people. Do you want anything?"

"Yeah, would you bring back a couple of bottles of water?"

Pete gave him a thumbs-up and left. Matt watched the news by himself flipping through channels and he stopped when he saw the president and Hannan. To Matt it was an even more intense of a display of the demon gasbags than ever before. They swirled around the president and there were at least six of them all around Hannan, taking turns whispering to her. The gasbags were excited and they wove in and out of the audience and the press. The demons were in a frenzy. It made Matt nauseous.

165

Matt prayed to keep a clear head and to be able to continue looking at the evil. He knew he was following God, so he prayed for strength to go the distance, where ever God would lead. He continued to watch more news. A Democrat strategist on CNN said – "Anika Hannan is the obvious and I will say brilliant choice by the president. She is ready for this job and with Anika Hannan I'd feel totally comfortable if the president died or …excuse me, I mean if for some reason, God forbid, anything happened to the president. I think she will lock up the White House for the Democratic Party until 2024. I am thrilled with her and can't wait to have her confirmed and sworn in." Matt laughed out loud.

A Republican senator said – "Anika Hannan looks like a smart choice for the president. She has been out there with him for weeks helping him with his plan for the economy and they appear to work well together. I do not foresee any major hurdles for her in the confirmation process."

On MSNBC, Rachel Maddow said – "Today is a great day. A day I've dreamed of for a long, long time. As a woman I'm proud of the president's choice of Anika Hannan to be the next vice president, the first female vice president. As a lesbian woman I'm even more proud to have Anika Hannan as vice president because of her caring sensitive, compassionate nature. She cares about people. People who need help, the homeless, the unemployed, minorities, our immigrant families who have come to the Unites States to breathe free. I know in my heart – and yes for the three of my viewers out there on the right, I do have a heart, I know that Anika Hannan as vice president will succeed in making our world a better, more peaceful and tolerant world."

Matt flipped over to another network and heard an atheist blogger say – "I'm happy to say, thank God for Anika Hannan."

On FOX, Greta Van Susteren was interviewing Henry Kissinger. Greta said "Former Secretary of State Henry Kissinger is here to go "On the Record." Now Senator Anika Hannan, if confirmed, is about to become our next vice president. How does Dr. Kissinger, the most respected foreign policy expert in Washington think she will do? Well, let's ask. Secretary Kissinger is here live in Washington. Always nice to see you sir."

"Good to be here Greta."

"All right. Mr. Secretary, have you met Senator Hannan?"

"Yes I have met her."

"What do you think of her?"

"She is very intelligent and uniquely suited to foreign policy, especially now in 2009. We have an entirely different global dynamic than we did before September 11th, especially in the Muslim world."

"What role could a Vice President Hannan play in foreign policy? Does she have a good grasp of it?"

"Well, we have one of the most complicated international situations because so many things are going on simultaneously. You have a huge financial crisis, which has the foreign policy effect in that we are losing the economic leverage we used to have. You have the shift of the center of gravity of international affairs toward the Pacific, so that China and India are emerging as very significant countries. You have problems like global warming, environment, which can only be done on an international basis. Then of course, you have North Korea, the jihadist problem, Iran and their nuclear program and the Iranian elections coming up. Regardless of who wins their election, Ahmadinejad or Mousavi, the United States must avoid sending the wrong message to Iran. America must support free, fair elections. If the election in Iran is close or disputed, and I believe it will be, the president must be ready to quickly support the voters and speak up against corruption and promote democracy and human rights. The same way Ronald Reagan supported Polish Solidarity leader Lech Walesa and the way Reagan spoke against the Soviet empire and the Berlin Wall."

"Isn't the role of vice president more domestic than foreign policy?"

"Traditionally yes, but this president should, I believe, take advantage of her ability to communicate and deliver the American message to our friends overseas. She speaks several languages and of course she speaks Arabic."

"Wouldn't a strong foreign policy vice president push Secretary of State Clinton into the background? How would Secretary Clinton react?"

"I would imagine privately she would not react well, but it is the president's responsibility to determine who is best to carry out his policy, as long as it sounds like one voice. The job of vice president is very flexible and the president can assign her or him as he sees fit. Secretary Clinton would still have a great deal of work to do."

"Did the president call you or ask you about his nomination of Senator Hannan for vice president?"

"No he did not."

"Dr. Kissinger, thank you for going "On the Record" with us. It is always nice to see you. I wish you'd come back to Washington more often."

"I look forward to it."

"Nice to see you sir." Greta said and went to a commercial.

***

Matt watched the video of the president and Hannan two more times and he was more repulsed each time he saw it.

Pete came back 30 minutes later with a bag of food. "Hey I found this great little hamburger stand. I brought you one. Cheese burger with everything. Want it?"

"No thanks. I don't feel right." Matt motioned toward his stomach. He was still sitting in the same spot where he was when Pete left. "Pete, this is really bad stuff. This woman Hannan is not good. I can't look at her anymore."

"Then turn it off. You don't have to watch it. What is it with you and her anyway? Just find something else to watch." Pete pulled the small table in the corner close to his bed where he would eat the burger.

"I'm sure it sounds weird, but I just see evil all around her." Matt took a deep breath. "I don't feel good. Really, I feel sick."

"What's the big deal? Actually she looks pretty good. That sort of Catherine Zeta-Jones look. Tall dark and handsome. Oh yeah. Can you believe who she's married to, that old guy? Kirk Douglas? Any way she's a lot better looking than most liberals." Pete unwrapped the burger and the smell of onions and peppers triggered something bad in Matt.

"My mouth is getting that watery feeling. Oh man. I'm gonna puke." Matt grabbed his travel bag and quickly made it into the bathroom and closed the door. Pete heard him losing a day's worth of meals. He turned up the volume on the TV.

Sometime later Matt came out of the bathroom brushing his teeth. "I guess you really were sick of watching her." Pete said and he tossed Matt a bottle of water that had brought back with the burger. Matt took it back to the bathroom. He rinsed his mouth and gargled four times with mouthwash.

Pete was now lying back on his bed with pillows propped behind his head. He had the remote in his hand and was flipping through the channels. "You're really worried about Hannan?"

"Yeah. Her and a lot of other things too. I know God works all things for good for those who believe, but there is so much happening so fast all over the world and I think she is part of all that. Look how fast the president came out of nowhere to get elected to the most powerful office in the world. We really have to pay attention to all this stuff."

"Matt, you know I agree with you. These are scary times. The economy heading for the dumpster and this trillion dollar bail out stuff. Where is your and my bailout? And how many trillions of new debt? I can't keep up with all this. Everyday there is something new that's just out of wack. More people are saying they are afraid of government. I feel like we are living in some other world. I'm just glad I know how this is all gonna end. If I didn't know the end of the Bible I'd be freaking out about now."

"Me too brother, Amen. Hey Pete, pray with me." They both sat on opposite edges of the beds facing each other. Pete turned the TV off and they prayed for the United States and the leaders in government. They prayed for wisdom and discernment for the President of the United States. They prayed for guidance for themselves, for Pete looking for a new job and Matt in his business, and Matt prayed for protection for themselves and their family. "Lord, keep your angels near them to defend and protect them from evil forces."

When they finished Pete said "Good one."

Pete moved the one large chair in the room closer to the TV and sat in it. He turned the TV back on. As if on cue, a local news report came on TV hyping Hannan's appearance tomorrow at Sorber Arena at Packard University in Detroit. She was scheduled to speak at 11AM and the doors would open at 9AM. This confirmed everything Matt already knew. Matt was lying on his bed on his side facing the TV feeling tired. It was a long day and he had been up since 5AM, drove ten hours and just spent some time being sick. "Pete, I want to go see her tomorrow."

"Are you nuts? She just made you puke and now you want to go see her in person. What will happen to you then? Will your eyes pop out and your head explode?"

"Yeah… bring a garbage bag. I'll be OK. I can hold myself together. I just won't eat any breakfast."

"What about those houses you want to see?" Pete said as he opened a bag of pretzels and he pulled a bottle of diet soda from his cooler. He was still hungry.

"It doesn't actually take that long to look at a house. I don't ever buy anything sight unseen. That's why I wanted to see these. I just need to confirm they actually exist and then do walk troughs, about fifteen or twenty minutes each tops."

"You drove all this way for a fifteen minute look?"

"Yeah. I don't know anyone in Detroit personally that I can trust to look at houses for me and if it's a good house at a good price and if I can

169

make at least $15,000 or $20,000 per house, I'm willing to spend two days to look at them. I really want to see Hannan in person. If she becomes VP you can say you once saw her up close. You'll thank me. Anyway it shouldn't take all day so we'd probably be out of there by 1 o'clock, plenty of time to do what we gotta do and head home." Matt felt guilty for telling this lie, and as he was talking to Pete he was mentally praying for God to forgive this. He just could not tell Pete everything.

"Oh man." Pete said shaking his head. "You know what kind of crowd that's gonna be? Not exactly of my political persuasion."

"Mine either. But you know… guys like us really need to have more open tolerant minds. We must be able to empathize with and appreciate those on the other side of issues. We must engage those on the left side of the world and be more accepting and open. We need to be enlightened…did I already say tolerant?"

"Yeah. OK, OK. Enough of that baloney. I'll go, but if I wind up wearing some PETA or tree hugger T-shirt, just leave me behind."

"I can do that. You don't eat tofu or wear Birkenstocks do you?"

***

It took several hours for the Arish-Asad in Detroit to get organized and into their car to make the hit on Matt. At 2AM they drove down the street where the Holiday Inn was located and they drove right past it. The driver said "I know it is here. I have seen it many times. Look at the address again!" They had the right address and they checked and rechecked the street signs but they did not see the hotel. "How can this be? A building cannot disappear!" They circled the block eight times and drove all around the area but could not find the hotel. They searched for an hour and finally called their superior to confirm the address.

He was outraged by their incompetence and told them to not come back until they did as they were instructed. "A child, a blind child could find such a large hotel, you are idiots!"

The men continued to search and argue among themselves. They switched drivers, got out of the car and walked the street in front of the hotel but could not find it. They asked the only two people they saw on the street and both said they did not know of it.

At 5AM they gave up and went to their homes. What the men could never know was that God had placed a veil of confusion in front of them. Later that morning they were all called to meet with their superior. They were going to meet Allah.

TUESDAY AT THE ARENA

Their wake up call came at 7AM. They showered and were out the door by 7:35. They picked up some McDonald's drive through breakfast and coffee and were at Sorber Arena at the university in plenty of time to get a good spot in line to get in. They arrived without incident. Matt wanted to get in and as close to up front and near Hannan as possible. When they were walking toward the lines already formed to go inside, he told Pete he thought they should try to look more like the rest of the crowd. He saw a man with the tie-dyed shirt selling t-shirts. Most of the shirts had Hannan's name on them. "Vice President Anika" "Hannan For America" "Vice President Hannan" and even "Niki For President" were the most common. Matt approached the man and asked "How much for an extra large?"

"The prices are listed over there on the sign in front of the table to your left." the man said pointing to his right.

He found the little hand written piece of paper he called a sign. All the Hannan shirts were $35. "You couldn't have just said - 35 bucks?" Matt asked.

"There is no way I'd pay $35 for something I'm gonna wind up using to clean up spills with. You might as well buy a couple of ShamWows and least you get your money's worth." Pete said while looking through the pile of t-shirts. "Hey, here ya go!" and Pete pulled out a CHANGE t-shirt and handed it to Matt. There were other people milling around and looking through the shirts.

"How much for this one?" Matt asked holding up the shirt.

"Ten bucks. We really bought into the whole CHANGE thing, bought way too much into them. It didn't turn out to be a great seller like we were told it would be. It was great during the election, then it just fizzled. Just can't sell CHANGE anymore."

"I'll take it." Matt said and he handed him the money. Matt put the shirt on over his long sleeved T-shirt and then carried his pullover fleece. He also wore jeans and a pair of work boots. Pete had on a gray t-shirt with ARMY printed across the chest in black. Over that he wore a royal blue long sleeved fleece that zipped up the front. He also had on cargo shorts, a pair of Nike running shoes and tennis socks. It was a pleasant morning, about 50 degrees, clear sky and sunny.

The event was scheduled to start at 11AM. The arena could hold 7,000 people for a basketball game and they expected it to be filled to capacity. A lot of the locals wanted to see their senator, home town girl "Niki" and now nominee for vice president, so they added another 1,000 seats on the floor. Yesterday's news added excitement and all the major media was there. It was an historic nomination. A woman had never been nominated to replace a vice president who resigned, and she was the first Muslim American ever to be nominated for this high an office, a heartbeat away from the presidency.

At 9AM the arena doors opened. Each person patiently went through two separate security checkpoints. The local police were there to handle traffic outside and the county sheriff's office provided security inside the arena. A small detail of Secret Service agents were there but only to observe and advise. No packages, bags, backpacks, and umbrellas were allowed in. Some people brought in homemade signs but 500 printed "Hannan for America" signs were provided by the DNC and distributed.

By 10:15 Senator Hannan had arrived at Detroit Metro Airport and now she was en route to the arena by limousine, escorted by two Detroit Police Department cars. Hannan always preferred to travel light and like this day, only brought with her Omar, Amy and one tall and one short male staffer.

The original purpose of her event was a town hall meeting to discuss the economy there in Detroit. Now the purpose was her first appearance in her home town the day after her Vice Presidential nomination. The arena was a one year old state of the art facility that Hannan had gotten earmarked federal money directed toward. There were bleacher seats on both sides of the basketball court and more of the same at one end as well as balcony seating on one long side. The main entry end of the arena had a large 30' X 20' Jumbotron style video screen hanging high above the doors. In the middle of the floor an elevated stage which was really just a platform assembled and decorated red white and blue. It was only two feet higher than the floor. Six padded folding chairs were placed at one end, along with a small table with bottles of water and one cordless microphone stand.

Matt could see a few dozen gasbags moving quickly over the crowd. They would stop and chew on the ears of people and move on and do it again. They seemed to patrol the crowd looking for any opportunity to agitate and excite the people.

The two of them easily made their way to seats near the front in the eighth row toward one corner of the stage. Matt put his fleece over top

172

of his CHANGE T-shirt when they sat down. Seats were filling in rapidly. Matt spotted four seats straight ahead of them in the front row that had plain white unmarked pieces of paper folded over the backs of them as if to save or reserve them. "Pete, we're gonna upgrade." Matt pointed to where he wanted to go and Pete followed him and they quickly moved forward and claimed the two seats furthest right at the end of the row. Two people in the second row glared at them and Matt said "Sorry we're late!" No one ever came to challenge them or to claim the seats.

As they sat and waited, an older couple soon came and sat next to Pete to his left. They were in their early sixties and the man's hair was nearly white and in a long braided pony tail down his back. He wore a "Niki Our VP" t-shirt with an open long sleeve paisley shirt over it. He also wore jeans and Birkenstock sandals with no socks. The woman he was with looked the same. The man leaned over to Pete and said hello and asked "Have you been following Anika for long? We just love her and what she stands for."

"Me?" Pete checked the man out with his eyes, "Oh yeah. I dig her. She is smokin' hot if you know what I mean. She's single, right?" Pete nudged the man with his elbow, nodded his head and winked at him.

"Yes, she's really dedicated to her constituents. She'll make a great vice president."

"She's not gay is she?" Pete asked him. "I mean, hey, whatever but geez would that be too bad, ya know? I'd love to see her in a nice short tight black mini skirt."

Matt overheard him and said "Pete, what are you doing?"

"Nothing, just goofing with the old hippie over here."

The man then asked Pete. "What do you think of her positions?"

Pete wiggled his eyebrows, nodded his head and gave him a big smile.

"I mean policy positions."

"I think she is wrong on just about everything." Pete said looking at him with the most serious face he could pull together.

"Well, why are you here? Are you a Republican?"

Pete stood up tall in front of the man, all 6-3" 260 pounds of him, then leaned down a bit to get closer to his face and said "Why? Do I look like a Republican?"

"Well, no...." he said softly.

"Cool, then enjoy the show." Pete said in a friendly light tone and sat back down.

As the crowd waited there was a real feeling of excitement, antici-pation, and a level of tension. There was a great deal of loud conversa-tion. Matt watched more gasbags appear swirling around over the heads of the crowd. Pete noticed the noise and said to Matt, "I've been to lots of concerts in buildings like this but why are these people so noisy?"

"Excited I guess. Maybe they think they are all gonna get a bailout check here today." Matt knew that the demons were now busy trying to fire up the crowd and stir emotions. The demons reminded him of film he had seen of tiger sharks swarming an area in anticipation of feeding. At one point, one gasbag swooped down very close to Matt's head and Matt ducked down to his left and bumped into Pete. The demon noticed Matt flinch and its head turned back toward Matt and glared at him with black hollow eyes. The demon kept going and did not stop.

"What's the problem?"

"Nothing, I'm just jittery." Matt said and he kept watch of the demons. He had not seen any angels since yesterday on the Pennsylvania Turnpike.

***

The Arish-Asad who were monitoring Matt's phone located him at the arena. The DC commander who had exploded with rage when he found out the Detroit team failed him, decided not to do anything at Hannan's event because of the security that would be there. However, he did order the men to be ready to track Matt afterward.

***

At 10:30 five technicians and stage crew were on the platform doing final sound and light checks and repositioning the chairs and table. A TV camera was panning the crowd and people were enjoying seeing themselves on the big screen. All of the press and news media were placed in two areas, in the balcony and on a higher raised platform on the floor, opposite the Jumbotron.

Matt sat there watching the crowd and he was praying and remem-bering the answer to his prayer yesterday morning "Seek her out." He was nervous not knowing what would happen or what opportunity he might be presented with. Then suddenly, half the lights in the arena flickered, and went out for a full three seconds, and then the lights came back on. This distracted the crowd and quieted them somewhat. Matt looked around and saw on the stage, standing among the stage crew, two

174

angels with tall folded white wings standing back to back of each other, holding Xiphos swords pointed down at their right sides. They were leaf shaped bronze swords, two feet in length. This was the first time he saw angels with weapons and it surprised him. Matt did not want to take his eyes off the angels and he leaned his shoulder against Pete to get his attention. "Pete, something's gonna happen. Keep your eyes open."

"What? The lights?"

Matt did not reply. He focused his attention on the angels. They remained motionless until together they raised their swords straight up over their heads and they extended their massive wings. Then an enormous, silent burst of light blinded Matt for a moment and the entire arena went black. The crowd groaned and became still and quiet. Every light was out. Only light from the exterior entrances let in some reflective sun light.

"This is good. I've seen this before." Matt told Pete.

Then a deep rumble lasting a long ten seconds was felt and heard from deep below the building. That was followed by the loudest noise of thunder Matt had ever heard from the sky outside. Inside the building the crowd was frightened and confused. They did not know if they were in an earthquake or a storm. The people still in line outside to enter the building heard the same sounds and were amazed as they had felt the rumble and now looked to the sky to see only the sun and bright blue.

Inside the arena the lights were powering up slowly and the Jumbotron's live picture was scrambled and jagged. The public address system gave a high pitched shriek like the sound of speaker feedback, but it was eerie and painful to hear. The sound mutated into desperate screams and wailing noises that frightened most people and made the rest nervous. At the same time the Jumbotron screen was filled with contorted gray gaunt faces pressed together side by side and each had soulless black holes for eyes. The screen made the images twist and screwed the faces sideways so hard that some people could not recognize them as faces. The crowd gasped and voices were raised as the discomfort among the people grew.

Then in an instant it stopped. All the lights were at full power and there was quiet. The crowd was relieved and a layer of peace covered everyone. Matt sensed it, but no one knew that the two angels had driven every demon and evil spirit out of the building and away from the grounds of the arena.

"Are you OK?" Pete asked the older couple to his left. They sat stunned with blank expressions.

"I think so. Did you see the screen?" the older man asked Pete in a stunned shaky voice.

"No, I had my eyes closed."

***

Senator Hannan's limo arrived just as security allowed the last people into the building. A police officer opened the limo door for them. The sunlight hit Hannan in the face and made her squint. They had been sitting behind tinted windows for the drive from the airport. "Great. Now I get a headache. I can't freakin believe this." Hannan said as she put her hand to her forehead and stepped out of the car. Amy never heard her swear before and was surprised and amused at the same time. Omar handed Hannan a water bottle and she batted it away.

They were led by sheriff's deputies into a waiting room area close to the main floor of the arena. "I'm nervous and I don't feel right. My head is killing me. Omar give me some water!" Omar gave her a serious sideways look. "Who are you looking at?" Hannan said as she glared back at him. "Amy do you have something for my head? How about you guys?" Hannan said looking at her other staffers. "Why the hell are you morons even here?"

Amy and the other two just looked at each other. This was not the Anika Hannan they knew and loved. None of them had ever seen Senator Hannan behave like this. She was extremely tense and was becoming more rattled by the minute. Hannan almost never used notes for these type of events but now was feeling so strange she said "I've gotta make some notes. I've got to write something down. I can't concentrate."

Amy told her "There is no time. The networks need you to start on time. They are going live out there on satellite. They also need the video for east coast noon news."

"Yes I know! Now back off and let me think." Hannan snapped at Amy as she stood and then leaned with her back against a wall with her head down and using both hands to rub her temples. "When I'm done here, I don't want any of you speaking with the press. I'll do it all myself right back here in this room. I only want one person from each network and one local TV. Let WDIV in here. Got that? And by the way Amy, why couldn't you for once in your life wear something that fits?"

Omar looked Amy in the eye and smiled. Amy gave him the finger.

***

The introductions had begun on the stage. There were two speeches. One from the congressman of the district and one from the county Democrat party chairman. Three unopposed Democrat judge candidates for the upcoming primary election were introduced to the crowd. The congressman was the master of ceremonies for the event.

***

From inside the waiting room they could hear the speeches on the speaker system. "Come on already!" Hannan said looking at the speaker mounted in the wall, "Nobody is here to listen to your crap. These people are here to see me!" She pointed to her shorter staffer and yelled at him "Get out there and tell them to pick up the pace or I'll kick someone's ass!"

Anika Hannan was unaware that for the first time since she was a child, she was not being controlled or protected by the demons that influenced her every thought. She was a raw nerve exposed and unfamiliar with her uncontrolled self.

SHOW TIME

The congressman took the microphone and began his introduction of Hannan. "This is a proud day for our great state of Michigan and it is an extraordinary time for the United States of America. Ladies and gentleman it is my distinct honor to present to you the next Vice President of the United States, our home town girl, Anika Hannan".

As he started speaking, the intro to the song "My Girl" by the Temptations, a huge Detroit and Motown Records hit from 1965 started to play. The crowd got right to its feet and cheered. People got into the music and sang along with the upbeat very familiar song. She walked into the arena to a big ovation and took the two steps up onto the stage. She shook hands with each of the five people on stage as they walked off. Hannan wanted to be on stage by herself, this was her celebration. The cheering lasted a few minutes while signs waved and the music played loudly. Hannan waved to the crowd. She did the, pretend to see someone she knew and wave at them trick in every corner of the room. She pointed at no one and gave the personal wave. She picked up a wireless microphone from the mic stand at the center of the stage and began her remarks.

"Thank you. Thank you everyone. It is great to be home!" The crowd gave another loud cheer. "Does everyone like this great building? I worked hard to get the funding for it but don't expect to see me playing any basketball!" she said and the crowd gave her a warm laugh. "I am extremely proud to stand before you today, here in the great city of Detroit and say to you that I am excited and I look forward to being confirmed soon as the next Vice President of the United States of America." That remark got her the longest round of applause and cheering of the morning.

Anika Hannan continued her comments describing how as vice president, she would work side by side with the president as he would lead the nation out of the economic crisis. She said the president is on the right course and is salvaging the ruined economy he inherited from the Republicans. She talked about how proud she was of him for reaching out to other countries like Venezuela and Cuba and the success of his trips overseas and the G20 conference. She also said she admired the president for reaching out to Iran to speak with no preconditions.

"Matt my gag reflex is going crazy. I feel like I'm being spoon fed a load of…"

179

"I know. You forgot to wear your boots." Matt said while breathing deep and trying to remain calm and ready for whatever may come.

Hannan finished her remarks and began taking questions from the crowd. Sound technicians brought out two wireless microphones on stands and placed them on the floor at opposite corners of the stage. One was placed only ten feet from where Matt and Pete were sitting. People got out of their seats to quickly form lines to be able to ask a question. Matt got up immediately and got in line. No questions were screened and the only instructions were for the person asking the question to state their name and where they were from.

Matt prayed fervently the entire time he was waiting. He prayed for a question to come to him to ask. He was so focused on his prayer he did not hear the questions asked before him. Matt was allowed to ask the fourth question. As soon as he took the microphone in his hand, Hannan recognized him from the photograph Omar had shown her of him. She was visibly shocked and she took a step back. Her demeanor changed instantly. She turned away from him and went to get a drink of water from the table on the stage. As she drank her hand shook and she listened to him with her back turned.

Matt said, "My name is Matt Davidson and I live near Valley Forge Pennsylvania." Hannan knew his name and was certain of who he was. He asked her "Senator, I know you are of the Muslim faith, Muslim background. How have you reached out to Christians like me, followers of Jesus Christ?"

She turned around and said "How did you get in here?" she pointed her finger directly at Matt. "Who do you think you are?" The crowd was astonished by what she asked and by the tone of her voice. "Do you come here with your holier than thou Holy Spirit?" The crowd went silent, and then people began to boo her.

"You came here to challenge me. Where is your Christian tolerance? Your Christian good will? You fear people like me, like us." She pointed at Matt again. "This man comes here to harass me." She said to the crowd "I want him out of here." There was loud booing at her and jeering. The crowd was turning quickly and loudly against her.

"Senator, I just asked a question." Matt did a good job of keeping his composure.

"Your questions are from whom? Were you sent here to embarrass me? Who do you work for? The Secret Service or the FBI? Do you work for the president? He fears me. I demand to know how you got in here!

Who are you?!" she screamed.

Samir Omar was standing thirty feet away from Matt when he started toward him. He came from Matt's right around the corner of the raised stage. He was almost running. Pete stood up and moved to get close to Matt when he saw Omar coming. Omar grabbed at the microphone but Matt avoided him. Omar tried again and got a grip on the mic and for a brief moment they both pulled on it. At that same moment Omar's keys and a computer memory stick attached onto the same key ring, fell off his belt carabiner onto the floor. Pete was now standing next to Matt. An invisible angel picked up Omar's key ring and put it in Pete's left side fleece pocket and zipped it closed.

Matt let go of the microphone and Omar almost fell down backward when he got control of it. The arena was loud with thunderous booing at Hannan. Two sheriff deputies walked up to Matt and asked him to go with them out of the arena. Matt calmly went with them. People were calling to Matt, "She's an idiot! Good job! Way to go! She should apologize!" Others were saying to each other "What just happened? Is she crazy? Did you see that? Did she lose her mind?"

People started throwing Hannan's printed signs at her on the stage. Other pieces of crumpled paper and debris were being thrown. Hannan said to the crowd "What is wrong with you people? He came to attack me! The President is weak and he needs me!" The booing and yells at her continued and got louder.

Back stage Amy grabbed a sheriff deputy and told him to go out on the stage and get her out of there. "She's gonna kill me." He said shaking his head.

"Just do it! Use your gun if you have to." Amy told him.

Pete looked in the direction where Matt was led and then went back to his seat. He leaned over to the shocked older couple and said "Some show, huh?"

Two sheriff's deputies walked out on the stage to the senator. One of them told her "You really should get off the stage."

"How dare you!" she said and she slapped him across the face. "To hell with you all!" she said into the microphone, and she threw it to the floor with a loud thumping rattle over the sound system. The deputies went to take her by the arms but she resisted their grasp and walked off the stage. That was it. She was finished.

Pete stayed behind for a while not sure what to do, and then he went to find Matt. The sound technician turned on the music again, "My Girl" and this time people booed.

As the deputies walked off the stage with Hannan, Omar jumped up on it to take a short cut across to follow her out. When he jumped he noticed the weight of his keys and carabiner was missing from his belt. He felt a rush of a cold panic across his chest. He searched himself, looked at the floor of the stage where he stood and then went back onto the floor to search where he had been.

The sheriff was there in uniform as Hannan walked toward the waiting room. He was an older man, 65, tall with white hair, thick white mustache and a deep voice. He stopped her and said "I should arrest you for assaulting one of my deputies."

"Get out of my way. I am a United States Senator! Who are you? The sheriff of dim-wit county?" Hannan said to him in disgust.

"Lady, you better get out of here before I have you cuffed and hog tied." The sheriff told her and he let her go to the waiting room. There, Amy Daly and the two other staffers kept their distance from Hannan. A deputy told them her car would be ready in two minutes. Hannan was not finished ranting. "Did you people set me up!?!" she picked up a telephone from a desk and threw it toward the two staffers. "Where is that little freaking Omar? I want to know how the hell that Christian got in here and how dare he ask me anything! Did one of you two idiots give him the microphone? Amy, call somebody. Find out where that man is and then get me a gun!"

The deputies took Hannan, Amy and the two staffers out to their limo. They all got in and Amy asked "Are we going to wait for Omar?"

"No! Forget him! Let's get out of here now and fast." Hannan shouted and the driver took off.

***

A deputy took Matt's name, address and phone number. They were very polite to him and several times the deputies told Matt "You are not in trouble. You didn't do anything wrong."

The sheriff came into the room and went over to Matt and said "Son, I am embarrassed as hell about all this." he said shaking his head in disbelief. "On behalf of the entire state of Michigan I want to apologize to you for that… whatever the hell that was."

"Thanks sheriff, I really appreciate you saying that."

"Son, I'm a Christian too, and I liked your question and I'm glad you asked it. I think the whole world just learned something here this morning."

182

The sheriff told Matt he could leave and he suggested that his men could get him out of the building first so no one or the press would bother them. Just then Pete came into the room. Matt saw him and said "The big guy is with me." and waved to Pete to come near him.

The sheriff said "Well let's get you boys outta here because we can't keep the rest of these people in here much longer."

They got to Matt's truck just as the deputies started allowing people out of the arena. Matt took off the Change T-shirt and got his hat out of the back seat and put it on. Pete put a hat on also and they both reached for their sunglasses at the same time. They did not want to be recognized. Pete got in from the passenger side and Matt drove the truck out of the parking lot. Pete was putting on his seatbelt when felt something in his fleece pocket on his left side. He unzipped it, reached in and said "What the... look at this. I just found this in my pocket." He held up a key ring with four keys and a memory stick. "How the... these aren't mine and they were in my zipped pocket. There is no way on the earth these were in my pocket before we went in that arena."

"We gotta see what's on the memory stick." Matt said.

"What do you care about some stick? What the heck happened back there? She acted like she hates you! Oh man, she just snapped! Does she know you?"

"I guess she does now. Do you think you can read whatever is on that memory stick?

"There might be a password but you never know. Why do you want to see what's on it?"

"Look, like you said, that thing wasn't in your pocket before. It was put there. You didn't bring your laptop did you?"

"No."

"Well then I guess we're goin' shoppin'. Got any money?"

***

Only minutes after Senator Hannan gave her meltdown performance, the president was leaving the Atlanta Convention Center when he was approached by reporters who asked if he had a reaction to what the senator had just said minutes ago. He had no knowledge of what had just taken place, neither did his staff.

"Mr. President, do you still support Senator Hannan as your nominee for vice president?"

"Yes of course. She has my full support. 200%. She is the best qualified person for the job. She can speak for me anytime. She is a

183

clear thinker, and articulate speaker and someone all Americans can trust. She and I have the same core fundamental values and beliefs. I'm looking forward to having her confirmed and sworn in as soon as possible." The president said this as he walked through the lobby to his Presidential Limousine.

Immediately after the president made his comments, the cell phones, BlackBerrys and iPhones of his staff started to explode with calls, texts and emails about Hannan and her imploding performance in Detroit.

Inside Cadillac One, Chief of Staff Boreland said, "Mr. President, we have a major problem." He said this without looking up from his iPhone as he continued to read the stream of messages.

"Problem with who? What did the Speaker of the House say this time?" He smiled and looked at the others to laugh at his joke but they were all intently looking at their phones.

"This is a disaster! Not the speaker sir. Senator Hannan. Apparently she freaked out at an appearance in Detroit about 15-20 minutes ago." Boreland said.

"Is that why CNN just asked me that stupid do I still support Hannan question? Why didn't you people give me some freakin heads up!?!"

"We didn't know sir. I'm just now getting calls and text messages." said Jim Dexter, Boreland's assistant.

"I don't believe this! What the hell did she say? Somebody better tell me fast or I'll throw all of you out of this limo without stopping! One of you idiots, turn on that TV!" Boreland dove toward the TV and tried to get some news.

"Mr. President I'm getting the video on my phone!" Miles Thompson said holding his phone in the air to get a better signal.

"Who has my phone? This can't be happening to me." The president said.

On his earpiece Dexter just heard the audio of what Hannan said. "Oh my Gaa... we are burnt toast."

"What? What? Give me that damn thing." He said while grabbing for his own phone. "Why can't we get this 20 million dollar limo TV to work? Are all of you guys useless?"

They could not get the limo TV to work so they all huddled together looking at each other's phone screens trying to see the video.

"Here it is!" Thompson said. The president and three of his staff crammed shoulder to shoulder while looking at the same small 6 square inch screen while Thompson held it against the ceiling of the limo to get a good signal.

***

Omar stayed behind at the arena. He reported his missing keys and memory stick to security. A few maintenance people helped him search but when he yelled at them they became less than helpful. The staff at the arena all took pride in their beautiful new building and now it would be known as the site of Hannan's low performance as a human. Omar traced his steps and searched everywhere he had been in the building. He finally found his carabiner on the floor under chairs near where Matt had been sitting. The titanium carabiner had been bent completely open allowing it to slide off of his belt. It was left curved in the shape of the letter J. Omar continued searching for the memory stick looking through trash cans emptying them onto the floor. The arena facilities manager threatened to call the police to stop him.

***

The president's motorcade arrived at their second stop, a speech for the National Education Association at the Grand Hyatt Hotel. He and his staff had looked at the complete video of Hannan's implosion. It was stunning and it made no sense to him. She was not provoked and it looked like she recognized him somehow and she just attacked him. They were still in the limousine and the president was slumped sideways sitting low in his seat. "What the hell am I gonna do? I look like an ass for picking her and Hannan is a raving loon! Is she on drugs or has she lost her mind?" the president asked.

"Mr. President, you have to let her go." Boreland said.

"I can't." he said with a frustrated half voice.

"What do you mean you can't? Excuse me sir, but she is your choice. Just tell her to withdraw. You can get Secretary Clinton for VP. She can pull you out of this one."

The president gave Boreland a blank stare. "Please, I wouldn't ask her.... haven't we been through this with Clinton a billion times?"

"Mr. President you will have to respond to this quickly. If you stick with this raving Christian basher they'll have to invent a new underwater polling machine because your numbers are gonna be lower than whale poop."

185

"Sir, no one in Congress will vote to confirm Hannan now. Not after that manic display. They would rip her to shreds. Even our side is looking for at least one thing they can resist you on and they'd love this. Sir, she slapped a deputy and she insulted you."

"Mr. President I can call her team right now and tell her to withdraw..."

"Let me think about it." The president's voice was weak and he had the body language of a beaten man. He was afraid to make any move against her. He thought of her as a cornered cobra and he had no way to know where she could strike.

"You've got to be kidd......"

"Not another word! When I'm done here with this speech, I'm not taking any questions from anyone. I've gotta go do this and then you guys better get me the hell outta here. And that freakin teleprompter better work!"

***

Jen called Matt "I've been trying to call you. Matt you're all over TV."

"Yeah, I kinda figured. Pretty crazy huh? I didn't know what to expect but that sure wasn't what I thought would happen."

"Marcia called me at the office. Her husband recognized you on TV. There is no cable TV at the office, just that big TV with the DVD player so a couple of us went over to the sports bar at the mall to watch the news. Are you guys OK? Did anyone hassle you or did the police keep you?" Jen was nervous and worried.

"We're out of there already. It was amazing. I had to talk to security, the sheriff's guys for about five minutes then they let us go. They didn't ask Pete anything. All they wanted was my name, phone number and address. No other questions. They were really good guys. Actually the sheriff apologized to me "on behalf of the entire state of Michigan". Matt tried to imitate the sheriff's voice. "He said he was embarrassed and ashamed of what Hannan said. The sheriff told me he is a Christian."

"Oh, Matt. Oh thank you Lord."

"Secret Service was there also but they didn't care about me. I think they were embarrassed by her too. I heard one agent say, "I really don't want to work for her.""

"Matt even MSNBC is showing this. It's a little hard to cover up a freak-out like that."

"Jen, we found something. I'm not gonna tell you what, but I'll call you soon."

"What? What does that mean? You found what?"

"I know that sounds all cryptic and mysterious, but I'll call you when we know what we have. Don't worry."

Pete leaned toward Matt's phone and said "Hi Jen! We're on a mission from God!"

Jen rolled her eyes to herself and thought – Two grown men? God please protect them.

"OK Matt. Call me and be careful."

Matt closed his phone and said "Pete, ya know I think we really are on a mission from God. I gotta tell ya, I didn't just decide yesterday that I wanted to go see Hannan. She is the real reason we made this trip. I've had a bad feeling about her for a long time and I felt led to be here today. And that memory stick didn't leap into your pocket and zip itself closed. It was placed there and I'll guarantee there is something on it we need to see."

"OK brother. You know I'm with you, but tell me why you felt led to be here."

Matt looked all around him to pull an answer out of the air. "I can't tell you exactly why. I will tell you I have been praying constantly about this, about today and about seeing Hannan. I just knew I had to be here." Matt could not tell Pete about the angels because he felt grateful to him for sticking with him so far. He did not want to risk having Pete think he was over the edge.

"Hey, I said I'm with you and it's been fun so far, plus I always did want my 15 seconds of fame." he laughed. "So I think we should pray and get to that computer store, get some gear and crack this nut." He said holding up the stick. "GPS says the store is just up here on the left."

"Thanks man. By the way, got any money? I'm a little light plus I've been feeding you for two days."

"Look, as the acting sidekick in this little adventure, I think it is the responsibility of the... oh, how shall I say... you to pay. And anyway, I'm unemployed."

"So am I, but I can't lay me off."

"I feel your pain." Pete said doing a good Bill Clinton imitation. "Don't worry, I've got us covered... in plastic." He pulled a credit card out of his wallet and waved it. I know exactly what we need. A middle of the road laptop, car power adaptor and a broadband card so we can get Internet from the truck."

***

The four Arish-Asad men were less than enthusiastic when they were ordered to follow Matt. They were told about the men who failed last night and where they were now. They decided to take their time and keep their distance.

***

When they arrived at the computer store, Pete changed his shirt and they both wore their sunglasses and ball caps. Matt saw their reflection in the large glass doors as they walked in. He said to Pete "Are we here to buy stuff or rob the place?"

They went straight to the computer section and Pete was greeted by the smallest, nerdy-est looking sales guy in the store. Matt watched and listened to Pete and the little guy speak the same techie language. He laughed at the physical contrast of the two. Pete told Matt "This will take a few minutes to get this stuff and set up the broadband card. I'll hang with my new pal here. You go play Guitar Hero till I'm ready for ya."

Matt wandered toward the new TV area and he was praying as he went. He prayed asking the Lord for help, guidance and a clear path. Matt had a TV at home that was on its last few weeks of life and he would love to surprise his kids with a new flat screen, but that was impossible right now. Matt felt a twinge of money related tension in his stomach. It reminded him that since he began seeing angels, he was feeling much less stressed by business. He felt that if God knew him and was using him, God would provide for him. He knew he had to work and fulfill his obligations, but his confidence was coming back.

There was an older married couple looking around the TVs and one young female salesperson changing channels on one of the large flat screens. All the TVs were showing the same thing, some aerial footage of the Great Wall of China. Matt asked her if she could get some news on one of the flat screen. "Sure, what channel do you like?"

"Thanks. How about FOX? I'm waiting for my friend to pick up a laptop." She got the channel and there were talking heads discussing what had happened less than two hours ago with Senator Hannan.

"...at her first appearance after being nominated by the president to replace Vice President James Peterson who resigned last Saturday due to a heart condition. The questioner in the video has been identified as Matthew Davidson from Valley Forge, Pennsylvania. He is in real estate. Let's turn first to Democrat Senator Beth Ann Burden from California.

188

Senator what is your reaction to what happened today? – "I've know senator Hannan since she came to the Senate in 1998 and I know her to be a kind gentle woman. A true American. I've seen the tape several times and I get the impression that the man was a right wing teabagger and his intentions were to provoke her."

A conservative radio talk show host said – "Wait a minute senator. All this guy did was ask a simple question that my twelve year old Girl Scout daughter could have answered. She should have said "I will do my best to represent every American of all faiths." Period. If she'd done that we wouldn't be here now looking at her buried in her own pile of smoking rubble."

New York Times reporter – "I guess we were watching two different tapes. The man from Pennsylvania attacked her for being a Muslim!"

Pennsylvania Congressman – "That's outrageous! That wasn't an attack! It was an honest question with a very revealing answer. Out of the heart the mouth speaks."

Matt had removed his sunglasses to get a better look at the video. He stood beside the sales girl and watched the debate. They showed the tape of Matt asking his question and Hannan's response. The sales girl looked at Matt, looked back at the screen and then checked her watch doing some time calculations in her head. Matt saw her do this and he stepped backward in between two display shelves and put his sunglasses back on.

Pete was ready to leave and found Matt standing there. Pete saw a shot of himself on the big screen. "Hey, I look good. Let's get out of here before one of these geeks blows our cover." Pete was enjoying their adventure.

The sales girl and one of her co-workers were watching them check out. Matt saw them looking and he could tell they recognized them. When they were finished at the checkout, and had their equipment in bags, the middle aged woman teller handed Pete his receipt. Pete told her "We're on a mission from God." Matt elbowed him in his back.

"I can always tell. Have a nice day." She said stone-faced. Pete burst out laughing.

They walked out of the store. Matt said "You aren't much for low profile, are you?"

"Do I look low profile?"

Matt told Pete he was sure two of the sales people recognized them. "Cool maybe they want our autographs. Ya know, depending on what might be on this memory stick, we could wind up selling our own t-shirts. Mine could say "Pete the IT Guy" yours could say "Matt the ...whatever". Maybe we could get a reality show. It could be about our wacky adventures. Ya know, like driving to Detroit, making a VP candidate self destruct... and then driving back home."

"You have no shortage of ideas do you? I should have partnered up with you years ago. Let's get out of here and stop someplace else to get the laptop working."

They drove a mile down the highway and pulled into a grocery store parking lot. They parked off to one side with a long cinder block wall directly behind them. Matt backed into a space. He wanted to be able to see everything in front of them and leave quickly if he had to. Pete got into the back seat of the truck where he would have more room to spread out and work by himself. He very quickly got the laptop powered up, loaded some software he bought, set up the broadband card and inserted the memory stick in the USB port. Matt then got in the back also and sat next to Pete to be able to see the screen."

"The dummy. Not even a password. This better be good because it's too easy." Pete said. To his amazement, everything opened right up for them. There were Word documents, some .pdfs, two Excel spread sheets and some photos. Pete opened the first document. It was two years worth of Senator Hannan's itineraries up through the next three days.

"Matt, this has got to be Hannan's stuff. Oh my good Lord. Wow. This is a miracle!" Pete was stunned. The next file had a list of bank account numbers with bank names for each account and the name Omar at the top of the page. They Googled omar hannan senate michigan and found out that Samir Omar was Hannan's assistant. They even found a photo of him.

"Holy cow! That's the guy who tried to grab the mic from me. Oh Lord thank you for this! Pete we have to take our time and get a good look at this stuff."

"I know and I'm gonna copy this all onto the hard drive." The third document had a list of email addresses. There was also a photograph of a very attractive thirty-ish blonde and a press photo of Senator Hannan. Pete said, "From the looks of this, this guy thought he would never lose this stick. What a goof. This guy was organized but lazy and stupid for ever carrying this around with those keys. This guy is in big trouble."

There was even more on the memory stick. Three documents were written in Arabic, and one in French. The rest of the information on the

190

memory stick was golden. There was a list of three URLs, websites that no one would recognize and a password for each. Pete checked one site and it was very sparse, all text and all in Arabic. "I'm not gonna go to any other websites because I don't want anyone to know where we're looking at it from. If something looks suspicious to them they'll shut it down."

Another file had an unorganized list of money amounts and dates with Hannan's name at the bottom. There was an Excel spread sheet that listed Omar's personal cash totals in nine different accounts and CD and mutual fund interest rates. They all totaled 1.1 million dollars. The last spread sheet listed 16 women's names. Each had a corresponding city, date, three initials and the abbreviation for the government title SEN, REP, GOV, AMB, SECT, PRES. Three of the officials had two women listed. There was also a column for a dollar amount. They were either $10,000 or $5,000. It was easy to understand that these women were paid a monthly sum of money for some association with their corresponding US government officials. They both saw it at the same time. PRES and the president's initials with two women's names.

"Pete, this is huge. This is unquestionably why we are here. We are supposed to have this. We have to tell somebody about this. We need to pray."

Pete pushed down the lid of the laptop. They were silent for a moment and Matt put his hand on Pete's shoulder and began to pray "Lord Jesus. Thank you Lord God for this miracle you have made us part of. Lord you guided me here and you gave me a good man to be at my side and I thank you. Lord I know there are evil forces at work and you have given us proof, evidence. Jesus help us to now know what to do, where to go, who to speak to and who to trust. Lord we ask that you protect our families. Surround them with your mighty angels and keep all harm and evil from them. And Lord we ask the same for us. We will watch for you guidance. Please lead us on your path. We pray in the name of our Holy Lord and Savior Jesus Christ. Amen."

"Amen. Good one." said Pete.

***

The commander of the Washington Arish-Assad recognized Matt's face and name on the news. He saw the first report at 1:45PM. He considered a strike against Matt's home and family just out of anger, but he was more disciplined than that. He also assumed Matt's family was still under the protection of the Secret Service. He was partially right. He told his men to continue to follow Matt and monitor his phone and to report anything unusual. The commander watched the video of Hannan and her self-destructive performance. He lived in the United states long enough to know that the American people could never accept someone like her as their vice president. He felt that the entire operation was a failure. Years of planning and development was wasted. He decided to wait a few hours longer and follow more news before taking any action.

***

"We gotta get on the road." Matt said. It was 2:20PM.

"Let's go. I can keep looking at these files while you drive and with the broadband card we should have Internet wherever we have a cell signal. We can keep up on the news. I love this! Hey man, any time you want to do a road trip, I'm in!"

Phone calls and text messages were coming in from all over the country. All of the media wanted to talk to Matt. No one really was sure of Pete's connection to Matt yet because he was not questioned at the arena and the video did not make it obvious that they were together.

Pete called his wife and updated her. He did not give her much detail, only what she already knew from watching the news. Debbie did not do well with trouble or stress. What she already knew was more than she could handle.

Matt spoke to Jen and told her they found something interesting and they would bring it home. Then as he was speaking he remembered what happened at Home Depot and the man who fell at his feet. "Jen I gotta go. I just remembered something so I'll call you later. Don't worry, just pray. Love you. Tell the kids I'll be home late. Give Debbie a call too."

He had not thought about the possible connection between the man at Home Depot and Hannan for a few days but now he thought that they should be very careful. His caution meter went wild and he prayed to himself while he drove. He did not want to spook Pete, so he did not say anything to him. He just drove a little faster.

***

It was 11:30PM in Tehran when the leadership saw the CNN news report about Hannan. There was anger among them as the news spread. Everyone wanted answers.

***

192

Matt's cell phone started to go off every 30 seconds. The whole world now knew him and they all started calling. It was easy for anyone to Google Matt's name and find his phone number and information about him. A call came in and his caller ID said FOX NEWS NY.

"I'm taking this call." Matt told Pete and he put it on speaker.

"Hello, Hello Mr. Davidson?"

"Yeah, this is Matt Davidson."

"Sir, my name is Amelia Kane. I'm a producer with Fox News and WABC Radio in New York. Mr. Davidson we would like to get your comment about what happened today between you and Senator Hannan in Detroit. May we interview you? Have you spoken with any other press or TV?"

"No, I haven't spoken to anyone. I've had everybody calling but I'm on the road right now. I'm heading home."

"To Valley Forge sir?"

"Yeah." At that moment it sunk in to Matt that now everyone knew who he was.

"Mr. Davidson we have a studio on Market Street in Philadelphia. Could we interview you there?"

"We won't be home till late. You want us for TV huh? Which show?"

"We'd like to get a taped interview to use on all of our news programs. We hope you'd agree to do a few live interviews with us also."

Pete signaled Matt to cover the mic on the phone. Matt asked her "Can you hold on a minute?"

"Tell her you'll do it exclusive if you can get on with Sean Hannity, I love his show. Matt we've got all this stuff, big time stuff, Watergate big. Let's get on Hannity and blow senator what's her face out of the water. Let's show them the whole load. God didn't drop this in our laps for nothing."

"You're right. Let's do it." Matt said.

"Hello FOX... I mean Miss..."

"Yes sir, Amelia Kane here."

"Amelia, if you can get Sean Hannity himself to call me back I'll give you so much stuff his head will explode."

"Oh wow! I mean yes sir! Thank you so much Mr. Davidson. I'll call you back as soon as I can."

***

Immediately after the Detroit event ended, Senator Hannan went to her parent's home in Ann Arbor. This had been arranged prior to the event and it would have be a good place to do some family and home town interviews as the vice presidential nominee. Hannan's staff that made the trip to Detroit with her, all separated to either go back to Washington or elsewhere.

Omar had walked the grounds and the parking lots around the arena still searching. He realized he would never find it so he called for a cab to take him to the airport to go back to Washington. There was nothing for him to do in Detroit and Hannan did not call him to ask where he was. He knew they were finished. He also knew the information on the memory stick was devastating to Hannan and to other operations that were already under way. There was the possibility that it would never be discovered. Perhaps someone had picked it and the keys up and throw them in a trash can somewhere else. That was his only chance. He made his way back to Washington alone.

***

By the time Erika and Abby got home at 3:15, TV News trucks and vans were already at their house. Abby had to blow the horn of her car to get reporters out of the way so she could get onto their driveway. They were pleading with her to talk to them and six sets of reporters and camera men followed her up to their garage and surrounded her car as she got out of it. "What are you people doing here? Get off our property!"

"Are you the daughter of Matthew Davidson? What do you have to say about your father?"

Abby got worried. She had not seen or heard any news today and for all she knew he might be hurt or worse. "What happened? Is he OK? Where is he?" They quickly told her what happened with him in Detroit but she could not process it with all the people pointing microphones at her face. She worked her way into the house and locked the door behind her.

Erika got off the school bus along with some of her neighbor friends. One of the neighbor moms told Erika what happened with her dad and explained why the TV crews were all over the place. The mom said she called for the police to come and keep the reporters off everyone's property but they had not arrived yet. She suggested that Erika hide out at her house for a while. Erika said "No. I've got to get home. I can see Abby's car and if I don't get home she'll be worried. I'll go around those guys and in the back way."

Erika called the house from her cell phone. "Abby unlock the back patio door. I'm coming through the Burn's back yard and I'll sneak around through the trees and run through the back yard into the house."

"OK. Do you know what's going on?"

"Yeah Mrs. Miller just told me. Open the door OK?" Erika was already halfway through the trees. None of the reporters saw her. She ran across the yard and straight into the house. "Do you think Dad would mind if I got the B-B gun out and shot at these creeps to chase them out of the yard?" She locked the door behind her and put her book bag and purse on the floor in their usual spot.

"We gotta call Mom. Mrs. Miller said she called the police to get these people out of the yard." They both looked out their front window at the media mob. Just then the house phone rang, it was Jen. Erika put her on speaker.

"Do you girls know what's going on?" Jen was calling from her office at work.

"Yeah now we do. Why didn't you call us? There are reporters all over the road. Mrs. Miller called the police."

"Really? I've been trying to call both of you all afternoon. I left messages for you both on your phones."

"Well my phone was turned off in my locker all day. You could have called the school office." Erika said.

"And mine wasn't charged and I left my car charger in my bedroom." Abby told her.

"Of all the days... car charger in your bedroom? Why would you... forget it, anyway make sure Tommy gets in the house and don't talk to anyone. I'll be home as soon as I can. Take care of Tommy."

The doorbell rang. It was the local police chief at the door. He told the girls he had moved the reporters off their yard and onto the street. "If anyone comes on your yard my guys will shoot them, OK?" he said with a big smile. "I'm going to keep at least two of my patrol cars out here the rest of the night." He handed them three of his business cards with his phone numbers on them. "If you girls need anything call me. If you need pizza later, we deliver."

They told the chief their brother would be on the school bus at 4:10PM and they asked if he would make sure Tommy got in the house safely. The chief had one of his officers pick up Tommy in a patrol car and drive him down the street and up the driveway. Tommy loved it. The girls told Tommy what was happening and all three of them turned on the TV and watched their father make news.

195

ON THE RADIO

Matt was driving and Pete was looking for news about the Hannan event on the Internet. It was 4:31PM when Matt's phone rang. It was Fox News calling again. He put the phone on speaker.

"Hello, this is Matt Davidson."

"Mr. Davidson my name is Sean Hannity. You spoke earlier with one of our producers Amelia Kane."

Matt and Pete recognized his voice and they both got big excited grins on their faces. Pete pumped his fist and quietly said "Oh yeah!"

"Hi Sean. Yeah, we've had kind of a crazy day and she said you'd like to talk to us."

"You said us. Would that mean you and the big guy with dark hair and beard standing next to you in the video we've been looking at?"

"Yes. That big guy is my friend Pete. We were at the arena together." Pete flexed both his big arms across his big chest and laughed.

"Mr. Davidson I only have a few minutes. I'm on a bottom of the hour break from my radio show, but we would like to interview you as soon as possible. Would you agree to do a phone interview in the next 15 minutes?"

"Yeah, we could do that, but I gotta tell you that we have some information about Hannan... uh Senator Hannan that you'll...I mean everyone will be interested in."

"What kind of information?"

"Well it's pretty heavy stuff and I think we need to show it to a lawyer before we give it to anyone."

"Mr. Davidson, Fox News has the best attorneys in the business. We could review the information with you and give you their counsel. We deal with these types of situations every day."

Pete leaned over to Matt's phone and said "Not like this you don't."

"Well OK. How about if we get you on air with me in the next half hour and we won't mention your other information until you're comfortable with talking about it?"

"Sounds good." said Matt. "We can pull over some place where we have a good cell signal and wait for your call back."

"Excellent. I want to thank you gentlemen for talking with us. We will call you back in about ten minutes."

***

The Arish-Asad men listening in, contacted the men following Matt and Pete, and instructed them to watch for their truck stopped somewhere ahead of them. They gave them the approximate location and told them they should be near them in the next few minutes. Their orders were to kill both men and seize Matt's vehicle and everything in it.

***

Matt pulled over and off the road about thirty feet to the right at a wide emergency stopping shoulder along the highway. They were in Ohio between Toledo and Cleveland. He left the truck running because the weather got much cooler and they had the heat on. Matt also wanted to leave his headlights on to make sure he was visible by the cars speeding by. He made a few fast notes of answers to questions he thought Hannity would ask."

"Pete, do you want to talk on the radio with him?"

"Not really, but I guess we're in this together. If I think of something good I'll chime in."

"No jokes, OK?"

"Dude, you know me. Serious as a myocardial infarction."

"Great. How many years of med school?"

"I didn't do med school but I did stay at a Holiday Inn last night." Pete smiled.

***

Jen got home from work and pulled onto their street. She proved to the police who she was and they cleared the path for her to drive up to her garage. She went up a few feet then stopped when she remembered to get her mail out of their mailbox at the end of the driveway. She opened the door and stepped out of the car and told one of the police officers what she wanted. "That's OK ma'am. We already took your mail up to the house. These knuckleheads were snooping in the mail box. I gave one of them a ticket for unlawful trespass. It was great." He laughed.

"Oh thank you so much. Thank you for being here!"

"Really it's our pleasure ma'am. Your husband did a great job today. Tell him we all loved it."

The reporters got close to them and were pressing in on her. She was almost back in her car when a reported yelled "Does your husband think he's like Joe the Plumber?"

Jen knew better but she answered anyway "My husband is an honest man who asked an honest question."

"Would you describe your husband as a Christian extremist?" The question stopped her in her tracks.

"What kind of a ridiculous stereotypical prejudicial shallow minded question is that?" Jen asked. She thought to herself – I gotta get away from these people.

"Is your husband a Republican?" another yelled. Jen closed the car door and went up the driveway into her garage.

***

Amelia Kane called Matt and said they would be on air with Sean Hannity in four minutes and asked Matt to hold on. They both listened to Hannity's broadcast through the phone while they waited. Hannity was talking up their "exclusive" interview. "We will have Matthew Davidson with us, the man who asked the question that sent vice presidential nominee Anika Hannan off the deep end today in Detroit. We've been watching the video all afternoon and now we are the first to have Matthew Davidson with us coming up in about two minutes here live on the Sean Hannity Show."

Matt was sitting in the driver seat. He had set the seat back as far as it went so he could stretch out and try to get comfortable. "I can't believe we are doing this."

"Strap in Buddy. This is just the start of a wild ride." Pete said sitting beside Matt and was looking at his laptop.

"I feel like I've been on this ride for a long time now."

"We gotta pray." Pete said and he began to pray. "Lord Jesus, you know what we're doing, but we don't. Please don't let us sound like morons or escaped mental patients. Give us, Matt especially, the words you want him to speak. And Lord if there is a book and movie deal in this, I'd like to play myself in the movie. In the name of Jesus, Amen."

"Good one. I feel better already." Matt said with a hint of sarcasm.

"Mr. Davidson, Sean will be with you in 30 seconds." Amelia Kane said.

"OK, thanks." He said feeling his mouth getting dry. He took a sip of some old cold coffee and made a gag face at Pete.

"Take some deep breaths... but don't hyperventilate. And whatever you do, don't say um and uh." Pete told him.

'Uh, thanks coach." Matt said and shook his head.

Hannity did the introduction to the segment, "Ladies and gentlemen thanks for staying tuned in to us because right now on our newsmaker line we have Matthew Davidson, the man who asked a pretty simple question that caused Democrat senator and vice presidential nominee Anika Hannan from Michigan to self destruct in front of about 8,000 people and the rest of the world live on TV. Mr. Davidson welcome to the Sean Hannity Show."

"Thanks Sean." Matt said. They were live on the air.

"May I call you Matthew?"

"Call me Matt, please."

"Matt, we've all seen the video today and it's probably the most striking melt down ever recorded of any politician caught on tape. What happened?"

"Sean... I got the opportunity to ask a question. They placed a microphone right near me so I just stood up and got in line. It was a very nice crowd of people, polite. They were happy to see her and excited. Her staff or whoever, weren't screening questions and obviously my question wasn't planted by her people. I wanted to ask Senator Hannan about something that was important to me. I'm a Christian, a believer in Jesus Christ and I wanted to know what she has done or would do as Vice President of the United States to reach out to people like me."

"A fair question. We all saw her reaction to your question. What was your reaction to what she said to you?"

"I was stunned. I asked an easy fair question. I think her reaction to me, a Christian, speaks to the rest of America... to all of America as to what she really feels and who she really is. I don't think this was just a bad day for her. This should have been one of the best days of her life but instead she revealed herself to all of us. I'll definitely say that I do not want her as the next Vice President of the United States of America."

"I agree. This was the biggest day in her political life and she had a meltdown. She acted like she knew you, as if she recognized you."

"I've never met her or even been within miles of her ever as far as I know before today." As Matt said that, he hoped he was factually correct.

Pete gave Matt a thumbs up and whispered "You're doin good."

"Did you intend to challenge or attack the Senator as she claimed?"

"No. I wanted to see her in person. It was an historic thing. How often do you get to see a President, Vice President or soon to be Vice President? I didn't know there would be an opportunity to ask a question. It just happened."

"You live in Pennsylvania. Why were you there?"

"I went to Detroit to look at houses to buy." At the last instant he decided not to mention Pete. He thought it might be in his best interests to stay out of it for as long as he could.

Hannity continued, "You are in real estate, correct?"

"Yes, I have a small company. We own single family rental properties and we repair and sell houses."

"How has the burst in the housing bubble and the home mortgage crisis affected your business?"

"Business has ground to a halt. Mortgage money is not flowing. Credit is much, much tighter, especially for first time buyers, which is most of our market. Every loan is being scrutinized way beyond what used to be normal. Appraisers are scared and appraisals are much lower than a few months ago. Even insurance companies are more cautious about issuing new policies. It's as if all the rules affecting our business that were in place before September 2008, were thrown up into the air and only half of the rules have landed and those that did land are upside down."

"Senator Hannan asked if you were sent by the Secret Service or the FBI, and I'm sure the Secret Service agents that were there loved that question. Matt, do you work for either agency?"

"No sir. I admire them both but no, I don't work for them and they didn't send me there."

"Matt, Are you a racist?"

"No. I'm sure anyone who knows me would say I am not a racist nor do I belong to any groups really, other than my church and some business associations."

Pete waved at him and pointed to the NRA sticker on his back side truck window. "Oh yeah, I am a NRA member."

"Do you support Second Amendment rights?"

"Yes sir. Yes of course I do, absolutely."

Two cars pulled right in front of Matt's truck and parked side by side 100 feet away. They were clearly visible in Matt's headlights. Four Arish-Asad men got out of the two cars. Matt was trying to concentrate on speaking with Hannity so he looked down and not at the men. Pete watched them walking all around the parking area and they appeared to be looking for something. One of them had a flashlight and shined it all around where they were and away from the road toward a high chain link fence used to keep deer off the highway. The other men walked right alongside Matt's truck and never looked at it or in it. He could recognize the men as mid-eastern looking and Pete could see a hand held GPS device one of them was looking at. Pete heard them speaking Arabic. That was enough for Pete. He tapped Matt on the shoulder "Time to say bye-bye. We gotta go!"

Hannity asked Matt "Do you think what happened today will affect Senator Hannan's nomination for the Vice Presidency?"

"Yes of course. She smacked a law enforcement officer in the face and she said the president fears her. What could he possibly think of that? I've seen the video and I saw the look on her face in person. I think that anyone who watches it will see the unknown side of the senator. The President has to see that she can't be Vice President."

Pete tapped Matt on the back of the head and pointed to the men. Matt looked out the truck window and saw the men and as many demons with them sniffing around like hungry dogs. Matt also saw four angels standing between them and the men.

"Matt, let's get moving! Say goodbye and call back later." Pete said as he began write down the license plate numbers and a description of the two cars.

Matt covered the phone and said "Yeah, I see what you mean." Then he saw the angels attack the demons in a furious swirl of dark and light. To Matt it looked like a dog fight in the air, fast and furious. Then he saw four bright white, silent explosions twenty feet in the air and it was over, and the angels and demons were gone. Matt pulled the truck out onto the highway and hit the gas "Mr. Hannity we really have to go now. We have to take care of something. Can I call you back?" The interview ended well but Matt could not remember what he said. Now he had a surge of energy and all he wanted was to get some miles between them and the men they saw. He knew they were trouble and the angels protected him and Pete.

"Do you remember the mile marker back there? We should call the Ohio State Police and tell them those guys gave us some crap or threatened us." Matt said.

"Yeah, I wrote down the marker number and the license plate numbers of both cars. Do you really think we should call the police?"

"Well pardon me for profiling, but considering where we were today and whose day we ruined...."

"What's all this "we" stuff?" Pete said trying to tease Matt.

"I believe those guys were looking for us, me at least."

"Why did they act like they didn't see us?"

"Maybe they didn't. We prayed for protection, well, maybe we just got some. How do you think they found us?"

Pete said "Unless they have a GPS locator on this truck, and I really doubt it, the only other way I can think of would be your cell phone. Everyone now knows your name. They could Google you and get your phone number off your website." As he was speaking Pete was doing just as he said. He went to Matt's website from the laptop. "Bingo. That's your cell number right?" Pete pointed to Matt's number. "Anybody can buy cell phone spyware."

"You're kidding..."

"Nope. Give me a minute, I'll show you." Pete searched for cell phone spyware. "Boom. Look here are ten companies that do it. Install in as little as five minutes... check any phone you want... cheating husband... daughter still going out with that jerk.... This one is $99.95"

"Holy cow. Talk about invasion of privacy. Is that legal?"

"I don't know but here it is. Big brother huh? And for a price, big brother can work for you. If any Joe Schmo can buy this stuff, what do you think the feds or serious bad guys can do?"

"Well if we take out the battery that should kill it, right?" Matt asked.

"Yep that's the only way. Give me your phone. Ya know it is possible to activate a cell microphone remotely also and listen to whatever the phone can pick up."

"Fff...fantastic. We are... we were sitting ducks. That's it. Call the Ohio State Police. Tell them those two cars pulled up on us when we were parked and threatened us with guns. They must still be behind us so they should be easy to find. And we need to call Fox and Hannity back."

"Yeah, I'll call and get an email address. We can talk to FOX by email and stay off the phones. We can do the same for Debbie and Jen. We can let them know what's going on." Pete said as he dialed 911 on his phone.

"Well, we can tell them most of what's going on. They would be worried to death if they knew what we got involved with today. We better call the Valley Forge Police and let them know we had some difficulty on the road and ask them to stay around our houses. There's probably news people all over them anyway. Boy, what are we in for?" Matt said.

Pete called the Ohio State Highway Patrol with his cell phone and told them that men in the two cars threatened Matt and Pete with guns. The OSHP was very interested and took Pete very seriously. They said they would dispatch a unit to investigate. Then by email, Pete and Amelia Kane arranged to get Matt and him to their New York offices the next day to look at their information and do some in studio interviews. FOX would send a car for them to pick them up 8AM and arrange for anything else they might need in the city. FOX News also offered to arrange security at their homes and they took them up on the offer. Matt knew they really did not need it but it made Pete feel better.

FOX replayed the recorded radio interview with Hannity on all their TV broadcasts with a photo of Matt from his website and pieces of the video in Detroit. All the networks showed the video of Jen and reporters in her driveway by the mailbox.

***

Ten minutes after Pete spoke to the Ohio State Highway Patrol, two of the OSHP cars without their flashing lights turned on, rolled up behind the two vehicles of the Arish-Asad men as they were moving at 75 miles per hour. They were traveling east on Interstate 80, the Ohio Turnpike, ten miles behind Matt and Pete. The OSHP troopers confirmed the license plate numbers and hit the lights to pull them over. The two Arish-Asad cars accelerated and a pursuit began. The Arish-Asad opened their car windows and fired at the OSHP cars. One car took several .44 caliber rounds through the grill and radiator and disabled the engine. The other OSHP followed alone but backed off to a safer distance. As soon as the radio call went out that their troopers were shot at, every trooper in the area was at alert. By radio the OSHP coordinated a spike strip point 15 miles ahead. The plan was to blow out the tires of the two cars and get them to stop. Troopers quickly got into position and laid down five sets of spike strips to stop the two cars. Beyond the spike strips five OSHP cars blocked the two lanes of the highway.

Both cars hit the strips within seconds of each other while speeding at 95 miles per hour. All four tires of each car were blown out and they continued on out of control, the one car hit the side of other and sent them into opposite guard rails where they stopped in clouds of dust. Four trailing OSHP cars stopped 100 feet short of the two crashed cars. They directed their head lights and spot lights at them. Troopers approached from both directions with shotguns and pistols drawn. AK47 fire erupted

204

toward the troopers from inside both crashed cars. Troopers scrambled for cover and they responded with shotgun blasts that took out all the windows of both cars. A full blown gun battle was in progress.

Ten invisible angels arrived and stood in front of the troopers as the gun fire continued. The angels had shields and their wings were extended giving cover to the troopers. An OSHP helicopter arrived and shined a powerful spot light at the cars in an attempt to blind the Arish-Asad. As the battle raged, two of the Arish-Asad men were shot and killed. The other two were knocked unconscious when an angel banged a sword against his shield and the concussion rocked all the cars and shook the ground and surrounding trees.

"What was that!?! Did they drop a hand grenade?" a trooper yelled. The firing stopped and the Arish-Asad men were all on the ground. Troopers approached and secured them.

***

While nearing Pittsburgh, Pete asked Matt, "Do you really believe in angels. I mean... I do, but I'm not sure how they work or what they really do on earth. Last night, when you prayed, you asked for angels to protect our families."

"Yes I do believe in angels. 1000% yes. With every bone in my body I can tell you they are real. Angels are ministering spirits, and I know they aren't those little cupid looking chubby things with the little bows and arrows either. Think about it, the angels in the Bible. People were terrified of angels when they saw them. What did they do when they saw an angel? They fell to the ground in fear and almost every time the angel has to say "Do not be afraid." In First Chronicles, one angel killed seventy thousand men of Israel. In fact the same angel was also sent to destroy Jerusalem and was so destructive that God had to tell the angel to stop. One angel annihilated all the fighting men and the officers in the camp of the Assyrian king. At the first Passover one single angel brought death to all the first born male children and animals of the Egyptians. Angels are warriors, protectors, rescuers. They carry weapons if they need them. They battle evil spirits. They're more like Navy SEALS, and you will defiantly not see anything close to a real angel on a Valentine's day card."

Pete asked "Back where we were parked, when it looked like those guys didn't see us... do you think angels....?"

"Why not? We prayed. Angels are protectors that do God's will. I don't think those guys suddenly got stupid and blind, unless God wanted them to act that way."

Pete was quiet for a moment imagining what could have happened miles back to prevent those men from seeing them, and Matt's truck when they were inches away from them.

"Do you think angels have wings?"

"Yeah, but not always. They have them if they need them. You gotta remember that they are God's created beings. God can give them any power, shape or form they need to carry out His purpose. And they're big guys. I've never seen a female..." Matt caught himself and his voice trailed off.

"You mean in books or drawings?"

"Yeah, definitely, that's what I meant, books." Matt laughed at himself.

Matt pointed to a sign along the highway that said - Welcome to Pittsburgh Home of the Six Time World Champion Pittsburgh Steelers. "God's angels make the Steel Curtain look like a lace doily."

"I hope you're right."

"I know I'm right."

***

Omar got back to his apartment in Washington DC at 7PM. There were no messages for him on his home answering machine, no email messages on his computer and he had not heard from Hannan since being at the arena. No one from Arish-Asad contacted him, and that was very unusual.

***

They got off the Turnpike in Valley Forge at 11:30PM. Mat dropped Pete off at his house. There were no reporters. Pete's name sill had not gotten out to the media. There was one car parked in front. When they pulled up, two men in suits and ties got out of the car and approached Matt's truck.

"Excuse me sir, do you live here?"

"Yeah, this is my house. Are you the guys FOX sent?" Pete got out of the truck and grabbed his things from the back seat.

"Yes sir. Your wife told us you would be here soon. We will be here until midnight then we have our third shift team coming on. If you need us for anything your wife has our phone number."

"Thanks. Thanks for being here." Pete said. They nodded and got back in their car.

"Matt, get home and go to bed. We've got another big day tomorrow."
Matt saw two angels in Pete's front yard and he waved to them. Pete
saw him wave, looked in that direction and looked back to Matt and
asked him "Who are you waving at?"

"Couple of angels standing guard over your home. God knows you
and Debbie. God bless you man. Thanks for being with me on this." Matt
got a little choked up and he felt his eyes moisten. "You're a good
friend."

Pete could see Matt's eyes and he understood what he meant. "Hey.
I had nothing better to do. Tomorrow, 8AM." They shook hands and Matt
drove off for home.

Matt pulled into his own driveway ten minutes later and there were
still four TV news vans parked outside. The police recognized him and
waved him in. The private security men were there also. It was good to
be home and he was relieved. He told his family the story of their adventure. The kids were impressed and proud of him. He told them the plans
for tomorrow and how he needed to get to sleep. He told Jen the unedit-
ed version later when they were alone. Pete had been emailing Debbie
and Jen the whole way home so everyone was up to speed on what the
plan was for the next day.

Matt took a shower and got into bed. He set his alarm for 6:30AM.
Jen got in bed with him and they talked about everything. Jen asked him
"Does Pete know about the angels?"

"He asked me if I believe in them. I told him what I know about
them, but I didn't tell him I see them. I just couldn't. Maybe sometime,
but it's a big leap on my part and it would be the same on his part to
believe me."

"It's about faith and trust. You'll know if you should. Hey you
looked pretty good on TV, my little celebrity."

"Want me to autograph something for you."

"Want to autograph some checks for me? There are some things we
have to pay." The conversation completely changed direction.

"I know there are." Matt dreaded talking about this.

"I got a call today from a credit card collection company."

"I'm sorry you had to deal with that." Matt told her. He hated that
he put her in this position.

"The guy was really rude and thought he could intimidate me or
something. He said "Well how do you intend to resolve this matter?" I
told him I didn't even know about it and that he should call you."

"I'll call him. I'll call tomorrow. Well maybe not tomorrow."

"Oh, and he was actually looking at our house with the satellite view on Google maps. He started saying something like "It looks like you have a very nice home, very nice neighborhood, and I see that you are current on your mortgage payments. Is there some reason this account is past due?" Jen imitated the man's voice.

"Oh brother. What is that supposed to do, scare you? Oh, we know where you live." Matt was felt a little angry but he knew he was responsible for Jen having to take the call.

"I'll take care of it Jen. Just let me focus on getting all this stuff with Hannan behind us first, OK?"

Jen agreed and they prayed together in the dark laying side by side on their backs thanking God for His faithfulness and His provision. Matt's last thought before he fell asleep was –thank you Lord for my good wife.

WEDNESDAY – ON TV

Matt practically jumped out of bed when the alarm clock went off. He was instantly awake and ready to go. He shaved and took another shower and was dressed in fifteen minutes. Jen made him take a suit and tie with him to New York so he would look "respectable" on TV. He had some breakfast with Jen and the kids. He took Erika's phone for the day so Jen could call him. Erika said "Dad if you get any texts from my friends, don't read them or send some goofy reply."

"Why not? They'll probably be messages for me anyway, ya know, wanting interviews and autographs and stuff."

"Dad, please don't answer, OK?"

"Yes dear." Matt learned to say – yes dear a long time ago, living with three women. Tommy learned to say it also.

The limo picked Matt up at 8:05AM. Pete was already in the car when it pulled up. Pete was wearing his sunglasses when he lowered the window and said to Matt, "Hey man, how do you like the way I roll?"

"Pretty sweet." Matt said. The driver laid Matt's suit in the trunk.

The kids were excited to see the limo and Tommy wanted to get in it. Matt told him there was no time and he had to get going right away. Abby took some pictures with her phone. Matt said his good-byes to them all with hugs and kisses.

Jen said "You two be careful, and be nice to the media moguls."

Matt laughed at her and kissed her one more time. The police made the way clear for the limo to leave through the crowd of TV news teams that were still in front of their house. A few of the news crews thought about following them but they could not gather up their equipment quickly enough. The limo driver took off pretty fast to make sure no one was behind them. The drive to New York seemed to not take long. They spent the time drinking coffee and reading the five morning newspapers FOX instructed the driver to have in the car. They arrived at FOX News through the New York City morning traffic at 10:30AM and were met on the side walk in front of the building by Amelia Kane and two FOX lawyers. Amelia made the introductions. The lawyers were specialists in verifying facts and protecting FOX against slander and libel issues.

Amelia said "Matt and Pete these are two of our attorneys…"

Pete said "Hey great to meet you. I see Dewy and Cheatem, where's Howe?"

209

"Yeah, Three Stooges, 1930 something. You know we have to sue you every time you say that? Copyright infringement." They all laughed and shook hands "My name is Rich Bender and..."

"My name is Ken Sanders. It is really good to meet you both and I'll say we admire what you men are doing. We will do anything we can to give you counsel concerning your protection, your free speech rights and what can or cannot be done with the information you have in your possession."

Matt said "Sounds good, let's get to work." and they followed Amelia inside the building to the elevator.

A few people recognized Matt and Pete as they made their way through the office to a conference room that had five TV monitors on the walls and two laptop computers on the table. There they met Brian Smith a computer and Internet expert. He was setting up two laptops to be sure they were ready.

Pete placed his computer bag on the table and got his laptop out and working. He said "Look, I just want to make it clear that nobody copies anything off this stick. Understood?" He held it in his hand in front of them. Pete was the biggest guy in the room and he made sure they all agreed.

They decided to look at the entire list of files and then each document one by one in order and evaluate what they were looking at. They linked the two FOX laptop screens so it was easier for them all to follow along. Matt stood back and let them go to it. Pete was in the mix as he was guarding the material until he felt comfortable with the lawyers.

Matt spoke to Amelia and drank coffee. He was struck by how pretty she was and she reminded him of Jen. Amelia was in her twenties, short blonde hair, brown eyes and Sarah Palin style eyeglass. She told him she was a journalism school graduate and in her fourth year of working at WABC Radio for Sean Hannity's show and doing some producing at FOX NEWS.

"I really love this work and this is the perfect job for me, a newsaholic. If they didn't pay me I'd be here working for free and waitressing at night. Don't tell anyone that, OK?"

"I won't say a word. Why don't you get a good look at those files? You don't need to entertain me." Matt said to her as he took his coffee and sat down on the opposite side of the table where all of them were working.

It took less than five minutes for Ken Sanders to say "Guys, I've got goose bumps. This is some very serious material we are dealing with. Brian can you start authenticating these files for date stamps and such? And go ahead and check the origin of those websites. Don't go looking at them but can you find out where they are from?"

"No problem. I'm on it and I can peek at the websites from a server we have in Istanbul, Turkey. It's undetectable; we look at Al-Qaeda and Al-Jazeera stuff from there all the time."

Rich Bender said "Matt and Pete, can we go back to yesterday and would you tell me how you got this memory stick?"

Matt said "We found it at the arena after Omar grabbed the microphone from me. We were sure it belongs to him. We saw his name on at least one file. We checked some stuff yesterday just like we're doing now."

"Do you think he dropped the stick?"

"Yes. That makes sense to me." Matt said.

"Did you pick it up?"

"No." Matt and Pete both said at the same time.

"Then why do you have it now?"

Matt asked "Can we just say we discovered it after we left the building?"

"Well OK, but where did you discover it?"

"In my pocket. End of discussion. Is that OK with everyone?" Pete said with his - that's the way it's gonna be voice.

"Works for me, you OK with that Ken?" Rich said. Ken nodded vigorously.

At 12:00PM they decided to take a quick lunch break after getting through all the files one time. They gave the list of the women's names to Amelia to see if she and some assistants could confirm links to the men implied.

They all returned to the conference room at 1:00PM. They talked about the list of women. "Is this a blackmail list? Vice President Peterson wasn't on it." Matt said.

Ken said "Maybe he was. The list was updated since he resigned. I gotta tell ya, this list is bigger than some blue dress with a stain. Hang this list out in the wind and see who starts dying."

"You aren't going to believe this!" Amelia said "A woman who worked for Jim Peterson was found dead this morning. Quick, go to the FOX website and pull up the story."

Brian got the site and found video of the story. The reporter said "Lindsay Holden, a former employee of former Vice President James Peterson was found dead this morning at about 7AM along a jogging trail in Fort Marcy National Park, in a Virginia suburb just across the Potomac River, south west of Washington DC. The cause of death has not been disclosed. She was reported missing last evening by her husband. Fort Marcy Park is best known for being the location of the 1993 suicide of President Clinton's White House Deputy Counsel Vince Foster. That case in the opinion of many, was never fully resolved."

Pete said "Whoa, guys… this is big. This is no coincidence. She was killed, I'll guarantee it. What did she know about Peterson?"

"She wasn't on Matt's list." Brian said.

"Hey, not my list. We just bring the bad news." Matt said pointing to himself and Pete.

"You know what I mean."

Ken said "Well Peterson wasn't on the list but the president is and he has two women's names attached to him and we know for sure at least one of them used to work for the president. This is some really heavy stuff we have our hands on here, and you guys have to decide how far you want to take it or who to give it to."

***

The Arish-Asad killed Lindsay Holden last night. She was no longer of any value so she was taken off the payroll. They had to ensure she would never speak about her role in the resignation of Vice President Peterson.

***

Sean Hannity stopped in to meet Matt and Pete and hear about the information they discovered. The lawyers told him what they had and they all discussed what they were prepared to go on TV and radio with.

Hannity said "Do you guys really want to do this? There will be a lot of people who will think you guys created this, that you are a couple of crazy Christians, or that there is some plot to take Hannan and the President down. You gotta be ready for what people will say about you."

Matt said "I know, and I've been praying about this. I feel strongly led to make sure the public, the American people get this information. I want this stuff made public before the government can stop us. I believe there is safety if the truth is placed out in the open."

"OK. I've seen a lot of people get overwhelmed in this type situation and you have to know what to expect. What do you guys want to talk to me on-air about?"

For radio they agreed Matt could re-tell what happened in Detroit with Hannan. They would also say they found Omar's memory stick after the confrontation at the microphone. They would tell how they looked at it out of curiosity, found the files, found Omar's name on a file and his link to Al-Qaeda and they were now prepared to give it all to the proper authorities. Hannity would also tease that more information would be revealed tonight on TV. For TV they planned to also describe the list of women's names and that the President is linked to two of the women.

"And what about the woman found in Marcy Park? Should we mention the Al-Qaeda websites?" Matt asked.

Ken said "We can't say there is any connection to her death and the vice president, not yet, and you should hold off on telling about the websites until the Feds can check them out. Remember that as soon as you get off TV the Department of Justice or FBI should be calling you."

"Can they be trusted? I remember Janet Reno and I wouldn't trust her even if she was my mom. Is the new attorney general any different? I know a couple of months ago he said that America is a nation of cowards. It's very hard for me to trust a guy who says that. Look I don't care what happens as long at the truth gets out and Hannan is stopped from becoming the next vice president."

"Matt, don't worry about her. She's dead meat." Ken said.

Rich said "We gotta be concerned about the women on the list. As far as we can tell they are all alive. I'd suggest we call the FBI as soon as you are off TV tonight." Rich continued "This is what should happen. After you go on TV, and on behalf of FOX, I truly hope you do because the ratings will be crazy. I will call D.O.J., they will probably call you also, or the FBI will. When they call, all you have to do is fully cooperate with anything they want. You can give them the files, all of it and just let the light of truth shine on it. The rest should take care of itself and we here at FOX News will keep the pressure on them to do the right thing. Gentleman this is important, historic and the national security implications are major."

At 2PM Matt and Pete both taped a long interview with Sean Hannity that they could cut up and use for promos that Hannity could play over two days. They ultimately decided to say they found the information belonging to Hannan's assistant Samir Omar that gives compelling evidence he is connected to a militant Muslim group in America. They also said there may be a connection between the death of Lindsay Holden and the militant group. At 4PM they went on Hannity's radio show and gave up some more information and Hannity teased that they would talk about it even more on his TV show at 9PM.

That evening both Matt and Pete gave separate sworn statements to Rich Bender as to what they knew about the memory stick they found. They knew they would be asked for statements and thought this would save them a day or two of meetings with the FBI or Department of Justice.

Pete's wife Debbie went over to Matt's house to watch them on TV. They loaded up with snacks and drinks and Jen invited a few of their friends from church to come over to be with them. All the DVRs and TiVos in their neighborhood were ready to go.

The show went well and both Matt and Pete were on together. Matt wore his suit and Amelia Kane found a shirt with an 18 inch neck and a tie for Pete. They were nervous about being on TV, but being there all day and being familiar with so many faces made it easier. The lawyers practiced the interview with them, asking the most likely and important questions they would be asked.

***

The leadership in Tehran, including President Ahmadinejad and Ayatollah Khamenei, was awake early to watch Matt on Sean Hannity's show via satellite. They quickly agreed to terminate all of operation "Planted Garden" and everyone involved outside of Arish-Asad command. The DC Commander received a communication within minutes of their decision, and then he gave his men their instructions.

***

Matt and Pete were finished at the FOX studio at 10:15PM. They said their good-byes to Hannity's producers, the lawyers and crew. Everyone at the studio had a feeling that they were witnessing important political history. Arrangements were made to stay in touch. Sean Hannity said to them "You men have had a long couple of days and I wanted to tell you that I appreciate you coming on my show with me. You're doing the right thing. You are great Americans." He advised them to do interviews on other TV news networks to build their credibility among the media. He also hinted at who to avoid. "Don't bother with those two who interviewed Sarah Palin, and I wouldn't waste a second of my life talking to the peacock network."

They got into the limo for the ride home and there was food and drinks for them, more than enough for two hungry grown men. "Very nice. I guess this is what first class feels like." Matt said as he settled in for the two hour drive home.

"I'm starved. If this stuff wasn't here we'd be stopping for pizza." Pete said as he looked to see what was there to eat.

"Amen brother. Hey Mr. Limo Driver, what's your name? Are you hungry?" Matt asked. It was a different driver than the one who picked them up in the morning.

"You can call me Vince. My mom calls me Vincent. I'm not hungry sir, but I wouldn't mind something to drink." The driver was a native New Yorker and he lived on Staten Island.

"Is a Coke OK? There's other stuff." Matt asked.

"That would be great sir, thanks." Vince said, and Matt handed him the soda. "Sir, if you don't mind, I just wanna say that I saw you gentlemen on TV and I think you guys did the right thing. I'm as American as apple pie and I gotta tell ya, the way that Hannan talked to you and what she said, it was disgusting. If I was there I would not have been as nice as you were, that's for sure."

"Well thanks Vince. We really appreciate it. I just hope this all works out for the good." Matt said and he opened a bag of Doritos and a Diet Coke.

As they were leaving Manhattan, Erika's phone in Matt's pocket rang. DEPT. OF JUSTICE D.C. was on the caller ID.

"Oh boy, look whose calling." Matt showed it to Pete.

"Here, let me handle it." Pete reached for the phone.

"OK big boy, talk to them."

"This is Mr. Davidson's office. To order a Matt Davidson T-shirt or schedule a personal appearance at your birthday party or garage sale, please press one. To request an autograph …"

Matt dove at Pete to grab the phone from him. "Give me that! Are you insane?" Matt said laughing. It was a very long day and they were punchy.

"I think they pressed one!" Pete said.

"Hello. This is Matt Davidson. Who's calling?"

"Is this Matthew Davidson?" a very serious gray haired male voice asked.

"Yes. It's me, Matthew Davidson. How did you get this number?" Matt turned the phone onto speaker so Pete could hear.

"Mr. Davidson, my name is Ray Lawrence. I am United States Assistant Attorney General in Washington DC. Sir, Mrs. Davidson gave me permission to call you. We are very interested in the information you discussed tonight on television. We would like to review it because I believe it concerns national security."

"I think so too. Come and get it. You can have it all. I'll gladly give you copies of everything. I'll even give you a copy of my sworn deposition that I did today in New York with our attorneys."

"Mr. Davidson we would be most grateful. When can we get this from you?"

"Tomorrow morning?" Matt asked.

"Could we get it from you tonight sir?"

"Well, we only have one copy of the information with us on a memory stick."

Pete started shaking his head no, with his mouth full of a bite of a hoagie. Matt asked Lawrence to hold on. "I have an extra copy here on disc." Pete said with his mouth still full and he pointed to his computer bag. Pete swallowed hard. "I made copies last night when I got home. I brought one copy with us. We have another copy on the hard drive and another on the memory stick. There's also one copy hidden at my house and Debbie put eight copies in our safety deposit box at the bank."

"Good job Pete. You just qualified for bonus pay."

"You can call me Mr. Backup or Mr. Redundant, I like Backup better... maybe Mr. Duplicate?"

Matt got back on the phone with Ray Lawrence. "Mr. Ahh... sorry, I forgot your..."

"Lawrence."

"Mr. Lawrence we do have a copy with us on a disc now that we can give you. Could you meet us? We are heading back home right now, leaving New York City. We just came out of the Lincoln Tunnel a couple of minutes ago."

"I could have a chopper meet you in 30 or 40 minutes. We can pick up your disc and not have to bother you gentlemen in the morning."

"I can't believe this! This is so cool!" Pete whispered. He was as excited as a little boy on Christmas morning.

"Wow. Yeah we can do that. Can you just make sure your guys bring lots of ID? I want to make sure I'm giving this disc to the right guys." Matt said and he felt his pulse beat a little faster.

"The chopper won't be enough for you? I'm just kidding. We will absolutely be able to clearly identify our people. Thank you very much for your cooperation Mr. Davidson. You will be called back to coordinate a meeting point."

***

Omar watched TV that night and he now knew that Matt somehow had his memory stick. As a soldier of Al-Qaeda, Omar knew he must face the consequences for giving up the information. He contacted the Arish-Asad commander and told him that the information that Matt Davidson had made public was from his memory stick. Omar told him that he would make things right and travel to Pennsylvania early tomorrow morning to kill Matt. He offered to do this as a desperate attempt to restore himself. The commander knew that whatever Omar did would not matter and Matthew Davidson was no longer a concern to them. All the damage was done. Their information was being made public and the operation with Hannan and others linked to it were all in ruin. Omar's offer was feeble at best and he knew Omar had no skills to take on such action. The commander and his superiors were now only concerned with damage control.

***

The limo driver continued south on the New Jersey Turnpike toward Trenton. Matt told the driver what the plan was and he was happy and excited to help out. They arranged to stop on a long straight stretch of the Turnpike just north of Hightstown. The New Jersey State Police met their limo at 10:50PM. The troopers stopped traffic on the south bound side three minutes before the chopper arrived and they lit road flares to mark their location. Matt, Pete and Vince the driver, got out of the limo to wait for the chopper and to stretch their legs. It was a clear night and they could easily see it approach from a few miles out. The troopers asked them to get back into the limo during landing. Right on schedule a Blackhawk helicopter from Willow Grove Naval Air Station in Pennsylvania, landed in the middle of the two lanes in front of them. A crewman jumped out a side door and ran to the limo. He identified himself and Matt gave him the disc. Then he ran back to the chopper and 30 seconds later it was in the air.

"I bet James Bond feels like this every day." Matt said to Pete.

217

The flight crew took the disc directly to Andrews Air Force Base in Washington. Assistant Attorney General Lawrence had it in his hands 20 minutes later.

Matt and Pete got home to Matt's house a little past midnight. Debbie was still there with Jen and the kids. They had lots to talk about and it felt good to all be home.

THURSDAY – CLOUDY ALL DAY

United States Assistant Attorney General for the National Security Division, Ray Lawrence, was a long time veteran at the Department of Justice. He started there in 1988 when he was appointed by Ronald Reagan in the last year of his presidency. Lawrence survived at Justice through the Clinton years and now in 2009 he was the head of the division. He was ready to retire but since he did not see any talent coming to the Justice Department with the new administration, he felt he should stay. He expected to be fired when the Democrats took over, but no one ever came knocking on his door to tell him to leave.

A Navy lieutenant delivered the disc to Lawrence at his Justice Department office at midnight. He went right to work analyzing all the files. Those that needed to be translated were sent out and done in less than 30 minutes.

Lawrence called Deputy Director John Sheeler of the FBI. Lawrence and Sheeler had worked on many cases together over the last fifteen years. Sheeler was a real professional and he was the only person at the FBI Lawrence would trust with something like this. "John its Ray Lawrence. Sorry to call you so late but it's real important."

"No problem Ray. If you're working I guess I should be too." Sheeler had been sleeping on a lounge chair in his living room where he fell asleep watching TV. His wife turned it and the lights off when she went to bed an hour earlier. Sheeler had his cell phone in his pocket and it woke him when Lawrence called.

"John, I sent you a list of names and I need everything you can give me on each one as fast as you can."

Sheeler was already on his feet walking through the dark heading to his computer in his home office. "OK. I'll go look at it right now and get people working. I'll call you ASAP. Hey, how about some golf next week?"

"You got it. Talk to you soon."

Lawrence sent the website addresses to the CIA and they confirmed back to him that they were secret Al-Qaeda sites that contained coded information. They felt that finding these sites could have great value in the war on terror and they worked to mine them for information as fast as possible before they were shut down.

At 2AM, Sheeler called Lawrence. Sheeler recognized what Lawrence saw and he wanted to make contact with each woman on the list because he felt they and possibly family members may be in danger. Lawrence agreed and told him to find them, and observe them but wait to make contact. It was possible there was more they could learn from these women before they spoke to them.

***

At 3AM an Arish-Asad cell captain got past the locked front entry door of Omar's apartment building in Washington. He went to Omar's second floor apartment door and hung an ordinary white plastic bag, the kind commonly used at food markets, on his door knob. The contents of the bag weighted .90 kilograms.

***

By 4AM Lawrence completed reviewing all the files and he had received good data back from FBI and the CIA. The information from the FBI included a transcript of the tip line phone call Matt had made to the FBI about Hannan. It also linked Matt to the low level "unusual incident" report that was created after Matt made the 911 call at Home Depot when the Arish-Asad boss tried to kill him. Lawrence knew Matt was not in Detroit at Hannan's event by chance, but nothing else about Matt was unusual. Matt, Pete and their wives all checked out clean, right down to the movies they rented on-line. Lawrence would want to speak to Matt soon, but for now his main concerns were Omar and Hannan. At 4:10AM Lawrence made a phone call to the attorney general.

"Sir, this is Ray Lawrence at National Security Division. We haven't met yet sir."

"What time is it? Are you working late or early?" He was in bed with his now awake wife lying next to him.

"Late sir. Sorry to bother you at this hour but this morning at 12AM I received a copy of information supplied by Matthew Davidson, the gentleman who was in Detroit with Senator Hannan."

"Oh brother, what a disaster."

"Sir, Mr. Davidson was on FOX News last night and revealed some of the information he found on a memory stick at the arena in Detroit. I already emailed you my summary, but the information clearly implicates one of Senator Hannan's staffers in a conspiracy against the president, members of congress and others. There are also links to Al-Qaeda. I have already gone for an arrest warrant for Samir Omar, Hannan's staffer."

"You said the president and Al-Qaeda?"

"Yes. There is a list that connects 16 women to 13 men and all the men are US government officials. The women either work for these men now or they did in the past or there is some other close relationship. The list also indicates that the women are being paid substantial sums of money every month."

Trying to conceal a yawn, the attorney general said "What do you think we should do? Is this something I can sleep on or...."

"Sir, I would never call you at this hour just to tell you a story. It is my opinion that this information is genuine and presents evidence of a legitimate threat to the United States, the president, and the others I mentioned. My advice is to tell the president immediately. I also suggest that you advise the president to withdraw Senator Hannan's nomination for the vice presidency."

"He's going to hate this." The AG said as he pulled his blanket away and sat up on the edge of his bed in the dark.

"He will hate it more if Hannan gets confirmed and sworn in as vice president and then this information hits the fan. Sir the cat is out of the bag concerning Hannan. After that thing in Detroit and Mr. Davidson on TV last night, the president can't keep her as his nominee. Sir this information also leads me to suspect the resignation of Vice President Peterson last week was part of this. If I am correct, there is now an opportunity to prevent damage and possibly save lives."

"I'll read your report and call the president. Don't go to bed yet, I'll probably need you in a couple of hours."

***

Omar woke at 5AM and prepared to leave his apartment. He did not own a car so he phoned for a taxi to take him to Alamo car rental at Union Station. He packed a travel bag and took with him a Glock 27 handgun, $40,000 in cash, his wallet, passport and cell phone. By using the Internet, Omar printed maps and directions to where Matt lived. His plan was to simply go to Matt's home, wait for him if necessary and shoot him dead. Afterward he planned to drive to Montreal and take a flight to France.

Omar turned off the lights in his apartment, unlocked his door and pulled it open. The explosion destroyed all of his 750 square foot apartment and the apartments above and below him. A fire started but it did not spread far because the District of Columbia Fire Department arrived quickly. There was not one piece found of Omar's remains that was larger than a tennis ball. The bag placed on his doorknob contained a motion detecting detonator and .75 kilograms of the explosive C-4. Neither of Omar's neighbors was at home when the explosion rocked the neighborhood. One neighbor was away at a Christian writer's conference and the other neighbors, a husband and wife, had car trouble out of town that delayed their return home. Only Omar was killed, no one was injured and Omar's cash was blown out onto the street.

***

At 6AM the attorney general called the president at the White House. "Mr. President. Good morning sir."

"Kinda early for you, huh?" The president took the call in the White House residence. He had just gotten dressed to go workout with five Secret Service agents.

"Yes sir. I have some important information regarding a staffer of Senator Hannan."

"Oh man, Hannan is just killing me."

"Sir, we are convinced that her assistant, Samir Omar is involved with a conspiracy to blackmail members of congress, and others in elected and appointed offices. He also has connections to Al-Qaeda."

"I was worried about that." As soon as he said it he braced himself to be questioned. There was no way he was supposed to know about any of this. How could he say he was worried about it?

"Pardon me sir? I didn't quite catch what you…"

The president hesitated and then said "Can you prove this? Do you have evidence?" He had to plow through, change the subject and get past his slip.

"Yes we have evidence. It would need to be proved in court of course. We already have a warrant for Mr. Omar's arrest and we have copies of his electronic files that were recovered in Detroit by the man who asked Senator Hannan the Christian question."

"Is that a coincidence that the same guy shows up with information? How did that happen?"

"It is not entirely coincidence and I'm not exactly clear the sequence of events but I will tell you the information Mr. Davidson gave us is substantial and we have confirmed the validity of much of it already."

"He just gave it up? Why would he give it up unless he wanted Hannan out? Who does he work for?" The link from Hannan to Matt made no sense to the president and he felt a twinge of conspiracy.

"Sir, everything about Mr. Davidson checks out clean and he is not a threat. He was on FOX News last night and described some of the information but not all of it. He has been extremely discrete and very cooperative."

"FOX News, great. Like I need this."

"Mr. President, your name was included in the recovered information." The attorney general waited for a reaction from the president. There was none. "Sir, is there anything that you are aware of, any pressure being put on you that may be connected to any women who do now or may have in the past worked for you?"

The president remained quiet, his brain reaching for unused lawyer muscles. For a flash he though - It depends on what the meaning of the word "is" is. Then he felt an even greater force of pressure than the one Hannan had put him under. He did not know what to say. His long silence became awkward and then the attorney general gave him a pass, for now.

"Sir, I strongly advise that you ask Senator Hannan to withdraw her nomination for vice president."

Finally the president said, "When can you get in here to the White House? We gotta talk."

"I can be there in less than an hour. I would like to bring Ray Lawrence from my group and the FBI Director with me also." .

"OK. Get over here." the president said as exhaled and his shoulders dropped.

***

The President sat at his desk in the Oval Office. He did not change out of his workout gear and went straight there after getting off the phone. He never really liked being in the Oval Office. He felt restrained and he was uncomfortable with the heaviness and formality he felt while being there. The president knew this meeting would be the only opportunity he would get to work his way out of this mess and he had to be careful about what he would say regarding what he knew. The men arrived and they all sat on furniture in the center of the office with the President in a chair in the middle.

"Gentlemen, you all probably know more about these developments with Senator Hannan and her man Omar than I do." He took a long dramatic pause. "There is one part of this you all do not know. Senator Hannan spoke to me privately about a week ago while on board Air

223

Force One flying back from New Hampshire. She told me that she and people with her had scandalous information about Vice President Peterson and that she would reveal it if I did not force him to resign from office. The information she had about him turned out to be true. She also said she had similar information about me. All faked of course, but she said it was embarrassing and I could not afford to have my administration knocked off course. Part of her demand was for me to nominate her to replace Peterson. I decided to wait and keep this to myself, let it play out and eventually Hannan would reveal herself. It turns out I was right and here we are."

"Mr. President did she tell you who she was connected to or working with?"

"No, but she showed me an extremely compromising photo of the vice president and she was very convincing."

"Sir, it appears she has ties to Arish-Asad in the United States and Al-Qaeda. The operation which she is part of, is extensive and has been underway for years."

"I thought so." The president said nodding his head. Ray Lawrence and the FBI Director looked at each other.

Lawrence said, "Sir, there are things we suggest that you do right away. First you must tell Hannan to withdraw her nomination. We would like to arrest her later today and dump a mountain of charges on her. We can give a good bit of information to the media right now to support the move."

"Did you get Omar yet? Pick him up?"

Lawrence answered him, "Sir, Mr. Omar is dead. There was a very large explosion this morning at his apartment here in town."

The FBI Director said, "Mr. President there were other members of congress and other parts of government, thirteen men total who have women place near them to provide similar blackmail scenarios. Right now my people are making contact with these women to provide protection for them and their families. They are in danger. We are assuming there was some force or coercion used to get them to cooperate. We will find out all the details over the next several days."

Lawrence told the President, "Mr. President, as Assistant Attorney General, I am concerned about the criminal side of this problem and making sure we proceed properly. In regard to you politically, and I will speak frankly sir, I advise you get your legal council on this. The Department of Justice can assist you with damage control where it is legal to do so and the attorney general will have control of what information we release and discretion in terms of who and what charges he chooses to prosecute. But sir, I want it to be clear that we are going to do this by the book."

The president looked at the attorney general who looked him in the eye and nodded his head in agreement. The attorney general said "Mr. President this is new ground, unprecedented. If this is done properly you will not be damaged."

The FBI Director added. "Mr. President, on the way here this morning I contacted the Chairman of the Joint Chiefs, the Homeland Secretary and the National Security Advisor and I suggested we informally, not publically, raise our terror threat warning level. We already sent all of our embassies a threat warning. We should be on guard against Al-Qaeda lashing out."

"Gentlemen, thank you for your swift work. I'd like you to be here with me when I call Senator Hannan."

***

At 7:45AM Hannan's BlackBerry rang. She was lying in bed already awake for an hour when the call came. She looked at the caller display and she knew what to expect. She got out of bed and stood up so her voice would sound as strong as she could force it to be. She was wearing white flannel pajamas.

"Senator Hannan. This is the President."

"Yes sir."

"I'm on a speaker phone and with me are the Attorney General, the FBI Director and Assistant Attorney General Lawrence. We are recording this phone call. Senator I am calling you to tell you to withdraw your nomination for vice president. I'll expect it by noon today."

"Sir, may I meet with you to discuss this please?"

"That would not be a good idea. The last time I spoke to you it didn't go very well."

"I understand." She pushed the off button and sat down on the side bed. She looked at her reflection in the mirror that hung on the wall in front of her. She felt as if she had aged 100 years overnight.

***

Matt and Jen slept in. They put Abby in charge of deciding if any incoming phone calls were worth taking. The three kids watched TV.

225

Church friends had done some grocery shopping for them the day before so they had plenty of food and no good reason to go anywhere. Tommy was playing peek-a-boo with the press photographers through the windows from inside the house and garage.

***

It was a gray cold misty Ann Arbor morning. The news media was all over Hannan's father's neighborhood and in front of his house. They were there overnight and most had been there since her stunning performance at the arena. Hannan had been held up there in the house ever since. She had not given any statement or comments to anyone.

The police kept the news media at a reasonable distance from the house and off of their property. The home had a long driveway, 100 feet from the street. News vans with satellite dishes, pop up tents, lights and cables were everywhere. At least one hundred people mingling around. There were a few dozen protestors who objected to Hannan's tirade against Christians. There were only three people demonstrating their support for her.

Early that morning Hannan's father received a message by cell phone. The caller spoke in Arabic and said, "Your humiliation must end. May Allah bless you."

By 10AM Anika Hannan had not yet sent a resignation letter to the president. She sat at one end of a couch in a numb daze watching her father's TV in his living room. She was still wearing her white pajamas, her black hair in a pony tail and she was barefoot. Her mother sat at the other end of the couch also staring at the TV. The news about the information Matt revealed on FOX last night was on every network. She held her BlackBerry and looked at the phone calls and emails pouring in but she did not respond to any of them. All of the curtains in the house were pulled tight to keep out the telephoto lenses of the press.

Her father came into the room and said to her in Arabic "I must speak to you." They went to the kitchen. Her mother stayed seated on the couch and looked at her daughter with a detached gaze.

Anika sat down at the kitchen table. She had taken this seat many times before when he thought he needed to correct her. He stood across the table facing her. His voice started calmly. "I have sacrificed so much for you. Your entire life I worked hard every day to provide your education, and provide opportunities for you. I took you, a girl, to Iran to learn from the Ulama. The Mu'allim taught you sunnah, the way to be followed. They taught you respect for the Sharia."

226

"Mu'allim!?! I was a child! Father, you let those men rape me!" she shouted at him.

He leaned across the table and slapped her hard across the face with his right hand. Her left cheek turned red and her nose began to bleed. He yelled at her pointing his finger in her face, "You are the whore! It was you and your loose ways. You brought it upon yourself! You have taken the honor from me. You are a disgrace and now you have ruined our best opportunity to extract justice from America! You lay more shame on me!"

Softly, through her tears Anika said "Father I did everything I was told to do. I gave my life to Allah, to Al-Qaeda and to Arish-Asad to restore your honor. Forgive me father! I only wanted to please you. I wanted you to love me."

"I cannot love the unclean." He said in disgust.

She put her head down on the table and cried a bottomless, mournful cry.

On the kitchen counter behind her was a towel folded lengthwise. He stepped toward it, lifted a corner of the towel back and with his right hand he picked up a long knife that was hidden inside the fold. He turned to her and from behind her he quickly took hold of her hair with his left hand while saying "May Allah forgive you." and he pulled her head back against his chest and cut her throat from left to right deep to the bones in her neck. He held her head against his chest for a moment, and then pushed her nearly severed head away from him onto the table. His daughter's last beats of her heart poured blood across the table.

He dropped the knife to the floor and went to her mother who was still seated in the living room and told her "Your daughter is dead. Call the police."

The 911 operator received the phone call. Anika's mother in a calm monotone voice asked for police to come into their home right away, and then she hung up.

The police, who were stationed in front of the Hannan home, got the radio call seconds later. Several reporters overheard it and the buzz spread among all of them. Four police officers took off running up the drive way and across the front yard to the front door, the press was right behind them, video cameras capturing every moment. When the police were half way, Hannan's father charged out of the house with blood all over his right arm and the right lower half of his blue shirt. He held a handgun and pointed it at the police firing several shots, one hitting a

CNN reporter in the leg. Police drew their weapons and returned fire hitting Hannan's father four times in the chest and once in the face. Anika's father was dead.

***

Jen slipped out of bed an hour before Matt woke up. The smell of cinnamon rolls baking down stairs in the kitchen nudged her awake. One of their special occasion morning treats was a cold cardboard tube of cinnamon rolls that the kids liked to bang open and bake. When they came out of the oven, they would fight over who got to spread the canned icing over the top of the rolls. Jen could not resist the smell and she went downstairs to eat one and be with their children who were watching news on TV. Tommy was counting how many times they saw the video of Matt and Hannan. They averaged three replays an hour on all the news networks. Today they all stayed home from school and work. Breakfast was something they rarely made time to eat together during the week, so Abby made pancakes from Matt's grandmother's recipe. She wanted to wake her father up to have some because they all knew how he loved pancakes floating in butter and syrup. Jen told her to let him sleep and he would be awake soon on his own. He rarely ever slept in and they all knew he had to be tired this morning.

It was 10:40AM when Jen ran up to their bedroom to wake Matt. He had just gotten out of bed and he was looking out the window at the news vans and people in front of their house. There seemed to be some commotion among them.

"Matt, Hannan is dead! It's all over TV. Her father killed her just this morning. Less than half an hour ago. That poor woman. The police shot her father and he's dead too. Oh Matt this is so sad."

"No. I can't believe it." They both ran downstairs to see the news coverage.

Pete called a few minutes later. "Matt, you saw what happened?"

"Yeah. I'm kinda stunned. I'm watching it now. I just got up, can I call you later?"

"OK brother. I just want to let you know I've been praying for you and praying about this since I saw the news. I have a peace about this and I'm not surprised it happened. I'm gonna keep praying. God bless you man."

Matt watched the video on TV and he saw three demons come raging out of the house with Mr. Hannan as he fired his gun. He saw the police return the fire and kill Anika's father. After his dead body hit the

228

grass, the demons rose above the group of police and reporters that surrounded Mr. Hannan's body, and they calmly circled the area and then vanished. Matt described to Jen what he saw. He was quiet for a while then said to her "This sort of makes sense. Really, what else could have happened? Hannan go to prison? Satan used her and I guess he had no further purpose for her. I don't know. I feel bad for her, for them. I'll pray that she had some redeeming element of her life but it's up to God where her eternity lies."

Jen asked "Do you think there was a chance she was saved?"

"Yeah, of course. We don't know where her heart was when she died. I always remember the thief on the cross. He only heard the Gospel a few minutes before he died and Jesus told him, that day he would be in paradise with Him. We know it's never too late for the saving grace of Christ."

LOOSE ENDS

Michael Rashid learned about all of these events in the media at the same time the rest of the world did. When he heard Matthew Davidson's name in the news, he became nervous and very paranoid, especially while at work at the FBI. He tried to lay low at his office. He had explained his burnt eye by saying a gas barbeque grill accidently ignited in his face. He used that to also explain the pair of crutches he used to nurse his burned foot. He said the flame scared him and he fell backward and broke his ankle. Friday, the day after Hannan was killed by her father, Rashid was killed as he left his apartment at 7AM to go to work. He was shot in the head by an Arish-Asad sniper using an explosive bullet. His headless body fell down his front steps onto the sidewalk.

***

Victoria Renard was in Paris the entire week when the American vice president resigned and Hannan was nominated to replace him. She watched all the news and she was frightened when she saw that the woman she recruited to be with Vice President Peterson was found dead. She thought that might happen, but it gave her a sad cold sense of guilt when she heard it was true. Victoria knew that all the work she had done with the women, and all the activity set in motion long ago was out of her control.

Jules Aimee had once casually joked to Victoria that he wished Anika Hannan was one of their girls. Now she knew that was almost true, and all the dots were connecting for Victoria. She was worried that because Hannan was dead, the women placed close to the president as well as all the others, would meet the same fate. Everything took a deadly tone. She worried about herself and her sons. She considered going to the police but she knew she was also guilty of many things. Victoria hurried to make plans to get herself and her sons out of France to spend a few weeks with friends and then decide what to do next. She also began carrying a gun with her everywhere she went.

At 11PM Paris time, on the same day Rashid was killed, an assassin broke into Victoria's apartment. Her sons were not with her, but a gentleman friend was and the two were sharing a bottle of wine. The assassin overpowered the man and knocked him unconscious. Then he disarmed Victoria who had retrieved her gun from her purse. The assassin overwhelmed her with his size and strength. He forced Victoria's hand onto the trigger of her gun as they stood directly over her friend. The assassin shot twice into his heart while he lay on the floor. Victoria screamed and fought him as fiercely as she could. He pinned her up against a wall. As she weakened from the struggle and with the gun still in her hand, the assassin guided it slowly, turning it toward Victoria and pressed the muzzle against her chest. She pleaded for her life as he fired one bullet that ripped her heart to shreds. Her last thought was of her sons. She died and fell to the floor. The assassin created the look of a murder suicide.

Investigators of the French Police Nationale, who were called to the scene of Victoria's death, found some of her notes relating to operation Planted Garden, but there were only two names that matched the list the FBI had. Al-Qaeda was all about tying up loose ends.

SUNDAY AT HOME

On Sunday afternoon, Assistant Attorney General Ray Lawrence rang the doorbell of Matt's home in Valley Forge. He knew Matt was home because the FBI had been keeping track of his movements since Thursday morning. When the doorbell rang, Matt was in the kitchen looking in their refrigerator because he was bored. This was the third day they had all been home without going anywhere and they were all tired of it. The press had finally given up stalking the Davidsons that morning and the last news van left 30 minutes before Lawrence arrived. Jen opened the front door.

"Mrs. Davidson, my name is Ray Lawrence. I'm with the Department of Justice." He showed her his identification. "May I speak with your husband please?"

"Yes of course Mr. Lawrence. Would you come in please?" Lawrence stepped inside the foyer and she closed the door. "I'll get Matt."

She found Matt browsing in the pantry looking for something bad to eat. "Matt, Mr. Lawrence is here to see you. He's the guy who called you about the disc and sent the helicopter, right?"

'Yeah, where is he?"

"In the foyer. Tuck in your shirt." Matt was wearing jeans, sneakers and a blue oxford shirt.

"Yes dear." Matt smiled at her and obediently did as he was told, then he went to see Ray Lawrence.

Matt found him standing where Jen left him. "Mr. Lawrence, I'm Matt Davidson. It's nice to meet you in person."

"Same here Mr. Davidson." They shook hands. "I hope you don't mind me just stopping by but I wanted to let you know what we will be doing next in the investigative process and ask you just a couple of questions. Could we go outside to talk for a few minutes?"

"Sure." Matt said and they went out the front door and walked around the house to the back yard. It was a warm sunny afternoon. "I'll have to cut this grass today or tomorrow." Matt said.

"My grass cutting days are long behind me. My condo association does all that stuff for me but I've mowed my share of grass, that's for sure."

"Yeah, I know what you mean." There was a moment of silence between them as they looked around Matt's big yard. "Mr. Lawrence, what can I do for you?" Matt knew that Lawrence would not come to his home to tell him something insignificant or ask a few questions that he could easily have done by phone. There must have been something important on his mind.

"Well, I do want to thank you for what you and Pete did. Your help and cooperation was remarkable and we, this government is very grateful to you." Matt did not say anything he just looked Lawrence in the eye and nodded.

"Matt, we know that several days before you were in Detroit, you made a 911 call from a Home Depot when a man collapsed at your feet. We know you never touched him. We saw the security video but we still don't know what happened to him. It turned out that the man has a drug problem and he was in the Unites States illegally. He also was on the Homeland Security watch list and he is still in custody and will be deported." As Lawrence was talking, the two of them started walking to the back edge of Matt's yard. Lawrence stopped and turned to Matt. "We also know you called an FBI tip line to call about Senator Hannan. You told them you saw patterns of activity around her that look bad. You also said you didn't think she was telling the truth when she speaks and there was something sinister about her."

"Yeah, and I also said I saw things around her when I saw her on TV."

"Yes you did. Matt, what did you mean by all that?"

Matt scratched his head and rubbed his chin. "It's very difficult to explain. I had been watching Hannan on TV, on the news for days and I had this feeling, a sense about her." Matt was not sure how much or what he should tell him. Then Matt added "I was being shown things."

"Shown what? By whom?"

"Mr. Lawrence, are you a Christian?"

"Yes I am. Since 1970." Lawrence paused and took a deep breath. "Matt, Let me tell you a little story. I was baptized as a believer on the flight deck of the aircraft carrier USS Kitty Hawk off the coast of North Vietnam. I was a weapons system officer, the backseater in a Navy F-4 Phantom. My pilot and I did a special delivery hop low over Haiphong where we should have never made it back alive. We took a surface to air missile right up our tailpipe. Somehow that didn't kill us and we stayed in the air. It shook us so hard we found out when we landed that our canopy locked up and we couldn't have ejected even if we wanted to. After the missile hit we took so much triple-A that our hydraulics and all our electronic were knocked out. We didn't even have radio and we had one huge hole, three foot in diameter in our starboard wing. We should not have been able to fly. When the wing got hit I saw the explosion and smoke. After that there was a constant bright white light outside the same wing. This was in the middle of the day and we saw it clear as can be. Well, we made it back to the Kitty Hawk and we even landed on deck without a tail hook. It was blown off and we didn't know it. And that light off our wing was with us until we landed, and then it was gone. Our aircraft literally fell apart when we landed on the carrier. Matt, I believe an angel brought us back to our ship. Unquestionably. Every man who saw that aircraft knew it was a miracle. When I figured out what happened, I surrendered to Jesus that very second. My pilot did too."

When Lawrence mentioned the white light, Matt knew he was telling the truth. "Mr. Lawrence, I don't know what to say other than I accept your story as true. I've had a few miracles in my life too. And I've seen angels, just like the way you described."

"Matt, why did you go to Detroit?"

"I felt I was led to be there. I needed to be there." Matt folded his arms across his chest and relaxed a bit. "I didn't know I'd be able to ask Hannan anything. I didn't plan it. I only know I received a word from the Lord, and that was to seek her out. I just went to that arena and did what I felt led to do and the rest just happened. I can't explain more than that. My wife knows, but I still haven't even explained this much to Pete."

"The things you saw around Hannan. What were they?"

Matt looked at the ground, shifted his weight and widened his feet apart to a more comfortable stance. He put his hands in the front pockets of his jeans and said "I'm trusting you with this, OK?"

"Matt, this is between you and me. I am officially off the clock."

"I could see demons around Hannan." As Matt spoke he watched for reaction in Lawrence's eyes. "Evil was constantly surrounding her, talking to her, influencing her. They were protecting her. I could see it on TV. It was so intense it made me sick. I prayed to know why I could see them, and God answered my prayer."

"What happened to Hannan in Detroit? Why did she... implode?"

"There were demons all over that place before she went on stage. And then I saw two angels clear the place of all of them. I think she was finally alone and she cracked. She revealed her true self."

"I believe you." Lawrence said. They remained silent, both feeling the moment. "For your information Matt, and this is classified, Hannan did blackmail the president into nominating her to become vice president and at some point later she or Omar was going to kill him so she would become president. We found some things, evidence in her office in Washington. Omar was part of it all. That's much more than I should say. But Matt, what happened with you and Pete most likely saved the president's life and who knows what else would have changed in the world if she had succeeded. I believe you Matt. You were shown things and you were led, and I thank God for that."

***

Because Hannan and Omar were dead, their trails ended with them. The only physical evidence found that linked them to anything, were the bandages and the tube of bacteria.

The FBI determined that Rashid had been connected to Hannan and Omar. Because he was careful, nothing was found at his apartment or at the FBI after he was killed.

All the women on the list were found and offered protection in exchange for information. There was considerable political pressure to keep the names of the men and women on Omar's a list secret. The women on the list led investigators to Victoria Renard, but not fast enough to save her life.

James Peterson stayed out of office, although he wanted the vice presidency back and had started making some comments to the press toward that end. The president had to call him personally and remind Peterson that his scandal was real and the president threatened to tell the press about it if he did not go away and stay quiet.

Colin Powell was nominated and confirmed as the new vice president.

No one was charged or prosecuted for anything linked to Hannan blackmailing the president. U.S. intelligence agencies gained some ground from the information Matt and Pete found on the memory stick, but no names surfaced in the subsequent investigations.

The president felt like he was lucky and was used to things always working out in his favor. He happily leaped into the role of the brave victim of the conspiracy and the liberal media adored him for it.

A MAN RESTORED

Matt stopped seeing angels and demons after Hannan was killed. He missed the comforting presence of the angels and it left him with a lonely feeling. He reasoned that God must no longer need him to have that ability because God's mission was accomplished. Matt knew the angels were not gone from his life and he knew they were always nearby and ready to serve God. He also knew that God would protect him and his family. God had been faithful and He always would be. Matt understood all of that in his mind, but in his heart he was sad to no longer have the angels as a regular reminder of God's protecting hand.

Shortly after the dust settled on Hannan and after Matt and Pete were interviewed several times by the Justice Department and the FBI about everything they knew, Matt began getting phone calls from political power brokers who wanted to meet him and discuss a political future for him. He was told that he should consider getting ready to make a run at congress in 2010. Matt and Jen enjoyed the meetings and talking politics, but he made no commitments.

Matt did a number of TV interviews retelling his story about Detroit and his reaction to the death of Anika Hannan. In the following weeks he would get calls to go on TV to comment about the president, Iran and some Christian issues. It was difficult for him to get back to work and focus on his properties. He felt pressure to stay current with all things political. Publicists, agents and lawyers wanted to represent him and cash in on his semi-celebrity status. They told him he should write a book. They advised him to prepare a speech about himself and the experience he had with Senator Hannan just in case they received some paid speaking offers for him. He and Jen did work together on a speech because he thought it was a good idea to be prepared for whatever might come his way. The speech included his personal testimony of his saving faith in Christ. Working on the speech also let Jen and him review together what had happened in their lives for the last weeks. They took a few days away alone together at a hotel in the Pocono Mountains where they talked, made notes about their experience and prayed together. It helped them close this chapter in their lives and get ready for the next.

***

At home in his office, Matt took a phone call. "Mr. Davidson, my name is Ollie Westmont. I've had a hard time reaching you."

237

Matt thought he recognized his name. "Well sir, I've been a little swamped lately."

"Of course you have. Ya know, I saw you on the news and I'm interested in investing in your company. Do you think we could meet sometime soon and talk about real estate? I understand now is a good time to find some deals." Ollie was an inventor and businessman. He held several cell phone technology patents. He also held leases on thousands of cell phone towers all over the US and Canada. He was a billionaire.

"You seem to me like a man of integrity and a brother in the Lord. I'll send you some information about my companies and some background about me. Can I call you again to set something up?"

"Are you the guy with the cell phone...?"

"Yeah that's me. Check me out and let's get together soon."

Doors swung open and several private investors approached Matt to invest in his business. He met a handful of Christian businessmen who helped him reorganize his company, restructure his debt at better rates and made even more investment capital available. He was a man restored.

A MESSAGE FOR THE KING

One month later, the White House called Matt's home. "This is the White House calling for Mr. Davidson. May I speak with him please?" the operator said.

Tommy answered the phone. "Is this really the White House? We get a lot of phone calls from all kinds of people."

"Yes this is the real White House. May I speak with Mr. Davidson?"

"I don't think so. Your phone number didn't come up on our caller ID. It says Private Caller."

" I really am the White House operator calling for Mr. Davidson. How can I prove it to you?" he said in a patient voice. He knew he was dealing with a young boy.

"I don't know. Telemarkets have the private number and they have the unavailable number too. My mom doesn't like telemarkets. She said they aren't supposed to call us because we are on a list of people who don't wanna be called. Lots of other people call us. Some are friends or people my mom and dad know. My mom says I should be polite when telemarkets call and just say we are not interested and hang up. I gotta go now."

"No wait! Am I speaking with Thomas, Mr. Davidson's son?"

"How did you know? I'm not supposed to talk about private stuff. Are you a stalker? My sister told me about stalkers. They creep her out. My dad was on TV a bunch of times. Is that why you called?"

"Thomas, I'm calling for the President's office. The President of the United States. It's very important."

The operator heard the clumping thud of the phone being put down on a hard surface and he could hear Tommy yelling in the background "Mom! The President of the United States is on the phone, should I tell him to call back?!"

Jen was in the basement doing laundry. "No! Don't hang up! I'll talk to him! Don't hang up!" and she ran to pick up a cordless phone. She got on the line and was connected with the president's secretary who invited the Davidson family to a private meeting at the White House so the president could meet them all and thank Matt and Pete personally.

***

The Secret Service was sent to transport Matt and his family, and Pete and his wife from their homes to the White House. They sent four agents in two black Cadillac Escalades to pick up them up. The Davidson's all wore their best clothing. For a week Jen thought about and planned what they all would wear. The day before the trip, Matt and Pete played golf together and ended the day by getting new haircuts. When Abby and Erika came downstairs to leave for the White House wearing their dresses and flip flops to meet the President of the United States, Jen looked at the two of them with an expression neither had ever seen before. It was threatening, frightening and much more severe than they had ever seen her look. Jen said "You will not wear flip flops to the White House. You will wear shoes. Now." The girls turned around and ran upstairs and put on shoes without saying a word.

The Secret Service agents treated them all very kindly and professionally. They gave Tommy a Junior Secret Service Agent badge and ID card that had his elementary school photo on it. Everyone enjoyed the trip and they had fun talking with the agents. Tommy asked "Can I see your guns? Do you guys have an Uzi? They're cool. Do you guys have bulletproof stuff? Can I try your ear radio? Do you guys really have a microphone in your wrist?" Agent Maloney, who was in charge of this detail, told Tommy that he would make an excellent agent one day if he worked hard in school. "Whoa Dad. That would be the coolest ever!" Tommy said with as much excitement as a nine year old boy could control.

Jen said to the agent, "Well I guess that's one career decision out of the way."

Pete loved every minute of the trip. He and his wife Debbie rode separately in one of the Secret Service vehicles. Pete talked one of the agents into letting him use their radio to talk to Matt in the other Cadillac. "This is Big Monkey One to Little Monkey Two. Do you read me? Come in Little Monkey. What's yer 20? Over."

From the front seat Agent Maloney said "Mr. Davidson, I think this is for you." and handed him a microphone.

Pete called again "Whiskey foxtrot tango. Do you copy?"

Matt took the microphone and reluctantly said, "Roger Big Monkey. Yes we copy." Everyone in the Davidson vehicle was laughing at Pete. Tommy loved it.

"Little monkey can you roger the recon at the big WH in T minus zero 200 niner niner?"

"You goofball." Matt laughed and then added "Hey civilian, get off this secure channel!"

"Roger that. 10-4 good buddy. We got a Secret Service convoy. Oh crap I shouldn't have said that! Over and out bravo charlie delta."

"He knows just enough to be dangerous." Matt told the agent while handing the microphone back to him.

Erika said "Hey Dad, we need code names. Can we have code names like the president and his wife have?"

"Yeah, why not? As long as we clear it with Agent Maloney."

"Sir, that is an excellent idea and it would enhance the level of security we hope to achieve." Maloney said.

They had a good time coming up with names for each other. They decided to call Pete – Big Guns; Debbie – Little Pistol; Erika – Drama Queen; Abby – Text Girl; Tommy – Special Ops; Jen – Miss Manners and they called Matt – Plot Killer. The Secret Service agents enjoyed the trip as much as their passengers did.

***

They all arrived at the White House at noon and went through security. They were supposed to meet the president at 12:30PM. The president was a half hour late when he met with them in an office outside the Oval Office. They were disappointed not to get inside to see it. The President thanked them for coming and he thanked Matt and Pete "for your service to our country". The White House photographer took several photos of them all and they brought their own cameras. Pete winked at Matt as if to tip him off to something. Then Pete stepped up to the president and said, "Mr. President would you mind taking a picture of my wife and me?" and he handed his camera to the President of the United States. "Just point and click." The president took their picture and they all had a good laugh.

Matt had been praying about this trip to the White House since it was arranged. He wanted to tell the President that God was responsible for how this all played out. He had been praying for just the right words to say this to him but so far no great lines were coming to him. In front of everyone he asked the president, "Sir, may I have a word with you privately?"

"How do I refuse a national hero?" the president said with a big smile. "Let's go into the Oval Office. Just give me a minute first, OK?" then he, Boreland and Press Secretary Albert Jones went in ahead of Matt.

Jen whispered to Matt, "Do you know what you are going to say to him?"

"I'm not sure but he needs to understand that God saved his presidency. Pray for me, OK?"

Inside the Oval Office the president said to Boreland and Jones, "Look, if this guy goes Christian on me, interrupt and say we have a meeting to go to." Boreland stepped outside and waved to Matt to come in.

Matt walked into the Oval Office and looked all around trying to take it in. He never imagined any occasion in his life that would bring him there. Matt got goose bumps thinking about all the great presidents that made history in this very room. He knew they would want to keep this brief and he was counting on the Holy Spirit to provide him with the right words.

"Matt, thank you again for coming to the White House. You have a beautiful family."

"Thank you Mr. President we're very glad to be here."

"I know you wanted a word alone but we have a new policy against me meeting with anyone alone. I am grateful that you came forward with your information. It's pretty amazing how you were at the right place at the right time. A miracle. Thank God for dumb luck, huh?"

Matt said "Sir, none of all that just happened. God was in control of these events."

"Like I said, thank God for that!" the president said with a flippant tone.

"Mr. President. God knows you and He knows everyone around you. It was God who made Senator Hannan reveal herself in order to protect you and this country. God gave us the information to save your life and end the attempt to take over this government."

Boreland interrupted, "Mr. President we need to meet with the commerce secretary in 5 minutes." The president turned away from Matt to look at Boreland.

At the same instant Boreland spoke, the brilliant angel Matt spoke to in the park weeks ago appeared next to him. Only Matt saw the angel who said to him, "Give him the message in your pocket." Matt felt his right side jacket pocket become very heavy.

The President said to Boreland, "OK. Right." then he turned back to Matt. "Matt I'm sorry we can't chat longer but... duty calls."

"I understand sir. May I give you this?" and Matt pulled from his jacket a solid gold, rectangular two sided tablet. It was the length and width of a letter size piece of paper and one half inch thick. Matt was amazed that he pulled the tablet out of his pocket without ripping it open. It was decorated on both sides with intricate designs and all twelve gemstones of the foundation of the New Temple of Jerusalem were imbedded into the gold. On one side of the tablet written in English were listed the Ten Commandments, and the other side was decorated with the profiles of two cherubim facing each other with outspread wings. Between them was written "There is no plan that can succeed against the Lord."

He handed the tablet to the president who was stunned by its beauty and the heavy weight of it. Boreland said to Matt, "How did you get this past security?"

The president said "Thank you Matt. Did you make this?" He needed both hands to hold it. It weighed nearly 30 pounds.

Matt said "No sir. It's not from me. It is from the Highest authority." The president and his two men stood there in amazement looking at the tablet. Matt turned to leave and he saw that the Oval Office was filled with angels.

ANGELS: A STORY ABOUT FANNIE & FREDDIE, THE PRESIDENT, BLACKMAIL AND MURDER

People want to and need to believe in angels. This is a story of hope, faithfulness, answered prayer and redemption. Matt is far from perfect. He is a faithful praying sinner who struggles every day with the same temptations we all do. This is a love story between a married couple with three children, taking them from their college days to almost 50 years old.

This story is political and I have pulled current national concerns into it, along with various personalities that all Americans are familiar with. I have portrayed some as the caricatures that I believe they really are. I have lived parts of this story and some events are my actual experiences. Matt Davidson's business problems are taken to the extremes that many real estate investors find themselves dealing with today. I consider myself an expert in my segment of the real estate market and I know firsthand the reality of what the credit and banking crisis has done to the American real estate market. This story was inspired by today's economic and political climate. Most Americans have been affected by this crisis and they will be able to relate to this story.

I always loved the thought of angels as mighty warriors and protectors. My "what if" questions are - what if a man could see angels everyday out in his daily life? What would he see and how would he deal with it? Who could he tell without being thought of as crazy? Most importantly - what would be God's purpose for allowing a man to see His heavenly created beings?

"Angels:" Is a story that says God is faithful and he is still in control of our leaders in Washington, no matter who lives in the White House.

John C. Bieber
2009

ACKNOWLEDGEMENTS

To Barb, I love to argue over semicolons with you. Let's do the next one in Punta Cana.

To Rachel and Lauren, You two are a gift from God. You have given me the best years of my life. I love you both with all of my heart... forever.

To all my friends who were my "reality check" readers. Thank you for taking the time to test drive this book. Your comments were enormously valuable and encouraging.

To my Lord and Savior Jesus Christ, thank you for connecting all the dots for me and giving me this story to write. My intention is to honor God with this book and to encourage some that, even as bad as your situation may be, there is always hope in our loving Father in heaven. And He is faithful!

The verse I pray for you all is, "That if you confess with your mouth, "Jesus is Lord," and believe in your heart that God raised him from the dead, you will be saved. For it is with your heart that you believe and are justified, and it is with your mouth that you confess and are saved. As the Scripture says, "Anyone who trusts in him will never be put to shame." Romans 10: 9-11

ABOUT THE AUTHOR

John C. Bieber is a Christian conservative opinion writer and blogger. He is a business owner and real estate investor who lives in southeastern Pennsylvania with his wife and two teenage daughters. John believes in American exceptionalism and he is a descendant of some of the earliest colonial settlers in Pennsylvania. "I believe I was born with a sense of patriotism and I have always known that the United States of America is the greatest nation in the history of the world. I believe America is still the last best hope for the world... second to Jesus Christ that is."

Visit John's web site at WWW.JOHNCBIEBER.COM.